For

Paul,

Sometime

Author's Note

All the characters and incidents in this novel are entirely fictitious. The Bron Eifion Slate Quarry does not exist, nor does Moel Eifion, nor the village of Nant y Bont. The mountain, Moel Eifion, has been placed roughly where Y Bigil is in fact, but I have done as little incidental violence to the topography as possible.

W.H.C.

W. H. Canaway

My Feet Upon A Rock

HUTCHINSON OF LONDON

HUTCHINSON & CO. (*Publishers*) LTD
178–202 Great Portland Street, London, W.1

London Melbourne Sydney
Auckland Bombay Toronto
Johannesburg New York

First published 1963
Second impression 1963

*This book has been set in Spectrum type face. It has
been printed in Great Britain by The Anchor Press,
Ltd., in Tiptree, Essex, on Antique Wove paper.*

My Feet Upon A Rock

Geraint Edwards is at the age when children discover that life and things and people—especially people—are seldom what they seem. The black-bearded, sinister schoolmaster he plans to shoot, when he can afford a gun, has a very human side to his character. Betty Mai Shafto is certainly not just a 'fat, toadying custard pie'. And the terrifying Englishman, Mr Maitland, is a never-ending source of shocks. But all grown-ups are unpredictable.

Gradually, as mature judgements take the place of the accepted notions of childhood, the boy grows up against the background of giant, craggy slate quarries and mountains which brood over the village and take their regular toll of human life. In these pages is the very spirit of Snowdonia.

What gives *My Feet Upon A Rock* its unique quality is the sense of wonder which W. H. Canaway has instilled from the first page and miraculously preserved to the last. It will appeal to an even wider public than the same author's now famous *Sammy Going South*.

1

HE WAS a small, dark-haired boy, red in the face from the long climb, thin bare legs muddy at the knees, his mouth and teeth stained purple from bilberries plucked and eaten on the way up.

'Well, here we are,' he said to himself grimly in Welsh, and sat down gratefully on the jumbled stones of the lakeside, near where the stream emptied out, its roar drowning his voice. The pewter expanse of Llyn Eifion stretched before him, its surface unruffled by any wind and broken only by the occasional spreading rings of a rising trout. The boy's gaze slid round to his right and up along the turreted black ridge of Crib y Geifr to where it disappeared in cloud under the north-west summit face of Moel Eifion, sixteen hundred feet above him.

He swallowed, and his small, thin fingers clenched at the rocks. But he forced himself to stand up, turn, and look down, following the tumbling white path of the stream towards the village far below: the haphazard toy cottages and smallholdings with the tiny white dots of sheep and the rather larger black dots of cows; the neat little toy council-house estate, the chapel, the school. His head swam.

The school. . . . He tore his gaze away. He looked left over Llyn Padarn, six hundred feet below, across to where the great ridge of Crib Goch soared up Snowdon, and over on Moel Eilio and Snowdon and up the Nant Peris he saw ridge and cwm, ridge and cwm piled unending, and all the topmost ridges passing into the secrecy of cloud. To his right, away over the village, the Menai Straits gleamed like a shot-silk ribbon, and beyond Anglesey was the sea again, and over the sea the long blue smudge that was the Wicklow Hills of Ireland. A flash from the windscreen of a car thirty miles away broke the spell, and he blinked, shuddering, then looked down again at the school, a twinge of a different sort of fear overcoming his fear of heights. He turned abruptly, and ran away from the edge along the shore of the lake to where three tumbledown stone walls marked what had once been a shepherd's hut. The sound of the stream dwindled to a whisper in the background, the only other sounds the boy's hurried breathing, the clatter of small stones dislodged by him as he pried with his hands at the bottom of the first wall, and the sudden amplified croak of a raven, which cursed the boy from its perch on a rock above the scree at the farther end of the lake.

The boy drew a battered aluminium tube from its hiding place, took off the cap, and extracted a fishing rod. He fitted its three sections together impatiently, attached a reel, which he took from a trouser pocket, drew cast and line through the rod rings. Then he fumbled in the other pocket and took out a matchbox, opening it and peering into it with a judicious air, forcing himself not to hurry. One after the other he selected three artificial flies, tying them on to the cast and testing each knot very thoroughly. His breathing calmed.

He moved to the water and began to fish, casting clumsily and inexpertly, so that the line fell in a snaky heap into the water almost at his feet. He clicked his tongue and cast again, then again, becoming absorbed in his occupation and unaware of his surroundings. He despised himself for his fear of heights, but doggedly braved the steep climb to Llyn Eifion nevertheless. His father was a good climber, and the boy would have suffered the pains of hell (a very real place to him, fire and devils and pitch-forks and all) rather than confess his weakness. On every visit to the high lake he compelled himself to a sickening ritual observa-tion of the view before he started to fish. Some day, he thought, he would look around, and there would be no fear at all. He would be like a falcon, proud and fierce and fearless, staring from its station at the little world below. Until that happened he had to live with his terror.

One day he had been inshore in a boat on Llyn Padarn with his father, fishing for the tasty red-fleshed char, when some pre-science had made him look up and he had seen, time suddenly suspended, the black spreadeagled figure of a man in the sky. Then the man had been falling towards them; the boy had screamed, pointing upward as the falling figure turned over twice in the air, slowly, and crashed into the water at the lake's edge twenty yards from the boat and eight hundred feet, vertically, from the gallery in the quarry from which he had fallen, drenching them.

His father had cut their fishing line with a swift flash of his knife; detached from events, the boy had experienced a vision of the line, thirty hooks baited with maggots, floating down, down into the green gloom of the lake, which everyone knew was bottomless. One part of his mind had wondered where those maggots would end up, while his father rowed with desperate splashing strokes of the oars to where the broken man was thrashing feebly in the water.

'Stay,' his father had commanded, and leaped out of the boat. The thrashing had ceased, and his father had remained a long time on his knees in the cold water, supporting the lifeless head till people had come, and his father had returned to the boat pale and silent, blood on his sleeves, and had taken the boy home. That had been five or six years ago; he must have been about five at the time.

He fished for three-quarters of an hour, catching nothing. His Uncle Tom was a wonderful fisherman, and might have taught him a lot, but he wasn't well, and it made him a bit cranky, somehow. The boy went back to give himself another dose of medicine, pouting at the view with assumed contempt and thrusting his sweaty, shaking hands into his trouser pockets. He *did* feel better: he was sure of it. Medicine was nasty, but it did you good in the end. He wiped his hands

9

on the seat of his dirty flannel trousers, grinning palely.

Down by the school the ant-like procession of his school-mates made its way along the lane as he watched. At the end of the lane the procession split up into small groups, or ones and twos, going their ways home. Well, let them. He hoped they'd enjoyed their afternoon, cooped up in school with Mr Griffiths. He put his hands on his hips and stared defiantly for a little longer, then went back to the lake, picked up his rod, and began fishing again. When he got home he would be leathered, and when he turned up at school next morning he would be leathered a second time, so he might as well try to catch a fish meanwhile.

He hated Mr Griffiths. When he had enough money he was going to buy a rifle with a telescopic sight, and come up to this very place, waiting till Mr Griffiths had done his marking and emerged from the school. He would raise the rifle slowly to his shoulder, then, so gently, squeeze the trigger and observe with satisfaction through the telescope the sudden look of surprise, the suddenly goggling eyes above the thick black beard, the crumpling of the colossus; no more Mr Griffiths. A national hero, that is what the boy would be.

He sighed, reeled in his line, and took off the tail fly, a wet Black Gnat, replacing it with a Kingfisher Butcher. He knew the name of the Black Gnat, but called the Kingfisher Butcher a Blue and Orange. He began to cast again, Mr Griffiths lowering in his mind like the cloud overhead, an impenetrable oppressive mass.

The boy had never come to terms with Mr Griffiths. He had enjoyed the previous years in the primary school, with fat and motherly Miss Jones Penrhyn; beautiful Miss Jones Heol yr Haul (who had since left and married a Liverpool dentist; she was sadly mourned by the boy, who had loved her frantically and brooded with despair over her fate: how could anyone marry a man who'd be liable to start pulling out your teeth at the drop of a hat?); melancholy, ginger Mr Richards, who lived in a golden mist of poetry and bothered no one who left him in it—all these had been fine; but then, in his last year at the primary school, to come face to face with Griffiths, Black Griffiths! It was like eating a pleasant enough meal and finding red-hot coal for afters.

All that year the boy had waged his losing battle. The first term he tried dumb insolence, standing when asked a question and looking stupid, oafish. It hadn't worked, for Mr Griffiths kept him standing till the tables were turned, and the class giggled and guffawed at *him*, not Mr Griffiths. The following term he had tried open insolence. When Betty Mai Shafto, the fat, toadying custard pie, brought Mr Griffiths a bunch of flowers, the boy came the following day with a razor-blade and laid it on Mr Griffiths' desk with a pointed look at the man's beard. And found himself using the razor-blade to sharpen half a gross of pencils after school.

His father was working in Patagonia. He knew that he couldn't see Patagonia from the edge of the lake, for he had tried many times, peering over to the left; that was its general direction. He could not tell his father about Mr Griffiths, for the battle was his alone. He sighed.

Suddenly a trout rose to one of his flies, and he forgot everything else in his passion to catch it. He cast and cast, bringing the flies back towards him, but the fish had cruised on elsewhere. Time went by as imperceptibly as the moving wreaths of cloud above his head, so that he did not hear the slow, heavy footfalls behind him until they were upon him. He looked incuriously over his shoulder, expecting merely another angler, and then remained transfixed, his mouth half open, the tip of his rod drooping into the water.

It was Mr Griffiths.

The man loomed above him. The trousers of his black suit were tucked into his socks, and he wore nailed boots.

Mr Griffiths looked at the boy for a long time, the eyes above the black beard dark and unfathomable. He was not even breathing hard after the climb.

He can't kill me, the boy thought desperately. Or can he?

Still staring at Mr Griffiths, he reeled in steadily and prepared for flight. But which way? Mr Griffiths stood between him and safety. If he ran along the lake he would founder in the bog below the scree.

Mr Griffiths said, 'Well, Geraint Edwards?' and continued to regard him impassively.

Geraint mumbled inaudibly, his fright giving way to a watchful sullenness.

'Say good afternoon!' Mr Griffiths roared suddenly.

The boy was so taken aback that he obeyed at once, in a whisper.

'That is better. Well, have you caught anything?'

Bewildered, Geraint shook his head. What was behind all this?

Mr Griffiths said, 'I should think not, to judge from the way you have been fishing. Like a baby waving a rattle. Here.'

He held out a hand imperiously.

Geraint thought, I've saved seventeen shillings towards that rifle. Oh, if he breaks my rod I'll buy a knife instead, straight away, and I'll cut his throat with it. . . .

Mr Griffiths took the rod, inspected the flies, grunted, and began to cast expertly. There was a splash, the tip of the rod bent, and in no time at all he was landing a good trout. He killed the fish, tested the knot of the fly which had hooked it, and cast again. This time he caught two fish simultaneously, one on the tail fly and one on the second dropper.

Geraint stared at Mr Griffiths, rubbing his chin.

'Watch.'

The boy needed no exhortation: he watched entranced.

'The trout doesn't think your flies are flies,' Mr Griffiths said. 'He thinks they are little fish. If they go through the water like express trains the trout says to himself, "What, rupture myself chasing *those*?" and he leaves them alone. You must work the fly, boy, make it hang in the water, then give a little jerk and a flutter, like this'—he demonstrated—'so the trout will say, "Ah, something the matter there, think I'll just put the little fellow out of his misery and get my supper at the same time." Now try.'

Geraint, puzzled and nonplussed, did as he was told, casting as far as he could and working the flies. Almost at once a trout boiled at the tail fly; Geraint missed it. Then it came again and was hooked. He landed the fish, trembling with excitement. He had caught plenty of fish with worms and maggots, but never one on the fly, though he had persevered all that season, and for a moment he was unfettered by Mr Griffiths' presence, his eyes shining with pride.

'Well, was that worth it?' Mr Griffiths said.

'Oh, yes!'

Mr Griffiths began to dismantle the rod.

'That fish was the reward of efficiency,' he observed. And then, sharply, 'Touch your toes!'

Startled, Geraint touched his toes. Mr Griffiths swished the handle section of the cane rod once.

Geraint yelped.

The man said in English, 'That was the bottom section of the rod. Highly appropriate.' And in Welsh again: 'That, my friend, was the reward for truancy. Next time you climb up here in full view of the school windows do it in disguise. Come.'

Geraint took the sections of the rod, put the reel in his pocket and the rod in its tube. But should he replace the tube in its hiding place? No; he would not trust Mr Griffiths as far as that. He carried the tube under one arm, and followed Mr Griffiths on the long descent to the village. Mr Griffiths said nothing, but set a hot pace, and Geraint's legs were soon shaky from the strain of hurrying downhill.

They reached the stone walls dividing the fields of rough marginal pasture, sheep yelling at them, and scrambled over the walls, still descending, till they came to the lane. Mr Griffiths was carrying the trout strung through the gills on a twist of reeds. He stopped outside Geraint's cottage, and said, 'It is late. You will get into trouble?'

Geraint hesitated, then nodded dumbly.

Mr Griffiths said, 'I will come with you to the door.'

Geraint's mother was a big woman with a loud voice. She had grown bigger, and her voice louder, over the years, but Gwen Edwards had been beautiful once, and you could see more than a trace of it still. Her hands were large and roughened and red, and thick mottled biceps bulged from the short sleeves of her print dress, but her eyes were a snapping blue, her cheeks full and pink as pippins, her hair smooth and dark and shiny as a starling's wing. She was a woman to command respect. And she was waiting at the front door of the cottage.

Geraint slunk up the steps behind Mr Griffiths.

'Where has he been, Mr Griffiths? In some trouble? You kept him in? I should think so, too!' And to Geraint: 'Just you wait, young man!' her voice vibrant with fury.

Astonished, Geraint heard Mr Griffiths, his voice muted to a winning rumble, say, 'Mrs Edwards, I have come to apologize. I am so very sorry. It was such a lovely evening, lovely.'

'Yes, it is lovely, but——'

'We have been fishing, Mrs Edwards. Couldn't resist it. To tell you the truth, to tell you the truth, Mrs Edwards, I had noticed that—er—Geraint, that Geraint was a keen angler, but not getting very far.'

Mrs Edwards sniffed and said, 'He has never caught a thing since he started with those old flies.'

'Well, yes. So I thought I might instruct him a little. Here.'

He held out the four trout, and Mrs Edwards took them, looking at them wonderingly, a half-smile lighting her face.

'Geraint caught all those?'

'Let us say we caught them together.' He looked at Geraint meaningfully and added, 'The reward of perseverance, one might call it. They will make a breakfast. Good evening now, Mrs Edwards, and how well you are looking, indeed.' He said emphatically to Geraint, 'A fine lady, your mother, a fine lady,' moving off swiftly with a brief wave, and Gwen Edwards waved back only half consciously, looking vague and a little roguish and completely taken aback.

Why, Geraint thought, Mr Griffiths played her like one of those old trout. She let him go without a word. He'd knocked her properly sim-sam. Her! And him, too, telling lies like that, and never a word about Geraint playing hookey.

He shook his head wonderingly, and followed his mother inside, sure that he'd get a leathering anyway, now that Mr Griffiths was gone. But his mother simply exclaimed, 'Men!' then rumpled his hair and said, 'You and your old fishing! Well, at least you have started to catch something again, anyhow!'

And she went into the kitchen and began to clean out the fish, while Geraint heard her humming. Those trout were not for breakfast. She cooked them for him there and then, with a fried egg on top; Geraint ate the lot, while she stood over him proudly.

He was wondering whether you could buy a landing net for seventeen shillings.

2

WIL EDWARDS yawned as he jounced in the back of Shafto's van, grinding in second gear up the top road. Persimmon Hughes sat next to Shafto and cursed as he did every morning as he tried to roll his first cigarette, the jolting of the van spilling his tobacco and shaking his hands so that the cigarette, when finished, looked like a small white sausage. Shafto watched the road, black brows drawn down toward his big, hooked nose. It was twenty minutes past seven.

That Shafto, Wil Edwards thought. He only gives us a lift so that we pay for his petrol. And I'll bet he is in pocket on it by the end of every week. Still, it is a long walk up by the top road to Patagonia. And he thought, My Geraint is coming on, catching trout on the fly. Beginning to grow. A matter for pride, and for regret. One minute they were sucking their mother's milk, small, helpless bundles, and the next they were catching trout on the fly. Why, the boy's voice would be breaking any time. There were signs of it already.

Shafto said in his thick South Walian accent, 'Wil, boy, I bet you half a crown it rains by dinner-time.'

They had passed through the gates, and Shafto was reversing the van into a parking space alongside other vans and small cars. The three men got out, and Wil Edwards led the way to the parapet silently, while Shafto and Persimmon Hughes shouted greetings to other arrivals. The three leaned on the parapet, the hard slate under their elbows, and looked casually out across the vertiginous drop, across the two-mile expanse of

Llyn Padarn like a puddle of blue ink below, and out to sea. Then Wil turned his back on the view and glanced briefly over to the summit of Elidir Fawr, where a small plume of cloud was hanging.

'Done,' he said with finality. 'It will not rain before dinner.'

Persimmon Hughes said, 'Great God, are you two at it again? Like a pair of kids.'

Shafto laughed and said, 'Mother wit, boy, that is what I got. Mother wit. Half a crown: a pint of beer, a packet of fag papers, and a bag of crisps, boy. You can do a bit with half a crown even yet. What's crisps in Welsh?'

'*Ysglodion*,' said Wil bitterly. 'You southern half-caste. You cannot even speak Welsh properly, and you have been here how long, ten years? And yet you think you can tell me, when I have been here all my life, that it will rain before dinner. You will eat your words yet.'

Persimmon Hughes said placatingly, 'Well, we shall see,' and the three men moved along the slate roadway in the cold early-morning air. It was half past seven as they entered the big cabin.

The big cabin was built of slate bricks, roughly plastered and whitewashed inside, roofed with logs and slates. Men were sitting at benches by the trestle tables, rolling cigarettes and waiting for the kettle to boil. Wil Edwards sat down and sulked, annoyed with himself for having allowed himself to take on the bet with Shafto merely out of a desire to contradict him; he knew that it would rain before the day was out. Dear God, he said to himself, Thou knowest I attend chapel regularly and am not really a betting man at all, except with Shafto, so please send the rain after twelve o'clock, and let me do that piece of drilling as well.

He added the last bit to his prayer as an afterthought. Then he felt better, and the heat from the rusty swag-bellied stove began to warm him up. Men drank tea, and Wil fetched his mug from the ex-Army respirator case which held his sandwiches. He sat sipping the hot tea.

Persimmon Hughes said, 'What time shall we start? It is ten to eight. Shall we start without Tom?'

'No hurry,' said Shafto. 'I got half a crown extra coming, anyway. Tom will be along soon.'

'Perhaps,' said Wil. 'And perhaps he will not.'

Shafto said, 'He is your brother, Wil boy.'

Wil said, 'And I am not my brother's keeper. He is troubled with his bronchitis.'

'It is the stone on his lungs,' said Persimmon Hughes morbidly.

Wil leaped to his feet angrily.

'It is not! I will not have you say that, Simeon Hughes.'

Shafto said, 'Aw, there's stupid you are. What harm does it do to face facts?'

Wil Edwards swallowed and said, 'I have tried and tried to get him to see the doctor, but he will not. And, anyway, it could be the bronchitis. It could be. He spends so much time at the river and in the wood.'

'Poaching,' said Shafto.

'You tell him that when you see him. Now I will go to the shed and ask Cledwyn Cil y Mor. He will know where Tom is. Wait now till I come back.'

He strode off and left the big cabin. Twenty yards along the roadway was the shed. Not very many men had yet started work, but the power was on and the noise tremendous. Wil stood by the entrance for a moment and looked round about. Along the far side of the shed were the saw-beds. Two early starters were working there, cutting rough-dressed blocks of slate into thick sections with the powerful circular saws, great-toothed, screaming at the bite into the slate, roaring impotently after the cut had been made, dribbling water. Cledwyn Cil y Mor was not at the saw-beds.

Suddenly Wil saw Cledwyn over to his right. Along this side of the shed were the stalls where the workmen split and trimmed the slate to the required dimensions. Wil walked past the whining, clacking rotary cutters, which they called 'threshing machines', to Cledwyn's stall. Cledwyn was a hard worker, and already a neat pile of freshly trimmed roofing slates lay at the front of the stall. The slates were counted in threes and 'hundreds', a misleading measure, for a 'hundred' of slates is made up of forty-two threes and a two: one hundred and twenty-eight.

Cledwyn had not yet seen Wil Edwards, for he was absorbed in his task. He was sitting on a broad, low stool, six inches from the ground. He had just drawn up a block of slate against the side of his left knee. He placed a wide chisel along the middle of the top edge, exactly along the line of cleavage of the slate. He hit the chisel very hard with a metal-bound mallet, and a perfectly straight crack appeared. He beat the chisel farther in, dropped the mallet, and levered the chisel back and forth with both hands. There was a loud report, and the slate split into two equal halves. Working with extreme skill and precision, with a perfect eye, Cledwyn split the halves into quarters, the quarters into eighths. Then he picked up the slates and stood, seeing Wil Edwards for the first time.

'Hello, Wil, how are you?' he said, and moved to the rotary cutter to trim the slates. Swiftly he inserted them, one edge at a time, and the *clack-clack-clack-clack*—four times in quick succession, each edge trimmed exactly straight and bevelled, produced a square slate, each angle a right angle. Wil watched admiringly. Cledwyn took home on the average seventeen pounds a week; and he was worth it.

'Man, devil, you have a wonderful eye,' he shouted at the top of his voice. It was odd that a man who did not work in the shed had to bellow to make himself heard, while the shed workers could talk to one another at about half the volume Wil had to employ.

It would have been discourteous for Wil to broach at once the subject he wished to discuss, so he shouted for a while about the weather and the prospects for the coming football season, before asking, 'Tom didn't come in your car this morning, then?'

Cledwyn paused, another rough-dressed block of slate in his hands.

'He has a bad cough,' he said, shaking his head and sitting down on the stool. 'He is not coming this morning, Wil.'

Wil nodded and left the shed, leaving Cledwyn to get on with his work and going back to the big cabin.

'Well?' asked Shafto.

Wil said shortly, 'Come on, let us get started. Tom is not coming, and so we will do our best without him.'

Persimmon Hughes stood up, small and eager like a terrier.

Shafto said, 'Wage slaves, that is what you two are. When I was in the coal in the Rhondda there were people like you two. Always hard at it. Doesn't do on piecework, boys: you get the rate cut that way. Wait till nine, that's what I say.'

'You and your coal,' Wil Edwards said. 'You should have stopped with your coal.'

Persimmon Hughes said, 'Oh, come on, Shafto, I do not like sitting about all day.'

'No,' Shafto said. 'Too many kids, you have. Hard work on nights means hard work in the day to pay for it, eh?' And he winked. 'What do you say, Wil boy?'

But Shafto rose none the less, and the three men made their way out of the big cabin.

The roadway was of slate, the buildings were of slate, the mountain was of slate, blue-grey, grey-mauve, grey-black. The stark line of poles carrying power and light cables looked like a line of growing trees by comparison: at least the poles were not made of slate. Underfoot on the slate were rusty narrow-gauge rails; water gurgled in a rusty spillway at the side of the track. The men passed the shed and then turned up the slate stairway to Patagonia, the highest gallery in the Bron Eifion quarry, seventeen hundred feet from the bottom.

The shed was at the level of Top Hat gallery, and from Top Hat up to Monkey Brand there were a hundred and eighty-three slate steps; from Monkey Brand to Patagonia there were ninety-seven. In the winter, despite sweeping and salt, the stairway was an icy nightmare; if you fell you would not just bounce down to Top Hat. That would be bad enough; but below Top Hat lay Jim Crow, and from Top Hat to the bottom of Jim Crow there were three hundred steps; from Jim Crow to Moonlight there were two hundred and thirty-two. You would miss Y Senedd, a small gallery extending out to the Eifion Slabs and over the Big Cliff seven hundred feet above the lake. Below the left-hand end of Moonlight was an old rock fall, and below its detritus lay The Haymarket, where you would finish up. Eight hundred and twelve steps, plus a hundred and forty feet without any steps at all. It was a long way from Patagonia to The Haymarket, and even then the tattered bleeding rag, which had been you, would by no means be at the bottom of the quarry.

When they reached the roadway of Patagonia the three men were scarcely breathing hard. They turned right towards the fire cabin, a little beehive hut of slate bricks with a log and slate roof, reinforced with steel girders at its entrance, and sat for a moment by common consent on the narrow bench running round the inner wall of the cabin. The men were as fit as mountain goats, but, after all, it was only right to have a rest after climbing those steps.

Shafto said expansively, 'This is what I like about the quarry: the freedom of it, aye. Nobody breathing down your neck after you.'

'I thought you did not like it after your old coal,' said Wil.

Shafto said, 'Well, that was just a manner of speaking. It's not so bad here, man, except the winter. That is when anybody in his right mind would wish himself underground; that's when you need to be a cross between an Eskimo and a bloody monkey to work up here.'

'You will get used to it in another ten years, perhaps,' Wil Edwards said.

Persimmon Hughes said, 'No sense thinking about the winter now. Leave well alone.'

Shafto said to Wil, 'That Geraint of yours. His voice isn't getting any better, is it?'

There was an undercurrent of malice in his tone. Wil Edwards looked at him sharply.

He said, 'A lad's voice is bound to break. This next year will see him through it, and he will be better than ever. He will make a fine tenor.'

'We'll see,' said Shafto. 'A girl, now, she doesn't have that trouble. Did you hear my Betty Mai in chapel on Sunday? Sweet as a blackbird. There's a voice for you.'

Wil Edwards said abruptly, 'Oh, come on, we have work to do,' and stood. They picked up their tools.

Patagonia gave a very high yield of slate, about one ton for every three tons of rock blasted. Wil Edwards climbed the hand rope to the top of the gallery, followed by Shafto. The top of Patagonia had no proper roadway and no narrow-gauge track: it was a rough rock ledge eight yards wide and a hundred and seventy yards long, in the shape of a bow. The thick hose of the compressed-air pipe, hissing at the joints, snaked along it. Arching above it on the left was the ridge of Crib y Geifr, and away on the right the ridge of Crud y Gwynt: the two ridges met at the summit of Moel Eifion, and the gallery lay dwarfed between their lower buttresses. Turning and looking down, a man felt godlike, thought Wil Edwards. Others became blasé, but he himself never lost the sense of wonder as he gazed down past the galleries, each one a row in an amphitheatre built for titans. To his right the immense stairway led down to Moonlight, and in front, a long, long way below, the truck incline arrowed down from the sheds on Moonlight to the main sheds at the bottom of the quarry, as far again as the length of the stairway. Down there, in the orchestra of the amphitheatre, lay the main sheds and offices; the biggest shed was a hundred yards long, but to Wil Edwards it looked like an oblong cube of grey sugar. Past these buildings lay the brickworks, its ever-present pall of dust partly obscuring it, and beyond the brickworks was the blue puddle of the lake. To the right of the truck incline, between The Haymarket and the main sheds, was the Twll Mawr, a hole like the pit of hell, with white dots of gulls wheeling over it. Often, visitors to the quarry, looking down from Top Hat—they were allowed no higher—to the Twll Mawr, suddenly sat down behind the wall, shaking, or were sick, or ran out of the quarry and down the top road as fast as they could. When the sun was in the right place Wil Edwards could see from Patagonia into the shaft of the Twll Mawr, where lay green, green water which no wind ever ruffled, its surface disturbed only by sudden hailstorms of rock from the blasting, and this no man had ever witnessed.

Wil Edwards tied his rope to a bar hammered into the rock, tested its hold, and let himself nonchalantly down the gallery face on a bowline. He had sized up the rock the day before, when the contract was agreed, and he was after a good fall of slate. When he reached the position he had chosen, he let himself down a little farther to a foothold, a ledge of slate a quarter of an inch deep. Balanced on this, he leaned upwards and hammered two metal pegs like pitons, formed from old gouges, into a crack in rock. The pegs were placed six inches apart. He took from his pocket a flat piece of wood, a miniature plank, ten inches by four, and set it on top of the pegs. He studied the arrangement, nodded with satisfaction, looked up at Shafto's head thirty feet above, and signalled that he was coming up.

He stood with Shafto for a moment and said, 'We will get a good fall.' Then he said, 'I thought Betty Mai was a bit shaky in her high notes. Why don't you train her for a mezzo?'

Shafto said blackly, 'A soprano she is, dammo. Anybody with any ear at all can tell that. You going down now? I ought to be helping Persimmon.'

Wil went down again, the white air line and drill accompanying him. He swung gently on his rope, then his feet found the tiny platform and he settled himself, leaning comfortably outwards against the rope, the drill hefted so that it balanced easily. Someone else had begun drilling far away, the thin pitch of the drill at that distance sounding like a demented woodpecker. Wil looked down and across unerringly to where Y Senedd began to give way to the Eifion Slabs, and, below them, the Big Cliff. There was a man drilling at the far end of Y Senedd: Wil saw the orange dot of his shirt near the straight white thread of the air line. A young man. Ah, yes, he knew who it was. Glyn Griffith. He was working close to the spot from which poor Emrys had fallen that day and nearly hit Wil's boat on the lake. Wil shook his head, recalling the occasion. Poor Emrys. He had died in Wil's arms. It was a dangerous place, that far end of Y Senedd.

And so he leaned back complacently, almost a thousand feet above the Twll Mawr, nodded up at Shafto, who then vanished, and switched on the drill. He was happy in sudden solitude, the position of his work and the sound of his drill encapsulating him completely. This was the work he enjoyed. The world could roll by. By now Shafto would be joining Persimmon Hughes, clearing up, rough-dressing the last few small blocks of slate left from the previous blasting three weeks before. Wil Edwards' father had told him of slate blocks in the old days as big as the chapel, blocks that took a year's work to cut down. His father understood the stone, and Wil himself knew something about it, but not his son. Geraint should go to no quarry. Geraint should have his voice properly trained, have an education. Why, there was no telling where you might end up these days with a good voice. In ten years Geraint might even be on television, with the George Mitchell Singers. Wil's father was a harpist, second to none in his day, but it had got him nowhere. Things had been different then, there were not the opportunities. The music had skipped a generation, leaving Wil Edwards out as a keen and appreciative listener, but no performer. Well, Geraint had real ability, and he should make use of it.

Wil thought of his father, by now sitting outside the cottage, his filmed blind eyes beginning to close in the sunlight, and of Geraint, up to the Lord knew what devilry at school. Then he gave his attention to the drilling, and the sound of other drills arose unheard about him. Down on Moonlight, a tiny locomotive was hauling a train of trucks laden with rough-dressed slate

24

to the incline. The trucks were uncoupled from the locomotive and sent down the giddy slope to the main sheds. They went down by the force of gravity, and were hauled up again by steam winch. Wil Edwards saw nothing but the face of rock before him.

His job was to drill in such a way that when the charge was fired it would shatter big blocks of slate from the stratum. On each side stretched the cliffs of slate, bounded at the upper extremity by the rock of the mountain ridges, and at the lower by the rubble and slate of previous blastings. The slate varied in colour almost imperceptibly to an untrained eye, but at the left-hand side of the gallery it was a grey-blue, good for roofing slates. In the middle, where Wil was working, it was rather darker, an inky mauve. Here could be obtained the big slabs for laboratory bench tops, the linings of fume cupboards. Over to the right the slate verged on black: polished, it looked like gleaming onyx, and was popular material for gravestones.

Wil drilled a hole three feet long and parallel to the rock face. Then, beginning four inches below the first hole, he started a second one, the drill held so that the holes converged and would meet at the farther end. It was hard work, and the dust made him cough from time to time. He did not notice that it was raining till the back of his neck was soaked, and one foot slipped on the wet surface of his platform. He looked up. Shafto was grinning down at him. He switched off the drill and went up to the top, putting down his tools and cursing silently and decently as he dug in his trouser pocket.

Wil held out the half-crown to Shafto.

'Ten to twelve,' Shafto said. 'Mother wit, boy, that's what it is, mother wit.'

'If you had one,' Wil said with suppressed fury.

Shafto went white and stared at Wil, who met him eye to eye. The two men glared at each other for a minute, and then Shafto spun on his heel and went to join Persimmon Hughes at the bottom of the gallery.

Wil Edwards was aware that he had forgotten himself. It was

the singing. If Shafto would only stop giving himself airs about his precious Betty Mai there would be no trouble at all. Her voice could not compare with Geraint's, of course. But Shafto was determined that Betty Mai should outshine Geraint, and bets like the one Wil had just lost were Shafto's way of saying, 'I won, so I'm a better man than you; therefore Betty Mai is better than Geraint.' There was no logic in it, no logic at all, but it hurt just the same. He went down and joined Shafto and Persimmon. The rain stopped at twelve-fifteen, just as the men reached the big cabin. Shafto beat his knees and howled with laughter outside the cabin door.

'What is the joke?' a man asked, pausing as he was about to pass by.

Persimmon Hughes took Shafto's arm just above the elbow, tightly. Wil Edwards watched silently, while Shafto weighed things up.

'You mind your own bloody business,' he said at last to the man. 'A private joke, see.'

Persimmon Hughes sighed and released Shafto's arm. Shafto looked at Wil Edwards inscrutably, then went into the cabin, followed by Wil and Hughes. The three men sat down together and ate silently, munching their sandwiches. When they were drinking tea Wil Edwards took out his tobacco tin for his first smoke of the day; he never smoked till afternoon. He opened the tin, considered a moment, then offered it to Shafto. Shafto hesitated, then took the tin, and rolled a cigarette. Persimmon Hughes lighted it for him, beaming.

Wil finished drilling early in the afternoon. He inspected the holes and found them good. Then he went up and disconnected the drill, taking it down to the fire cabin. Persimmon Hughes had walked to the top powder store, on the level of Top Hat but on the mountain a quarter of a mile from the gallery. He brought back twenty-four pounds of black powder. Again Wil went down the rope and packed twelve pounds of powder into each hole, inserting the fuse into the powder in the lower hole, then ramming the charges tight and tamping them with dirt and stones. The blue fuse trailed out of the lower hole like a length of disconnected electric cable.

The three men went for a mug of tea to the big cabin on Top Hat.

Persimmon Hughes said, 'We have the last lot all cleared away now, Wil, and we are ready and waiting. How will this one come, do you think?'

Another man said, 'Wil, you have been buzzing up there all the time like an old bluebottle. Will it be a big one?'

Shafto swilled the tea in the bottom of his mug and then said, 'Work for a month, we should have.'

Wil nodded in corroboration. Whatever divisions might threaten within, the team presented a united front.

'Man, devil,' he said, the strongest oath he ever permitted himself. 'We will have work for a month from this one, sure enough.'

The men idled and gossiped awhile. Through the little window of the cabin Wil could see framed the tip of Snowdon's summit and a three-quarter view of the hotel on top. He sighed, envying for a moment, but only a moment, the tourists transported to the hotel by the mountain railway, sitting drinking up there and perhaps even now scanning the quarry with binoculars. The blasting was a big attraction.

Eventually the men left the cabin and went up again to Patagonia. Wil Edwards roped down to where the fuse hung, and stripped the end of the blue cable till he had exposed the silver-white filaments of the timing thread which formed the inner core of the fuse, the thread itself encased in powder and the powder in turn contained by the outer cover.

Wil had employed a twelve-yard fuse. This would burn through in ten minutes. Quarrymen, like all good climbers, do not like to take unjustifiable risks; and their caution was heightened by the fact that they were exploding pieces of the mountain on which they climbed. Some genius long dead had invented the technique of using *papur poeth*, 'hot paper'. This was simply paper impregnated with a solution of saltpetre: a home-made safety device which enabled the worker to get clear in plenty of time. It was a fuse before the fuse, so to speak. A faulty fuse will blow through in no time, and without the *papur poeth* the shot-firer would have no chance at all. So Wil tore off a small rectangle of the paper and fixed one end in the timing thread. Then he waited.

Soon the warning whistle blew. Other shot-firers had finished preparing their fuses, and all was ready. The quarry suddenly emptied of men, it seemed: some were taking shelter in the fire cabins, some in the big cabins, some under fixed engine housings. The second whistle blew. Wil Edwards struck a match, lighted a cigarette which he had rolled while waiting, and touched the paper with the end. The paper ignited, and a glowing line began to spread slowly across the paper towards the fuse as Wil retrieved his pegs and his little plank, climbed up to the top of Patagonia, and went down to the fire cabin, ducking under the low lintel to join the others.

They waited quietly. There was a roaring explosion.

'Over on Y Senedd,' said Persimmon Hughes.

Another.

'On Moonlight,' said Shafto. 'Why they want to blast there passes my understanding. Enough work down there for ten years, there is.'

Another, ear-splitting to the three. But to observers under the crane housing on Jim Crow the place where Wil Edwards had been drilling suddenly bloomed into a brief stone chrysanthe-mum in front of a blue-black leaf of smoke; then the rock was falling and the smoke starting to drift away before the sound of the explosion came to their ears. After the detonation there was a rumble of echo. Something struck the roof of the fire cabin on Patagonia.

Wil Edwards smiled with satisfaction.

Stone and slate stopped falling, the crescendo becoming

diminuendo. A last rock fell, slithered, cracking harshly on slate, stopped.

Two more shots were fired, and then the all clear blew.

Shafto was first out of the hut, followed by Persimmon Hughes. Wil came after, slowly and modestly; he knew the shot had been a good one.

They gazed at the mass of rock and slate, the two northerners dourly pleased, while Shafto, the mercurial southerner, cackled with glee, talking non-stop.

They had work for at least a month, maybe even five weeks.

3

IT WAS six-fifteen in the morning, late July, the view from the cottage in the early light obscured by grey haze. Geraint slipped out of bed and went downstairs. His father was already up, laying the fire in the big kitchen. He laid a neat fire, economical balls of newspaper below a symmetrical arrangement of kindling sticks, of which he cut sufficient on Saturday afternoons to last the week. Wil Edwards did not look round as Geraint leaped up the steps that led from the dining-room to the kitchen; he continued to place small coal on the sticks, deliberately, as was his way of going about things. Then he took a box of matches from the floor beside him and handed it over his shoulder to Geraint.

Geraint lighted the fire. This was a morning ritual which he had performed every morning since he was five, missing it only during spells of mumps, measles, chickenpox.

'Thank you,' said his father, as he always did.

They both watched judiciously as the paper flamed, then turned away as the sticks caught fire.

'The kettle is boiling,' said his father, as he always did.

Geraint made tea while his father stripped to the waist and washed and shaved at the kitchen sink. There was no bathroom in the cottage, and the sink had to serve both for dish-washing and personal washing. Every week Geraint bathed in a polythene bath on a plastic sheet in the middle of the kitchen floor. Gwen Edwards washed clothes in a big electric copper. Even so, they were better off than many families in the cottages.

Wil Edwards was a freeholder. When he returned from

service with the Welch Regiment after the war he had bought the cottage with two hundred pounds saved from his pay as a company sergeant-major, and had used his gratuity carefully and wisely. The oil lamps had been the first to go; Wil had had the house wired for electricity before Geraint was born. When Geraint was six months old, and the nappies were beginning to make Gwen Edwards weary and irascible beyond all reason, Wil Edwards had said, 'We cannot have this,' and laid on the water. Along the opposite side of the road standpipes were fixed at intervals; the water main was thus only just across the road. But even an electric copper had to be filled, and it needed many buckets of water from the nearest standpipe. So Wil laid it on; it cost seven pounds ten shillings for the Council to bring a pipe under the road to the gate. They fixed a stopcock, and there they finished. Wil had a cousin in Caernarvon who was a plumber, so the rest of the work was done for him at cost. In no time at all there was a beautiful shiny cold-water tap over the sink. It was very cold water, too. Three years ago, succumbing to the inevitable, but proud as well, Wil Edwards had asked his cousin to install a water heater which worked directly from the pressure main, and they revelled in hot water. All in all, he thought, he had not done badly.

Geraint took a cup of tea up to his mother, who was wide awake and waiting for it, lying, Geraint thought, like a queen with her black hair spread on the pillow. He sat in the warm curve of her arm and held the saucer while she sat up and drank the tea. She sighed, replaced the cup on the saucer, rubbed her stomach below her heavy breasts, luxuriously, and gave a mock groan. She was always sweet-tempered in the mornings, so long as she had her cup of tea in bed, and the mood would last till after breakfast, till her husband and Geraint were safely out of the house. In his own interest Geraint had soon learned to make a cup of tea as his mother liked it: hot, strong, and sweet. Like his mam.

'Oh, well, time to get up,' she said, and Geraint left her to it.

His father had finished shaving, and it was Geraint's turn at

the sink. He washed his face and hands quickly, looked sur-
reptitiously over his shoulder, saw his father's eye upon him,
and resignedly washed his neck and ears. His mother came
down as he was brushing his teeth. Although Geraint was as
ready as the next boy to skimp washing, he brushed his teeth
with quite fanatical thoroughness, having a healthy fear of
dentists and a furious determination to avoid any more of their
attentions. He had seen things on the television commercials,
spiky demons of decay who sat in the gaps between your teeth
and chipped away at your enamel like quarrymen dressing
slate; and, though he was aware that their representation was,
to say the least, only approximate, he made a good job of
clearing them out. He spat them, invisible but deadly, into the
sink and turned the tap full on, filled his mouth with clean
water, just in case there were any stragglers left behind, and
chomped the water about in his mouth before blowing it in a
fine spray at the sink outlet.

Geraint then took a bag of meal from the cupboard under
the sink and went out into the backyard to the chicken run. He
fed the chickens and emptied the half motor tyre which served
as a drinking trough, refilling it with clean water which he
ladled from the rainwater barrel with a dipper. He watched the
fowls contemptuously, copying his Uncle Tom's attitude to
domestic poultry, which was one of searing scorn both for their
intelligence and for their qualities on the table. The hens
scurried about, clacking and quarrelling, while the old rooster
knocked a few of them about half-heartedly and then got
down to his breakfast.

It was time for Geraint's breakfast, too. When his mother
called he left the chickens and sat down at the kitchen table.
His father said a quick grace and then tucked in. You needed a
big breakfast if you worked in the quarry. Geraint's father ate
half a packet of cornflakes with a pint of milk, three rashers
of bacon with half a dozen sausages and a mound of baked
beans, followed by four thick slices of bread and butter with
marmalade. Geraint did his best, also.

His mother said to him, 'The amount you eat, boy, it is a wonder to me you are not as big as a tree.'

Geraint grinned.

His mother cut bread and made a pile of sandwiches, wrapping them in greaseproof paper and putting them in her husband's haversack.

Wil Edwards drank his tea, wiped his mouth with the back of his hand and said, 'Another cup, please, Mam.'

While she was pouring the tea he said, 'I do not like it, I do not like it one bit.'

'The tea?'

'No, no,' he said impatiently. 'I was telling you only the other day, remember? Every day since my last shot they have been blasting on Moonlight, blasting, blasting. There is enough work down there to keep them going for years without more blasting. They will be undercutting if they do not watch what they are doing.'

'They know what they are about,' Geraint's mother said.

Wil shook his head.

'You ought to be worrying about your brother,' the woman said.

Geraint asked, 'How is Uncle Tom, Dad?'

His father said, 'He has a cough from the bronchitis.'

His mother started to speak, but stopped at a small but decisive gesture from Wil. It was not lost on Geraint.

His mother sniffed.

'I know what you are doing, Wil Edwards,' she said. 'You are carrying Tom on your back, you and Simeon Hughes and that Shafto. What work is Tom doing for the money you earn?'

'That is a matter for us to decide. There is no better worker than Tom. You say we are carrying him; very well. That is as it should be.'

'Carrying him to the doctor, that is what you should be doing.'

There was a hoot outside in the lane.

'Shafto with his van,' Wil said gratefully, fetched his cap, picked up the haversack, kissed his wife, patted Geraint's shoulder, and went, breathing heavily with relief.

'That Shafto!' his mother said, and began to swirl round Geraint, collecting dishes and taking them to the sink.

Geraint fiddled with his teaspoon, tapping it on the cup and on the saucer.

'Mam?' he said tentatively.

'Get up, boy, if you have finished.'

'Mam, is Uncle Tom going to die?'

Gwen Edwards paused, dishcloth in hand.

'Whatever gave you that idea?' she said, amazed. 'No, of course he is not going to die. Hush now, and come and dry these dishes.'

Geraint dried the dishes and helped to stack them away, then slipped out of the kitchen, down the steps into the dining room, past the dresser with its ranks of willow plate, past the *tridarn*, that great cupboard with its secret drawers which not even Geraint knew how to open, and up the stairs to his grandfather's room. He turned the door handle stealthily and peered in.

His grandfather was still asleep. It was funny, you knew he was blind, but as he was lying there with his eyes closed, you forgot it. He looked like a picture of Abraham in a book at Sunday school. Geraint stole into the room and observed his grandfather, taking in the fragile texture of the wrinkled pale skin, blue-white, the sharp peaky nose, the patriarchal white beard with none of that nasty yellow in it. He looked somehow brittle, as though you could break off his ears like the handles of a jug. A faint rattle came from his sunken, parted lips, and then ceased. His teeth grinned at Geraint from the bedside table. Geraint loved his Taid deeply. Geraint's Taid knew everything and would tell you, if you cared to listen. He was so old and wise, though, that sometimes you had difficulty in keeping abreast of what he was telling you. Geraint loved him, certainly, but his almost geological age enabled Geraint to regard him

34

without any sentimentality. Ever since Geraint could remember, his parents had been diplomatically—they believed—preparing him for the old man's death.

How could Uncle Tom die before Taid? Taid was next. Why, Uncle Tom was Taid's son, incredibly, despite his stoop and his rheumatism and his cough and his peppering of white hair. And Dad was Taid's son. So Taid had to be next to go, it stood to reason. Otherwise it would make nonsense of things, the world would be sim-sam. Taid could be dying at this very moment. Perhaps he was. Geraint peered closer, interested, but his Taid was indubitably breathing.

Geraint was creeping out of the room when his grandfather said, 'Good morning, Geraint.'

Geraint halted, unastonished. They said old men's hearing worsened, but Geraint believed his Taid could hear a fly land on the ceiling, and he knew the old man passed from sleep to waking with none of the stretching, grunting, groaning and yawning which accompanied the awakening of lesser mortals.

'Good morning, Taid,' he said dutifully.

His grandfather said, 'I was not asleep. That van woke me up. It always does. Do you know, boy, a whole regiment of cavalry could thunder down this lane, and would not wake me, not one bit. But that van . . .'

His grandfather broke wind rudely, as he often did, and said, 'Butter will be cheap when grass grows down there.'

Geraint chuckled politely, though he had heard the cryptic statement five hundred times before, and said, 'Taid?'

'Well, boy?'

The words tumbled out.

'If Uncle Tom is going to die, because Dad says he has a cough from the bronchitis, but I know it is something worse than that, because I saw him shush Mam when she was going to say something, when are you going to die, because you are next, aren't you?'

'Boy, boy, whatever is in your head this morning?'

The old man heaved himself upright and got stiffly out of

bed, his blind eyes blinking. He gave a little yawn, no more than a bird's, then moved accurately to the window, lifting up the lower part of the sash and thrusting his head into the air.

'It will be a fine day,' he said, and stalked back. Abraham, the boy thought, white nightshirt and all.

'Now what is all this about Tom?' his Taid said, shivering and putting in his teeth. 'And hurry up. I want to get dressed. There is cold upon me like a vest made of ice.'

Geraint poured out his fears to the old man, who pulled his beard and nodded from time to time. As the upland morning chill struck harder he took a blanket from the bed and wrapped it round him.

'Well,' he said eventually, 'I can see it is time I got up. Listen to me, child. I have been told nothing of all this, but it will not take me long to find out. Now do not worry your head. Go down, and leave me to dress. And tell your mother I am coming down.'

Geraint went to the kitchen.

'Taid is coming down,' he said innocently. 'I told him about Uncle Tom.'

His mother raged at him, the breakfast mood suddenly gone as she rounded on him for interfering. He eluded her as she made a sudden grab at him, and dodged into the yard through the kitchen door, running past the squawking hens and up the steep path of the back garden, where small rowans and willows poked out of a wilderness of brambles and heather and bracken. He sat on a small rock outcrop and looked down at the roof of the cottage. He had done his bit; now it was up to Taid to sort things out. Even at that distance he could hear his mother's voice through the roof.

The blackberries were still green; Geraint tasted one experimentally, spitting it out with a grimace of disgust.

'I will go and see Uncle Tom after school,' he said to himself aloud. He plucked some white heather and took it down to the kitchen; his mother was nowhere to be seen and everywhere to be heard. Upstairs talking to Taid, he thought, without irony. He laid the spray of heather on the kitchen table and took his school satchel from its nail behind the kitchen door. Then he shouted, 'Good-bye, Mam. Good-bye, Taid,' and left the cottage.

He paused for a moment outside the gate, looking up at the window of his grandfather's bedroom. The front garden wall was seven feet high, and in the crevices of the stonework grew erica and ferns. Geraint grubbed for a small stone and threw it at his grandfather's window. He always did this as a final fare-well to the old man, who, after all, might be dead when Geraint came back. But when his mother's face, beautiful in anger, appeared at the window instead, Geraint gave a disappointed wave and ran down the lane to school.

Geraint quite liked school now. He had begun to work hard, and life had become a great deal more comfortable in conse-quence. He jostled and fought cheerfully with other boys in the playground, ignoring the girls for the most part, except to bait them, until the bell rang for morning assembly.

The headmaster, Mr Rhys, was a quiet man with a quiet voice. It was the sort of voice which never needs to be raised. The first few words were enough, and everyone stopped talking. Some people had to shout, and the result was simply that they shouted more and more loudly, vainly convinced that their one voice could make more noise than a hundred voices. They were wrong. But Mr Rhys just seemed to whisper, 'Good morning, boys and girls,' and everyone was as still as a bit of wood. The assembly began.

During the hymn Geraint's voice behaved oddly: it had taken recently to this eccentric behaviour. 'Your voice is beginning to break, Geraint,' they said, but did that help? Not a bit of it. It was disconcerting to be singing one moment in a pleasant treble, and then suddenly to slur a note like a record-player running down, croak like an old frog, and then pick up the treble again till next time. Geraint switched off his voice and opened and shut his mouth silently. He could hear Betty Mai Shafto two rows behind him, and could visualize her head bobbing with fervour, the open 'O' of her mouth as she gave the hymn all she had. *Ar Hyd y Nos*, hackneyed and inappropriate for a morning hymn, some might think, but Mr Rhys would not have cared. He knew it was a fine hymn, nothing like it for opening out young lungs before a morning at a desk.

After assembly Geraint nipped to the lavatory, and when he entered the classroom Mr Griffiths was sitting at his desk; the other members of the class were also seated.

Geraint explained the reason for his delay. Mr Griffiths nodded briefly, and Geraint made his way between the desks. He dropped his handkerchief with a studied air of unconcern by Betty Mai Shafto's desk, bent to retrieve it, flashed a glance, hissed, 'Pink knickers!' and sidled to his own desk, watching her blush as Mr Griffiths began to call the register.

Silly fat thing, Geraint thought. Betty Mai Shafto's blush was worth seeing, though. It started somewhere on her cheeks, but it spread like a fire, mantling her whole face, then her neck, with scarlet. Geraint watched it with satisfaction. That would teach her.

The first lesson was history. The class opened their notebooks, preparing for another dose of meaningless boredom. Betty Mai Shafto raised her hand.

'Yes, Betty Mai?'

'Please, sir, may I borrow some ink from Olwen?'

'Very well. Hurry.'

Betty Mai stood and moved behind Geraint, opening a safety pin as she went, and stabbed swiftly. Geraint howled with pain and fury.

'Geraint Edwards, stand up!'

Geraint was standing already, rubbing himself.

'Come out here.'

Geraint went, sheepishly, trying to think of a lie to explain his behaviour, but his mind was empty.

'Well?'

'Please, sir,' a voice piped up from the back of the class.

Billy Davies, Geraint said to himself resignedly.

'What is it, Billy?'

'Please, sir, Betty Mai stuck a pin in Geraint.' The voice paused a moment for effect, while Geraint stared, impassive as a clay model, at the blackboard beyond Mr Griffiths' shoulder. 'In his bottom.'

'Is that true, Betty Mai?'

A whisper.

'Speak up, girl!'

'Yes, sir. It—it is true.'

'Come out here, next to Geraint.'

Geraint heard Betty Mai come out and stand next to him; he dared not look at her.

'Face the class, both of you.'

They turned obediently.

Mr Griffiths said, 'You two are in your last weeks at this school, senior pupils, and yet you both persist in behaving like members of the babies' class. So I will treat you accordingly. Hold hands.'

This time, not only Betty Mai was blushing. Beetroot-faced, Geraint took Betty Mai's hand limply in his. To his astonishment she squeezed it; and, although he received a strange reassurance from the pressure, he tried to give a shout of protest, which came out as an unearthly croak. The class hooted.

Mr Griffiths said, 'Both of you repeat: "Little birds in their nest must agree".'

Betty Mai said sweetly, 'Little birds in their nest must agree.'

'Geraint?'

Geraint said venomously, 'Little birds in their nest must agree.'

'Good,' said Mr Griffiths through the laughter. 'Now, to your places. And let us have no more of this nonsense.'

During the last lesson of the day Mr Griffiths handed each pupil an envelope from the Education Office, enjoining them to take great care of it and hand it to their parents. Geraint knew very well what the envelope contained—a letter, and on that letter depended his destiny, for it would inform his parents whether Geraint was to be awarded a place in the grammar school that autumn or a place in the limbo of the local secondary modern school.

He stuffed the envelope into his trouser pocket.

School finished.

'Little birds in their nest must agree,' said Billy Davies in the cloakroom.

Geraint kicked him in the backside and said, 'Oh, lay an egg,' and emerged opposite the girls' cloakroom, where five girls were dancing round Betty Mai Shafto and chanting 'Little birds in their nest must agree.' She stood her ground tearfully but resolutely; Geraint fled.

His Uncle Tom lived on the far side of the village, north-west of the school. Geraint cut across the fields. You had to admit that Uncle Tom's house was terrible. It had only three rooms, for one thing; no water, for another; and it was very untidy and uncared for. Uncle Tom was a bachelor, and he didn't keep the place as trim as perhaps he ought to have done. Geraint pushed through a bank of tall flowering foxgloves, then kept carefully to the little path trodden through nettles and brambles to the front door, which was of weatherbeaten, spongy bare wood, except where a few streaks of sickly green paint still adhered. Geraint knocked, waited awhile, and then peered in through the dirty windows, knocking on the tiny panes and sending spiders scuttling for refuge.

Uncle Tom was not at home, so he would be either at the river or in the wood. The one advantage of Uncle Tom's place was its proximity to both. The river sang two fields below the cottage, and three fields above it the black brows of the wood frowned down. Geraint decided to try the river. He moved away through bleating sheep in the first field, and skirted the treacherous, boggy expanse of the second.

It was no use looking for Uncle Tom in the open. Geraint walked downstream on a small embankment, built in bygone days as someone's vain attempt to stop the bottom field flooding when the river was in spate. He continued till he came to a place where the bank was covered with bushes and small alders and willows.

You never saw a trout in the river; never the grey shape of a fish hanging in its feeding position, as in some other streams. Here the bottom was composed of countless small stones and fragments of slate. The trout lived in the cracks, shooting up from these to take flies and other food. This meant that if you fished a dry-fly you had to be deadly accurate: the fish's window of vision was maybe three inches in circumference, and you had to place your fly within that area; otherwise the trout just didn't see it. Visitors who thought they would try their hand at the dry-fly, since fish rose everywhere to feed on surface insects, generally gave up, cursing, because they didn't understand this; the locals for the most part ignored the rises and fished a leash of wet-flies downstream, philosophically hoping that the laws of probability would make up for the lack of skill. And they did. Uncle Tom, however, was not interested in trout at the moment when Geraint first caught sight of him, or of part of him. Uncle Tom's boots, showing brief, sockless sections of hairless white skin above them, were the only visible objects at that distance; good, strong, nailed boots they were, for upon his boots a quarryman's life could depend. They thrust incongruously out of the bushes, and Geraint thought with sympathy that Uncle Tom was losing his touch by letting them appear at all. He must be a sick man indeed. Coming closer, Geraint could hear the rasp of the man's breathing, and, craning his neck, could see his uncle lying on his belly, the upper half of his grey-shirted torso overhanging the water, his right arm in it up to the shoulder. There was a silver flash below the arm; the shoulder jerked convulsively, and Uncle Tom rolled backwards as his arm came up holding a gaff with a nine-pound salmon on it. He slipped the fish off the gaff, well away from the edge of the bank, then drew a knife and stabbed forward through the gills to the main artery, which lies under the tongue. He squeezed the blood out through a gill in a thin red jet, and the fish died quickly and quietly. Uncle Tom was panting, his face blue.

Geraint coughed; his uncle stiffened, and looked round.

'Did I give you a surprise?' Geraint asked.

The man said, 'You gave me a fright. Don't ever do that again, Geraint. The bailiff is over on Marchlyn Bach this afternoon, so we're all right.' He bent down to where his jacket lay among the bushes and took a large polythene bag from one of the pockets, coughing harshly as he did so.

'Dad said you had a cough,' Geraint said, looking keenly at his uncle for signs of impending death.

Uncle Tom tied the mouth of the bag with a loop of stout cord and slung the fish to his shoulder by the loop, so that the body of the fish in the bag hung at his side. Then he put on his jacket, tucked the head portion of the fish into the wide poacher's pocket in the bottom lining, and buttoned the jacket.

'What has your father been saying about me?' he asked.

'Well, not much, really. It was Mam. She said . . .'

He paused, embarrassed.

'Go on, boy. You can tell me.'

'Mam said—she said that Dad and the others were carrying you. I thought you must be ever so ill if they had to carry you, Uncle Tom. But you can walk. You must be able to, because you got down here, didn't you? And you caught a fish. I'm glad.'

Geraint was bubbling over with relief, but his Uncle Tom did not share in the gaiety. His mouth had tightened with a look of pain. He put a hand on Geraint's shoulder, heavily.

'Out of the mouths of babes and sucklings,' he said. 'Come, boy.'

He led the way back to his cottage. Halfway up the field next to it, he paused for breath and said, 'Look. A proper reception committee.'

Geraint's mother and grandfather were outside Uncle Tom's cottage. His grandfather was sitting patiently on the low stone wall and enjoying the late-afternoon sunshine. His mother was weeding the front garden, her wrists and forearms blotched with nettle-stings, and, as they approached, Geraint and his uncle could hear her muttering to herself. Geraint got behind his uncle and wondered which of them she would hit first.

'Here is Tom,' Geraint's grandfather said, without moving his head. 'And Geraint.'

The two of them had been walking on grass. Geraint stayed warily by his grandfather while Uncle Tom went a short way up the now considerably wider and neater path. Geraint's mother turned to face him.

'My, you have been busy,' Uncle Tom said admiringly. 'You——'

Geraint's mother cut him off at once.

'You ought to be ashamed of yourself,' she screeched. 'You are sick, are you? Sick! And we have been going out of our wits wondering where you were, thinking you might have dropped dead, indeed. And here you come as large as life with my Geraint (I'll have something to say to you later, young man)!'

Geraint wilted, edging closer to his grandfather.

Uncle Tom said, 'There is no need for this, Gwen. Calm yourself, love.'

'Calm myself, is it? Don't you understand that everyone is worried to death about you? And my Wil working himself to the bone to——'

'To carry me?' said Uncle Tom. 'Is that it?'

He paused, and Geraint's mother faltered, then tossed up her head and said, 'Yes. That is what I mean. It is not right.'

Geraint's grandfather said, 'Tom, my son, I did not even know you were sick until Geraint told me this morning. It is a hard thing, I know it myself, when a man becomes a burden to others. But it is in you to lighten that burden, and you must.'

Uncle Tom said, 'Yes. It was Geraint who told me also.' He said to Geraint, 'You have had a busy day, boy, all in all.' And to Geraint's grandfather again, 'I did not think. But there is no need to worry now. I will go to the doctor, and then I will apply for the disability pension, and then I will go before the medical board, and that will be the end of me with the quarry.' He grimaced, then made a smile out of the grimace, and said, 'It will give me more time for the salmons, and the birds.'

Geraint's mother exhaled and said, 'Well, I am glad you have come to your senses, Tom Edwards.'

'Leave it now, Gwen,' said Geraint's grandfather. 'It is time we went home. Wil will be back, and wanting his supper.'

Uncle Tom took off his jacket and slipped the loop of cord from his shoulder, holding out the salmon in its polythene bag.

'Here is Wil's supper, and a bit to spare, too.'

Geraint's mother made a gesture of refusal, but Uncle Tom insisted.

'Take it, Gwen. It is no more than his due.'

She deliberated.

'Coals of fire,' she said grimly, at last.

The man's voice softened, tenderly.

'Gwen, have you ever had your behind smacked with a salmon? Take it now, before I give you a good swish with it.'

The woman smiled suddenly, and took the salmon.

'Let me carry it,' the boy said, and his mother gave him the fish.

Gwen Edwards kissed her brother-in-law's cheek swiftly, touched his hand and said, 'Bless you, Tom,' then was leading Geraint's grandfather from the cottage, while Geraint bade his uncle a hasty good-bye and followed.

Carrying the salmon cradled in his arms, he soon passed the older people, and as he went he tried vainly to make sense of the events he had set in motion. He gave up finally, secure in the conclusions that everything seemed to have been sorted out, and that he was going to eat salmon for his supper.

All these happenings had caused him to forget the envelope which still reposed in his trouser pocket, but after supper his hand touched it accidentally, and he drew it forth.

'Dad,' he said, proffering the crumpled missive. 'I forgot to give you this.'

His father tore open the envelope, read briefly, then shouted, 'Gwen! The boy is going to the grammar school!'

4

AUGUST came, and Geraint left the primary school after his headmaster had given him a brief lecture about upholding the honour of the old school when he reached the new one. Mr Griffiths said no more than a casual word of dismissal to the class in general; there was no need of farewells, for Mr Griffiths lived in the village and would see his former pupils often. Besides Geraint, Betty Mai Shafto, Billy Davies, and seven or eight other of Geraint's classmates were going to the grammar school.

With August came the holidays, and the rain. Geraint spent much time fishing in the swollen river, hoping to catch a salmon. He did not succeed, but it whiled away the time, and once he caught a three-pound sea-trout.

August passed into September, and with September there arrived furious gales from the south-west, lashing the rain against the walls and roofs of the houses in the village. Geraint's father related how he had been swung on his rope like a spider on a loose thread of gossamer, then banged against the slate by a squall of wind which had spun him off his platform. But in the middle of September the winds dropped, the skies cleared, and the sun shone day after day. Geraint began to attend the grammar school, a co-educational establishment eight miles away, and a strange new world opened up: a world where the teachers wore academic gowns, where senior pupils were often taller than members of the staff; a world of algebra and French and Latin and similar mysteries. In the bus in the mornings and afternoons he sat as far as possible from Betty Mai Shafto. During the first week of the term he had a fight with Billy Davies, cheered on ironically by the older pupils. The fight seemed to clear the air, for Geraint and Billy became friends.

Billy's father was the Reverend Gwilym Davies, the minister of Moriah, which was the chapel attended by Geraint and his family. Mr Davies was a trifle vague in his manner, but he was well liked in the village, while Geraint had detested Billy as a telltale and a prig. The fight changed all that.

Betty Mai was blossoming out as a singer. Sometimes, infuriatingly, she would sing in the school bus, and Geraint hated her at such times. She had a reedy, true voice; at the new school she was learning to control her breathing and tone, and the results were already becoming evident; occasionally the bus conductor, dreaming as Betty Mai sang, would forget to ring a stop.

Geraint, on the other hand, was not doing so well in his singing lessons. His voice refused to settle down. His father insisted that it would do so in time, however, and so Geraint stuck doggedly to the lessons. His father was depressed by Geraint's apparent lack of progress, but was as stubborn as his son. Shafto needled Wil Edwards constantly by boasting about Betty Mai's prowess, and Persimmon Hughes was so preoccupied in keeping the peace between them that none of the men noticed, after they blasted in early September and after many more shots had been fired four galleries below on Moonlight, that a hair-crack appeared on top of Patagonia, so thin that it was almost invisible, but eighty feet long.

Geraint's Uncle Tom was awarded a one hundred per cent disability pension, and left the quarry, his place being filled by an amiable giant called Madog Parry.

September drifted into a golden October, days of grey morning mist through which the sun would break at perhaps half past nine, and would shine until it set in the silver strip of ocean visible from Geraint's cottage, away out in the Irish Sea beyond Abermenai Point. His grandfather no longer sat outside the cottage, for the early-morning sun had now left it, and did not touch it till almost two in the afternoon. The warmth began to fade, and the old man sat most of the day in the kitchen, close to the stove. Suddenly the peaks of Moel Eifion and Elidir Fawr, Glyder Fawr, Snowdon, Moel Eilio, and other of the highest summits were dusted with snow, which spilled down the less steep slopes. Geraint's father began to grumble as his output fell on account of the weather. The stars of winter came up over the horizon: Fomalhaut and Algol and the Square of Pegasus in the southern sky. A mild spell melted the snow on the mountain slopes, but not on the summits.

November, indeed, was a mild month that year. Geraint had scarcely the opportunity to notice the weather, except on his way to and from school, for he had a heavy load of homework, with the bases of new subjects to learn, and his father kept him hard at it. December, too, was mild, with much rain and blustery wind from the Atlantic, but it turned cold on the day Geraint finished his first term at the new school, and came home for the Christmas holidays clutching his school report.

That evening his father read the report.

'English: "Quite good. Spelling needs care." Welsh: "Good." Mathematics: "Good, though occasionally erratic." Latin: "Very good indeed." Handicrafts: "Fair only; tends to be slipshod." Music: "A good reader; voice has little promise"....'

Wil Edwards read no farther.

He looked up at Geraint, who was standing by Wil's chair, and repeated, 'Music: "A good reader; voice has little promise",' and then he said, in a growling voice, 'What fool wrote that of you?'

Geraint said, 'Mr Pickthorn. He is the music master.'

'He is an Englishman?'

Geraint nodded.

'I thought so. He must be stupid as well as English to have written that.'

Geraint said, 'No, Dad. He is not stupid. I think he is a good teacher.'

Wil Edwards said, 'Your voice is taking a little time to break, that is all. I have heard you in chapel, and I should know. There is nothing wrong with your voice. But your Taid shall hear you sing.' He said to Geraint's grandfather, 'Dad, will you tune your harp?'

The old man nodded at the fire and said, 'It is a long job, and I have not much inclination for playing these days. But I will do as you ask.'

He went down the steps into the seldom-used dining-room, and they heard him open the parlour door. They heard the faint scrape of a chair, and then the seemingly endless disconnected notes as the harp was tuned. At length Geraint's father made a gesture and led the way into the parlour.

The floor was of concrete covered with linoleum and a cheap Axminster carpet. There was a three-piece suite of imitation leather, and four cheap ceramic mallard, all drakes, flying in profile across the wall above the fireplace. In the far corner from the door stood the television set, in the opposite corner a grandfather clock.

Geraint's grandfather was sitting at a spindle-backed chair, the harp before him. He tilted it towards him and plucked a few chords; the notes rippled through the room, seeming to dance from the walls and the beams of the ceiling. Geraint's Uncle Tom had once said, 'Dear God, Dad, if you wanted to you could have the salmons jumping out of the water into your lap, and all the birds of the air clinging to your shoulders, if only you would go out and play to them.'

'Is Geraint ready?' the old man asked. 'What is it to be, Geraint?'

'Something with a bit of range in it,' Wil Edwards said. '*Ffarwel Mari.*'

Geraint sang the air while his grandfather accompanied him, occasional twinges crossing his face. Geraint was doing his best, anxious not to disappoint his father, but knew he was singing badly. He broke off, and a few notes of the harp hung in the air after him.

'I cannot go on,' he said. 'I am sorry, Dad.'

48

His father said stubbornly, but with an effort, 'There is nothing wrong with your voice. It will settle down.'

His grandfather said, 'My fingers are not as nimble as they used to be. Like a bunch of old twigs trying to pluck the strings.' He paused a moment and then said, 'Wil, that boy is a baritone, if he is anything.'

Geraint was biting his lip, trying to prevent himself from crying.

'May I go now?' he asked. 'I—I want to go for a walk.'

His grandfather said with understanding, 'Let him go, Wil,' and his father said wearily, 'Very well, but do not be late,' and Geraint fled from the house like a prisoner escaping.

There was no wind, and the moon had not yet risen, but the stars were bright above the peaks as Geraint trudged miserably along the lane. Why could his father not understand? he asked himself, and even as he asked the question he knew the answer in part at least, and intuitively felt something of Wil Edwards' disappointed pride. He knew nothing of Shafto's gibes and nothing of the intensity of the rivalry between the two men over their children's voices. He knew nothing of the way that rivalry had assumed a proportion out of all relation to its true significance, that for his father the honour of the north was at stake, no less, and that Shafto meant to show everybody that a voice out of the south was superior to a northerner's any day. But Geraint felt none the less that he had let his father down. It wasn't fair, he told himself. He would go and tell Uncle Tom about it, see what he had to say. But he was seeking comfort, not advice.

Uncle Tom was not at home. Geraint knew where he would be: drifting soundlessly through the black wood, his big catapult in hand, his pocket full of No. 5 pellets taken from twelve-bore cartridges. A bird, pigeon or pheasant, would be seen hunched black amongst the black branches, he would place a load of pellets in the catapult, and then, *swish!* and a dead bird. The method was much quieter and cheaper than using a folding gun, and no less effective.

Geraint made no attempt to find his uncle; for one thing, he would not welcome company, and, for another, Geraint had no desire to search the sinister wood. It was a frightening place by day and more so at night. Added to that, he might be shot by mistake.

Geraint turned from his uncle's cottage and ambled aimlessly on. In half an hour he had walked right up on to the eastern saddle; before him the road led down into the valley of the Nant Ffrancon, with Llyn y Mynydd a silver mirror down on the moor to his right. He halted, and sat on a wall, then heard music. He stood, listening, straining his ears, trying to fix the direction of the sound, and at length walked a little farther up the road and turned into a side lane. There was an expensive car parked there without lights, and beyond it a small cottage showing a yellow square at one half-open window. That was where the music was coming from. Geraint tiptoed through the gate and stood close to the window. He had heard plenty of music before, but never anything like this.

There was an orchestra playing, but for the most part he was hearing a violin, he decided, and got no further with rational thought, for the music took hold of him. He stood rigid, tears in his eyes, the glands at the back of his jaws reacting as though he had just taken a bite at a quince. It was less music than a miracle. That violin did things which Geraint's voice would never be able to do. It was singing, but more than singing, a melody which held him hypnotized, then a sudden delicate change which sounded like small antelopes dancing a minuet, then the singing again, up and up, soaring ineffably, but as controlled as, as . . . Why, it was like some sort of heavenly algebra, clear as the starlight.

A pair of jaws closed on his left hand, gently but very firmly, holding him round the wrist. Frozen with fear, he hardly dared look down, but when he did he saw the red eyes of a large dog. The music stopped.

A voice said in English, 'Bring him here, Hennessey,' and Geraint had to walk into the cottage as the dog pulled him forward. Inside, the light made Geraint blink. The dog was a big black labrador. Facing Geraint was a stout purple-nosed man in a dressing-gown, a shiny dressing-gown of deep blue silk patterned with gold dragons.

'Ha,' the man said. 'An intruder. What shall we do with him, Hennessey? Would you like him for supper, hey?'

Geraint said in Welsh, 'I meant no harm. I am not a thief.'

The man said, 'Speak English for God's sake, you unpleasant little brat.'

In English Geraint said, 'I did not mean to disturb you. I will be going now.'

'You'll be going, will you? Hennessey and I may have something to say about that. You Welsh, you're all the same. Sneaking about at night.'

Geraint said, 'I was walking on the mountain, on the road, and I heard the music. I would not have been stopping, but I heard the music.'

He paused, even now overcome by the memory of what he had heard, and the man looked quizzically at him, the stern lines of his face softening a little.

'The music?'

'I have never heard anything like it in my life,' Geraint said simply. 'I could not go from it.'

The man began to say something, broke off, and then started to laugh. Geraint was frightened and puzzled, but stood his ground while the incomprehensible laughter rang about him.

The man ceased laughing and said, 'Well, I verily believe, Hennessey, the little turd is telling the truth. Let go,' and the dog released the boy's hand. It was not even sore.

'So my old companion Mozart has got you by the short hairs,' said the man. 'And Hennessey, of course. An invincible combination. " 'Come into my parlour,' said the spider to the fly." '

Geraint wondered if he should run there and then, but the dog was sitting by the door, its mouth open and its tongue lolling out. Just waiting to grab him, he thought, and warily followed the gaudy dressing-gown.

The room had rough white walls of unplastered stone, a slate floor with small soft rugs scattered about, and horse brasses hanging near a curved sword above the fireplace. There was a sort of shield thing on one wall, and Geraint read on it '*Dominus Illuminatio Mea*'. Latin, he said to himself. 'The Lord My Light'. That unexceptionable sentiment reassured him a little. The man was mad, but perhaps not violent. As Geraint's eyes strayed from the man to the record-player in the far corner of the room, the dog came to him and sat beside his leg, leaning on it.

The man said, 'Hennessey approves of you. You may pat his head.'

Geraint did so, gingerly, and the dog acknowledged the attention with a brief thump of its tail, leaning more heavily on the boy's leg.

'So,' the man said. 'The music.'

He went to the record-player, opened the lid and switched on, lifting the pick-up and holding it poised.

'Listen again, then,' he said. 'Mozart. The G Major violin concerto.'

The music began, and Geraint stood there through it all, only half conscious of the man's gaze on him, the weight of the dog against his leg. When the music finished the record-player switched itself off. The click brought Geraint back to himself, and he let out a long sigh.

The man said, 'I'll be damned. It really has got you, hasn't it?'

Geraint said, 'Please may I sit down?'

His voice was small and shaky. The man indicated a chair, and Geraint sat, his leg suddenly beginning to quiver now that it was relieved of the strain of the dog's weight.

Geraint said with his best party manners, 'Thank you, sir, for letting me listen to the music. My name is Geraint Edwards, and I have been walking here from Nant y Bont.'

'Hennessey you know,' the man said. 'You and he have in a sense, ah, shaken hands. My name is Maitland. And now I think you had better be piddling off.'

Geraint said determinedly, 'That was a violin. The instrument playing the most, I mean.'

Maitland said, 'It's the usual thing in a violin concerto. The solo part.'

Geraint leaned forward eagerly and said, 'Oh, I understand. I have never seen a violin. Close to, that is.'

Maitland sighed and went over to a cupboard. He brought out a violin case and opened it.

It was beautiful, the boy thought, as Maitland lifted it out of the case and lights glinted from the patina.

'You can play the violin?' Geraint asked.

'Yes,' said Maitland shortly, replacing the instrument in its case and moving again to the cupboard.

Geraint swallowed and said, 'A long time ago I was saving seventeen shillings for something.' He picked his words carefully. 'I thought I would be needing it for something, but I have still got it. If I will be learning to play the violin from you will seventeen shillings be enough?'

Maitland paused at the cupboard door.

He said, 'My God, you've a cheek, haven't you?'

He closed the cupboard door without replacing the violin case, bringing it back into the middle of the room and taking out the violin again.

'Keep quiet,' he commanded, and tuned the instrument, his ugly, blue-veined face assuming the same rapt and far-away expression which Geraint had noted so often on his grandfather's face when he sat to the harp.

Maitland played a Bach bourrée, a thick roll of flesh squashed under his chin by the violin, and then regarded the boy.

Geraint sighed and then said, 'I would give anything to be able to do that.'

Maitland said, 'You will have to give everything. But seventeen shillings will be a start. What you don't pay for, you don't appreciate; there's too much spoon-feeding going on nowadays. I still think you're a cheeky young swine, but you're Welsh and I suppose you can't help it. I will divert myself. Come here the evening after tomorrow at seven. And now, for the second time, go away, before I tell Hennessey to tear the arse out of your dirty pants. I want to get drunk.'

5

GERAINT'S birthday was on 24th January. Two days
before, he was lying with his Uncle Tom in Prydderch's field of kale. They had crept on their bellies
under the broad leaves and between the rows of green stems.
The base of each leaf held perhaps an eggcupful of icy water
where it joined the stem, and, because he had shaken a few
stems in passing, Geraint's neck was cold and wet. He put up
with the discomfort, as Uncle Tom was after a pheasant for
Geraint's birthday.

Uncle Tom had made three previous daily visits to the field.
On each occasion he had taken with him a small, conical two-
ounce bag. He always bought peppermints two ounces at a time
for the sake of these bags. At a selected spot in the field he had
made a hole in the earth to fit the bag, and put a few brandy-
soaked raisins in the bottom.

'Look at it this way,' he had said to Geraint. 'Along comes the
old pheasant, says to himself, "This is very peculiar, very
peculiar: a raisin mine. What will they think of next?" and he
gobbles the raisins. Do it for him a couple more times, and he
expects the right to eat raisins from a bag in a field of kale.'

And they were now waiting for the pheasant. A new bag had
been placed in the little hole, and the raisins in the bottom.
Uncle Tom squeezed Geraint's arm, and they both froze. A
cock pheasant came strutting arrogantly along upwind through
the kale. He approached the hole where the bag was, pecked
uncertainly for a little while near it, and then suddenly put his

head in the bag to eat the raisins. But this time Uncle Tom had smeared golden syrup inside the top half of the bag, and the pheasant's head emerged with the bag stuck over it. Swiftly his foot came up to scratch it off, but too late. With a rustle and a heave Uncle Tom shot forward like an alligator. The tops of the kale swayed, water showered down, and then the pheasant's neck was wrung and the bird stowed away in Uncle Tom's pocket.

Geraint and his uncle walked wetly up the lane.

'That kale is no good at all,' said Uncle Tom. 'And Prydderch is a fool. He should have turned his beasts into that field months ago, and now the kale has bolted and it is beginning to rot. Still, it is good cover for the birds, whatever. This one cannot hang very long, if you are to have it for your birthday, but you do not like a bird to hang long, do you?'

'No,' said Geraint. 'I hate them when they are all green and smelly.'

They went into Uncle Tom's cottage, and Geraint drank hot tea while his jacket dried before the kitchen fire. The bird hung behind the door. Uncle Tom was breathing stertorously, coughing from time to time.

'Hell, devil,' said Uncle Tom. 'This cough is a plague of Egypt. I have my work cut out to keep myself from coughing when I am in the wood. But the coughing *is* the bronchitis: that much I know now. It is the squeaking and the heaviness in my chest that is the silicosis. The doctor said to me, "Dear God, man, you are carrying enough stone under your ribs to build a house!"'

Geraint announced importantly, 'I have been learning to play the violin.'

Uncle Tom said, 'It is the walk up here that brings it on. A council house, that is what I need, on the new estate.' He looked thoughtful. 'It would be farther from the wood, indeed, but closer to the river—on the other side, that is.'

Geraint said, 'Uncle Tom, I have been learning to play the violin.'

Uncle Tom stared into the fire and said, 'If I am honest with myself, perhaps I am getting a little too creaky for the wood. The salmons do not care if a man cough himself blue in the face, so it makes no odds so long as I know where the bailiff is, and I always do.' He paused, and then added, 'And the noise of the river helps to drown a man's cough. Up in the wood one cough does it: like a bomb in a cathedral. I will go and see the Reverend Davies, and he will help me to get a council house. This place is damp, too.'

Geraint said angrily, 'You aren't listening!'

'What did you say?'

Summoning up what was left of his patience, Geraint said, 'I have been learning to play the violin. Mr Maitland from that cottage, The Homestead, going over towards Tregarth, has been teaching me.'

'The violin? Maitland? A devil that man is, I tell you. I was at the back of his house one day and he set a dog on me.'

'Hennessey,' said Geraint. 'He is nice when you get to know him. Hennessey wouldn't really hurt anyone.'

'He had the seat out of my trousers as I was hopping over the wall. Just looking at a few raspberries, that is all I was doing; just looking. Well, well . . . the violin. Does your dad know?'

Geraint said shamefacedly, 'No. I have not told Dad.'

'He will have to know.'

'Yes.'

But how to tell him? Geraint had tried to bring himself over the past weeks to tell his father, but his courage had failed him every time. He had invented excuses for his frequent visits to Maitland's cottage: 'going for a walk', 'going to see Uncle Tom', 'going to see if Billy Davies is coming to play', and had hurried up the hill to Maitland's cottage, arriving out of breath, but with his keenness undiminished.

Maitland had given Geraint a hard time of it. He was a sarcastic and nagging teacher—'Not that way, you Welsh fool'; 'God give me patience, you hold the bow like a bloody butcher wielding a cleaver'; 'Why, oh why, did I ever undertake to aid a barbarian like you?' 'Christ, don't slap the bow on the strings and let it shiver there like a jellied eel. You can learn to play tremolo in a year or two.'

Geraint had borne up under the insults and abuse, and he was learning. He could play one or two simple airs. Maitland had used some of Geraint's seventeen shillings to buy a book of elementary exercises, and had expressed astonishment on finding that Geraint could read music. It was matter for wonder enough, he had said, that Geraint could read at all, let alone read music. Geraint endured Maitland, loved the dog Hennessey, and would allow nothing to deter him from learning. On the previous evening he had played a peasant dance, and to his surprise Maitland had said nothing derogatory.

'That was passable,' he had in fact admitted. 'Yes, I think that was passable.'

Geraint was not allowed to play Maitland's best violin, nor even to touch it. He had to make do with what Maitland called his 'third second-best'. The varnish was chipped and cracked here and there, but the tone was fairly good.

His Uncle Tom said, 'Well, you will have to tell your dad. If I were you I should speak to your Taid about it first, though.'

Geraint took home the pheasant, then sought out his grandfather and made a complete confession. The old man listened seriously, nodding as Geraint emphasized various points.

When Geraint had finished he asked, 'What shall I do, Taid?'

His grandfather thought, and said, 'It is your birthday the day after tomorrow.'

'Yes,' said Geraint. 'I am twelve.'

'This is what you must do,' his grandfather said, and told him. On the following evening Geraint visited Maitland's cottage, even though he had no lesson fixed.

On the morning of his birthday his parents wished him many happy returns of the day, but he was not allowed to see his presents until he came home from school in the evening. His mother had a slap-up tea ready, with trifle and jelly and *bara brith* on the table, and the pheasant a triumphant centrepiece. When Geraint's father came home they sat at table with the grandfather, Uncle Tom, and Billy Davies, whom Geraint had been permitted to invite to help deal with the pheasant.

After tea Geraint opened his parcels, which his mother handed to him. She had given him a heather-mixture sweater, knitted painstakingly and secretly over the previous weeks. He kissed and thanked her. His father's present to him was a landing net, and Geraint was overjoyed. He had tried in the autumn to buy a landing net with his seventeen shillings, but had been unable to find one cheaper than thirty. His Uncle Tom gave him ten shillings, while his father said, 'No, Tom, you should not do that, not on top of the pheasant, not out of your pension,' and his mother made protesting noises, and Geraint whipped the money into his pocket as fast as he could, in case they made Uncle Tom change his mind. His grandfather gave him nothing, but Geraint had not expected a present from him. Billy Davies gave him a packet of foreign stamps. Geraint was no philatelist, but appreciated the thought.

His mother said, 'There is this, too; it came with the post after you had gone to school,' and handed him a shapeless parcel.

'What is it, Mam?'

'How can anyone tell what it is until you open it, you silly cucumber?'

Geraint untied the string, removed the outer wrapping of brown paper, and the many layers of corrugated cardboard. Inside was Maitland's 'third second-best' violin, and a student-quality bow.

'A violin,' said Billy Davies. 'Here, let me see it.'

He grabbed the violin, held it like a guitar, and twanged the slack strings.

Geraint snatched.

'Give me that,' he said, and held the violin tightly to his chest, looking defiantly around.

'A violin,' his mother said wonderingly.

Geraint's father stood up.

'Who sent that?'

He moved closer, inspecting the instrument, and said, 'It looks a nasty old thing to me. Who sent it, I asked?'

Geraint said desperately, 'I didn't know he was going to send me this. He said I needed to practise at home, but I didn't expect . . . Oh, Dad, I have been learning to play the violin, and I am not going to sing any more.'

Wil Edwards took a deep breath.

He said to Billy Davies, 'It is time you went home, Billy.'

Billy said, 'But it is early!' He looked at Wil's stony face and said, 'Yes, well, perhaps I had better be going. Thank-you-very-much-for-the-tea-good-bye-everybody,' and vanished.

Wil Edwards said, 'Now then. We are all family here now.'

Uncle Tom said, 'Don't be hard on the boy, Wil.'

Wil Edwards turned to Geraint.

'What have you been up to?'

Geraint's grandfather said, 'I know all about it, Wil. Geraint has done nothing wrong.'

Emboldened, Geraint said, 'Mr Maitland The Homestead has been teaching me to play the violin, Dad. I thought—I thought it would be a surprise. Dad, my voice is no good. I thought this would make up for it, and would surprise you.'

'It surprises me right enough,' his father said grimly. 'You have been doing this without my knowledge.'

His mother said, 'Geraint, why did you say nothing about this? Your Taid says you have done nothing wrong, but you have deceived us.'

Geraint's lip trembled.

Uncle Tom said, 'Don't be silly, Gwen. If Wil had not been so pig-headed about the boy's singing this would never have happened.'

'So it is all my fault, then?'

Wil Edwards was pale with rage.

He went on, 'And where does this violin come from?'

Geraint said hopelessly, 'It is an old one of Mr Maitland's. The one I have been using. Mr Maitland must have sent it as a present so that I can practise at home.'

His father snorted with disgust.

'I shall have something to say about that. And I shall have something to say when I see this Maitland, indeed. A grown man sending presents to my son!'

What a birthday! Geraint was thinking. And he had been going to tell his father, anyway. Why couldn't things have worked out as his Taid had said they would?

The old man banged his foot on the floor petulantly.

'This is all nonsense,' he said. 'Geraint has told me all about his violin lessons. You should thank God he is having them, that is what I think.'

Uncle Tom said, 'Geraint told me about it, Wil, and I said he should tell his Taid before he told you. Why will you not leave the boy alone?'

Geraint's mother said, 'It seems as though his parents are the last to know.'

'It is natural enough,' said Geraint's grandfather. 'The boy should have learned the harp, but no, that was not good enough: he must be a singer. Before his voice broke it was not such a bad one, but now he has no singing voice. He should have been learning the harp. A violin cannot compare with a harp, but it is a stringed instrument whatever, and I will hear nothing against a stringed instrument.'

Wil Edwards said, shifting his ground slightly, 'I have not said anything against stringed instruments, have I? I am hurt and angry because my son has gone behind my back, and I do not know what else to think, either.'

Uncle Tom said, 'And we are telling you that the boy had no choice.'

Geraint said, 'I was going to borrow the violin to play for you and Mam, Dad. Taid told me to ask Mr Maitland last night, and I did, and he said I could borrow it. Perhaps it is not a birthday present after all; perhaps it is just a loan.'

Geraint was close to tears.

His father said, 'Well, we shall see. Get your coat. You and I are going to see this Mr Maitland.'

They walked in silence through the village. It was drizzling there, but as they turned right and moved up the hill out of the village, towards the saddle, the drizzle turned first to sleet, and then, as they climbed higher still, to snow. The night was dark, the peaks invisible; the only light came from the glimmer of snow on the ground.

They turned up the lane to Maitland's cottage, Geraint leading the way, and knocked at the front door. Wil Edwards was standing well behind Geraint, and Maitland did not see him at first.

Maitland said, 'Get back, Hennessey. Stay in,' and to Geraint, disgustedly, 'My God, it's you again. What the hell do you mean by it? You seem to think you can bust in on me any time you like, you little squit.'

Not knowing whether to be angry or relieved, Wil said in English, 'What do you mean, talking to my lad like that?'

'And who the bloody hell are you?'

'I am Geraint's father, and I want to know why you will be teaching Geraint to play the fiddle.'

'Come in, both of you,' said Maitland with resignation.

Wil Edwards went in, followed by Geraint, who bent and hugged Hennessey briefly. The dog licked his ear.

They shook the snow from their clothes and went into the parlour; Wil Edwards sat on the very edge of a brocaded chair, conscious of his big red hands, his enormous nailed boots. He twiddled his cloth cap.

Maitland said, 'So you are the father of this brat, and you have come here to protest most strongly about my teaching him the violin. You think it is quite outrageous, and you wish to forbid him to take any more lessons.'

Maitland was an impressive figure. He was dressed cleanly and soberly in a dark grey suit with a watered-silk tie and a light grey waistcoat. Geraint was glad, for Maitland might have been wearing the dragon dressing-gown and smelling of whisky.

Wil Edwards said, 'I did not say that. You have been teaching him. Why did you not let me know?'

'Good God, man, why should I let you know? The boy is your child, presumably; he should have told you himself. But it is of a piece, mark you: it is of a piece.'

'What do you mean?'

'Now listen to me,' Maitland said. 'What do you think I am, a retired music-teacher or something? I am not. Not at all. I am a retired tea-planter. But I used to play the violin six hours a day, and, though I say so myself, I play it well. I do not teach the violin. But your son, with whose qualities you appear, if I may say so, to be very imperfectly acquainted, virtually compelled me at pistol-point to give him lessons in the violin. I did not particularly want to, nor do I, and if you forbid him to have these lessons there will be no one happier than I, my good man; I shall dance with bloody glee; is that clear? The boy should have told you; it is of a piece that he did not. And yet I feel, in all fairness to him—in so far as it is possible to be fair to such an incubus in human guise—that I cannot be surprised he did not tell you.'

Bemused by this spate of words in a foreign language, Wil Edwards took refuge in rounding on Geraint.

'What have you been doing, Geraint?' he asked suspiciously.

'He has paid me to teach him,' Maitland said.

'Paid you?' said Wil incredulously.

Geraint looked important.

'Seventeen shillings,' said Maitland. 'All above board. Not what one would call a handsome fee, but a fee.'

Geraint said to his father, 'I had been saving the money to buy a gun—that is, a landing net. And then I heard the music from Mr Maitland's house, and I asked him to teach me how to play the violin, and I paid him. Oh, Dad, please let me go on learning.'

Wil Edwards was confused.

Maitland said encouragingly, 'Go on, man, forbid him.'

Wil Edwards said, reacting with hostility, 'No, I will not!'

'So he may continue to learn, then?'

Feeling trapped, Wil said sulkily, 'Oh well, I suppose so.'

Maitland sighed and said, 'Then that's that. For one moment of pure joy I thought I was going to get rid of him.'

He winked covertly at Geraint.

Wil Edwards said, 'He had a violin with the post today. Did you send it?'

'Yes, I did.'

'I will not have you sending presents to the boy,' Wil said, feeling on safer ground at last. 'It is not fitting that a grown man should send presents to a boy.'

Maitland said, 'The boy has told me that you wanted him to sing. Tenor, too. Well, I have heard him. The boy sings like a baritone bloody jackdaw, but at least when he was trying to sing he didn't have to buy a voice, and he was able to carry his voice around with him. You have to buy a violin, you understand, or beg or borrow or steal one. I couldn't see him buying one, though I could quite see him begging or stealing one, so I considered that he should borrow one. Why, man, do you think I would give away one of my violins? You must be out of your mind, and you owe me an apology.'

Nettled, Geraint said, 'No, he does not. It is my fault in a way. Today is my birthday, and when you get things in the post on a birthday you think they are birthday presents.'

'No,' said Wil Edwards. 'Mr Maitland is quite right. I have been hasty, and I am sorry.'

He was sitting up straight, his nervousness gone, and the monumental hands and feet suddenly seemed to lend him a monolithic dignity. Like a rock, Maitland thought: heavy and hard and dour and slow to move, perhaps, but there was something there all right.

He said courteously, 'That is handsome of you, sir.'

Geraint gaped. Mr Maitland had called his father 'sir'.

Suavely Maitland continued, 'I am pleased that we have come to an agreement. The boy will continue to learn. Now, to derive the utmost benefit from his lessons he must practise at home. Ideally, he should have his own violin, but he has not, and so it is best if he borrows that old one of mine.'

Wil said, 'How much does a violin cost?'

'You could have a good one made for fifty pounds. One not so good, thirty.'

'It is a lot of money.'

'Quite.'

Maitland paused as though struck by a sudden thought.

'He should have his own violin,' he repeated. 'Now look, Mr?—Mr Edwards, that old violin I sent—I would sell that. It needs a little attention, and you would have to buy a case for it.'

'Well, I don't know. . . . How much?'

'Ten pounds.'

Wil Edwards sat in deliberation, while Geraint held his breath.

'Very well.'

They walked home, side by side this time. It was snowing in the village now that the temperature had dropped, and the snow was drifting against the stone walls of their lane. Geraint thought, I've got a violin of my own!

He squeezed his father's arm and said, 'Dad?'

'What is it?'

'Dad, Mr Maitland called you "sir". Did you hear him call you "sir"?'

Geraint's father grunted, secretly pleased.

They went into the cottage, shaking the snow from their clothes in the doorway.

Geraint's mother and grandfather and uncle were sitting in the parlour; so was the minister. The television set was switched on with the sound cut, so that the figures on the screen moved and spoke silently; Geraint saw the reflected light flickering from the sounding board of the golden harp as he entered the room with his father.

'Oh, good evening, Mr Davies,' said Wil, who was taken aback at finding the minister present.

Geraint's mother said, 'Billy thought there was trouble brewing, and sent Mr Davies up to see if there was anything he could do. I have told him what has been happening.'

The minister said, 'What took place at Maitland's, Mr Edwards? You have not been indulging in violence, I hope?'

Wil laughed.

He said, 'I went up to Maitland's to punch him on the nose, and I ended up by buying a violin.'

He shook his head wryly.

Geraint said, 'Dad bought that violin for me. It was not a present after all, but it is now, from Dad. I have never had such a birthday before. Mr Maitland called Dad "sir".'

His grandfather said, 'You have done well for yourself, young man.'

'Then all ended well. I am glad,' said the minister happily.

The old man said, 'No, not yet. For now Geraint shall justify all this. He shall play for us.'

Geraint said, 'Dad, I was going to tell you today, and play for you as well; Taid said that I should. But—but—oh, all right, I will play.'

He fetched the violin and bow.

As his grandfather had advised him, Geraint played the air *Y Ferch O Blwy Penderyn*. He played uncertainly, and made several mistakes, but as he was finishing he noticed that his father had clasped his mother's hand.

Geraint's mother pulled her hand away and said, 'Old silly!' to her husband.

Uncle Tom and Geraint's grandfather clapped when Geraint finished.

Uncle Tom said, 'That was very well played indeed.'

'Very nice,' said the minister.

Geraint's grandfather said, 'It cannot compare with the harp, not for one moment. But it is an agreeable little toy, and you do not play too badly, Geraint.'

Geraint's mother said, 'And you are a cunning old fox, telling Geraint to play that tune. You had Wil in a proper hazz-mazz there.'

Wil Edwards coughed and looked sheepish.

The minister said, 'I am afraid I do not understand. Why?'

Geraint's mother said, 'Oh, come, Mr Davies, you know the song. *Y Ferch O Blwy Penderyn.* You know, it is the song a man sings about his sweetheart Gwen.'

'Be quiet, woman!' Wil exploded.

'Oh,' said the minister, who habitually missed every point going.

Uncle Tom sniggered.

Geraint's mother said, 'He used to try to sing it to me, poor dab, but his voice was never really up to it.'

The old man said, 'When he was courting Gwen, Mr Davies, he would drive us out of our wits with that song. Never off his lips; a terrible noise, like a dying bluebottle.'

Geraint's mother said to her husband, 'You should have learned the violin, Wil. I might have married you a year earlier.'

6

THAT February the ice on the rock outcrop in Geraint's back garden was four inches thick. The Council had salted the lane and laid down gravel chippings, but at the sides there were long stretches of ice which enlivened Geraint's journey down to the village to catch the school bus in the mornings; he could slide for yards at a time downhill, sometimes turning as he slid and falling into crisp, rime-crusted grass at the verge. The air was clear and still, and Moel Eifion's steeper faces, where the snow could not lodge, were black against the brilliant white of the easier slopes.

One morning Geraint found himself sitting next to Betty Mai Shafto.

'Move up a bit,' he said irritably. 'Taking up all the seat.'

My, she was fat, he thought, grimly squashing her sideways as the bus began to move off and the usual morning uproar began. He opened his school satchel.

Betty Mai said in English, 'You haven't done your homework, I assume?'

He answered in Welsh, 'Mind your own business,' and opened a book. He began to write, pausing frequently in thought; the bus bumped, making his hand swerve crazily as he wrote.

Betty Mai observed primly, 'No wonder Mr Watkins says your handwriting is akin to the marks made by a drunken spider which happens to have emerged fom the inkwell into which it has fallen, and wandered haphazardly over the page.'

'Oh, belt up,' Geraint said, 'and let me get on with this essay.'

He remembered a phrase of his grandfather's and added, 'You are enough to make a sow farrow.'

'We went to tea with Billy Davies yesterday,' Betty Mai announced. 'Mam and I, I mean. Billy played some Gigli records. At the beginning Mr Davies said, "Who is singing?" and Mrs Davies told him, "Gigli," and after the first song he said, "Who was that, Ritchie Thomas?" and she said, "No, Gigli." In a little while, after another song, Mr Davies said, "Well that one was Ritchie Thomas, wasn't it?" and Mrs Davies said, "No, I tell you, it's Gigli," and at the end Mr Davies said, "I think that was Ritchie Thomas. You know what, he sounds a bit like Gigli, don't you think?" And then he said, "That Gigli, he is a good basso, too"!'

Geraint said virtuously, 'You should not tell tales about a minister, even if he is a bit tone-deaf. It is not right. And will you shut up?'

Betty Mai asked innocently, 'And how is your singing coming on, Mr Gigli?'

She had wide blue eyes, fat pink cheeks, and a wide mouth with small white teeth. About a million of them, Geraint thought with revulsion.

He said, 'I have stopped singing. I thought you knew. I am starting to take violin lessons after Easter. Why don't you go on a diet or something?'

That shut her up, he thought with satisfaction as she began to blush.

'Fat thing,' he added.

Betty Mai turned her head to the window so that Geraint could not see the tears in her eyes, and he gazed past her across the lake to where the Moel Eifion brickworks sent up its pall of dust into the sparkling air.

On the following morning Wil Edwards was working at the bottom of Patagonia, dressing slate. The watercourses were frozen, the places on the cliffs of slate which had been wet with running water were now black with ice, and on every flat surface lay the snow.

Wil had begun working on a block of slate weighing perhaps four hundredweight. He studied the block carefully, then, picking up hammer and gouge, he hammered a wide dotted line down one end of the block, exactly at right angles to the cleavage plane of the slate. He dropped the gouge and took up a big, wide chisel and a heavier hammer. He placed the chisel again at right angles to the cleavage plane, adjusted it fractionally, and hit it very hard. Then he levered out the chisel and inserted a wedge, hammering it in until, with a loud noise, the slate split and the block was cut in half across the line of cleavage. Wil then cut each half into two parts along the cleavage line, and paused, his legs braced against the wind as he grinned over at Madog Parry.

'Come on,' he shouted. 'We will go up for the others and then have our tea.'

Madog Parry nodded, and the two men went up to the top.

Persimmon Hughes and Shafto were at the far end of Patagonia top, ostensibly clearing rubble, but in fact sitting cosily in a cranny of rock out of the wind, smoking. Persimmon Hughes waved as the two men approached.

'Time for tea, then?'

Madog Parry said, 'Well, there you are, sitting on your backsides, eh?'

Wil was tired, cold, and angry.

He said, 'Why could you not have come down if you were not working? You would have saved Madog and me our legs.'

Shafto said, 'There's good for you, a little bit of exercise. Warm you up, like.'

Wil said, 'You two are getting slack.'

'Don't be silly, Wil,' said Persimmon Hughes. 'We are the only fools working above Jim Crow today, you know that. It is too cold. I am not coming tomorrow if it is like this.'

Madog Parry said, 'We could ask to go in the sheds.'

Wil said, 'I would rather breathe this wind than the dust in the sheds.'

Persimmon Hughes said, 'You have been driving us like a slave-driver, Wil. What is the matter with you that you want to work like this when no one else is within three galleries?'

Wil said, 'If you are too soft you know what to do.'

Persimmon Hughes sighed and said, 'You are a hard man, Wil.'

Shafto said, 'Money, that's what Wil is after, isn't it, Wil? Going to train his lad at Covent Garden, maybe—with the voice that boy has it will be in the vegetable market and not the Opera, mind.'

Wil said quietly, 'And what does that mean?'

Shafto smiled.

He said, 'Oh, no, sorry. I am getting my facts wrong. Now what did I hear . . .? Oh, aye, that's it. The boy is sacrificing a fine singing career to play the one-stringed fiddle. That's right, isn't it, Wil?'

Madog Parry said, 'What are you talking about, man?'

Wil stood up, his trousers flapping about his legs in the wind, and said, 'He will not be talking at all, soon, if he says much more.'

Shafto said, 'Do I see him getting his rag out? Why, lads, don't worry: he is only pretending. He knows that he has been saved from a great shame, and he will no longer have to go around making out that kid of his can sing. The field is clear for the kid's betters.'

'Meaning?'

'Why, Betty Mai. Who else?'

'Get up,' Wil Edwards said slowly.

Shafto stood lazily, still smiling, and said, 'You croak like an old crow. How could you expect a brat of yours to do any better?'

Wil Edwards swung his fist; Shafto launched himself under it, driving with his shoulder into the other man's chest. Wil staggered backwards and fell with Shafto on top of him. Shafto hit Wil on the left cheek-bone and as Wil's head cracked against the icy rock Shafto jumped to his feet ready to kick, slipped, and fell in his turn, cursing. Both men rose at the same moment, and came together shoulder to shoulder, wrestling.

'Stupid fools!' said Persimmon Hughes.

'It will keep them warm,' Madog Parry said. 'They are evenly matched. Wil is bigger, but Shafto is broader.'

Wil and Shafto struggled, Shafto pushing Wil backwards to the edge of the precipice. Again they slipped and fell on the ice; Wil's head struck nothing but air, and he wriggled convulsively away from the drop, bringing his knee up at Shafto's crotch but catching him on the side of the thigh instead. They got to their feet and wrestled again, their nailed boots crossing and recrossing the long thin crack in the rock below the snow and ice: it was the thickness of a matchstick and a hundred and twenty feet long. Once, when Wil fell again and Shafto ground his nose into the surface, his eyes saw a tiny bared section of the crack, perhaps three inches of it, without recognizing it for what it was.

It was impossible for either man to keep his feet on the slippery surface for long, but still they fought, reeling, falling, rising again, falling again. They were panting now, and Shafto's lip was split; Wil's nose was bleeding profusely, and, as his head jerked, red drops spattered the snow round about. He rushed at Shafto, forcing him backwards along the gallery and raining blows to Shafto's ribs.

'Be careful!' shouted Persimmon Hughes, coming forward with Madog Parry.

Wil was past caution, thrusting Shafto farther backwards. Shafto tried to make a stand, grunting and hammering counterpunches to Wil's face, but he could not set himself properly. The ground began to slope away to the edge of the gallery, where it tailed off above Monkey Brand, which in its turn lay above the Eifion Slabs. Shafto slipped, fell, and then began to slide helplessly, so gently that it seemed like slow motion, while his hands scrabbled at the ice. Still slowly, slowly, his legs went over the edge, then his thighs. Shafto's eyes were staring straight ahead, his arms stretched out in front of him. He seemed to have stopped breathing, and to be concentrating on the slow progress of his fingers over the ice. They halted as his body momentarily balanced, but he could not move.

'The rope,' yelled Wil, and slid down full length after Shafto, his open knife in his hand. He slowed himself both by digging in with the toes of his boots and by thrusting the knife blade into the ice. His free hand touched Shafto's, and with the other he drove the knife blade in at an angle into Shafto's jacket sleeve, holding it there. For a moment the two men stared each other in the face, teeth bared and clenched, then mouths gasping like lovers in ultimate ecstasy. Wil felt his legs begin to slip sideways, once more in that unbearable slow motion, and he gazed past Shafto's shoulder, down over the Slabs to the lake below. On the roadway of Jim Crow he saw three black doll-like figures gesticulating. Then the rope hit him in the back, falling over him to Shafto, who grabbed it. The knife was jerked out of Shafto's sleeve and out of Wil's hand; he saw it twinkle two or three times as it fell, and then he had grabbed the rope too. His legs slid round and hit Shafto, who grunted but still held on. Persimmon Hughes had belayed the rope, and he anchored it while Madog Parry hauled the pair up to safety.

'The less said about that the better,' said Persimmon Hughes. 'Are you both mad?'

Wil said, 'It is a short way down from Patagonia that way, indeed. I have lost a good knife.'

He got to his feet and applied a handful of snow to his nose. Shafto said nothing.

The four men made their way silently down to the big cabin on Top Hat and drank their mugs of tea. They fobbed off the overseer, saying that they had had a slight fall, and that there was no need to make out an accident report. The few other workers in the cabin were unconvinced. They noticed that Wil and Shafto were not speaking to each other, and wondered amongst themselves. Never mind, they could wait. On Friday evening, when Madog Parry had drunk a few pints in the Prince of Gwynedd, they would find out what had been happening.

7

AND so the feud began. Wil and Shafto, though co-operating at work, spoke to each other no more than was necessary, and all the efforts of Persimmon Hughes to reconcile them proved useless. The two men were withdrawn and hostile. It had not taken Gwen Edwards long to elicit the truth when Wil had come home with a skinned nose and a bruised cheek-bone, and with the knees and elbows out of his clothes. Two days later she had encountered Mrs Shafto in the butcher's, buying a breast of lamb.

'Breast of lamb!' she sniffed.

Mrs Shafto bridled.

'And what is wrong with breast of lamb, might I ask?'

Mrs Shafto was a short, fair woman, who affected elaborate hats.

Gwen Edwards said, 'Oh, nothing at all, for those that cannot afford any better. Nothing at all. Have it by all means. Come to think of it, I will put it on your greengrocer's barrow for you.'

Mrs Shafto was wearing a large blue hat trimmed with artificial fruit. Gwen Edwards snatched the breast of lamb from the butcher's hands, said, 'Don't bother to wrap it, Owen, it will look a treat just as it is,' and slammed it down on Mrs Shafto's hat.

The butcher, a thin and earnest man with a clerical air, said, 'Dear me, Mrs Edwards!'

Gwen Edwards picked up the butcher's cleaver and shouted, 'You shut up, or I will have your head off with your own

74

cleaver, Owen, and this woman shall wear it on top of the breast of lamb. There is blood in my eye, Tabitha Shafto, there is blood in my eye.'

Mrs Shafto backed out of the shop, and passers-by were intrigued to see her with the breast of lamb on her head.

'Suits you a treat,' someone shouted.

Gwen Edwards stood at the shop door, brandishing the cleaver, and Mrs Shafto went fully fifty yards down the street, snivelling with fear and humiliation, before removing the breast of lamb from her head. Then, distance lending her courage, she turned and shouted, 'I will have the law on you, the law, I am telling you.'

'Don't be silly. You will want a witness or two for that. Who do you think will be a witness?'

'We have not seen a thing, indeed,' somebody said. 'Go home now, Mrs Shafto.'

'Go back to the south where you came from,' Gwen Edwards screeched. 'And take that ape of a husband with you, though what good he is to anyone I cannot imagine.'

The whole weight of village opinion was not on the side of Gwen Edwards in this episode, nor was it unanimous about the situation in general. There was a division of feeling. Owen the butcher, for example, sided with Mrs Shafto, and hence with Shafto. Firstly, he had been at school with Gwen Edwards, and she had always bullied him. Secondly, Mrs Shafto was a better customer than Gwen Edwards, who received much illicit game from her brother-in-law. And, thirdly, he never recovered the price of that breast of lamb. Mrs Shafto refused to pay for it on the ground that it had been soiled; and he dared not ask Gwen Edwards to pay. Only one-and-fourpence, to be sure, but who was he to turn up his nose at one-and-fourpence?

The chapel was equally divided among those who backed the Shaftos because of Betty Mai's voice, and those who backed the Edwardses because Wil was a big man in the chapel whereas Shafto went there only occasionally, to hear Betty Mai and not on account of the services. Within a month half the people in the village were not on speaking terms with those of the opposite half. Mr Davies, the minister, pursued a hopeful but ineffectual policy of non-alignment, rather like Mr Nehru before the Chinese invasion.

Much of this passed above Geraint's head. He was still visiting Maitland, but found that the skilled teaching in the violin which he received at school was of more value than Maitland's lessons. The music master, Mr Pickthorn, had been overjoyed to acquire a violin pupil. 'The violin?' he had said. 'Of course you may learn the violin, Edwards. I can get three choirs out of every form in this school, but apart from about twenty people at various stages of giving up the piano, and twenty trying to learn the electric guitar, you will be the only instrumentalist here. I will teach you myself.' More and more, Geraint encouraged Maitland to play, and watched his execution with absolute concentration. He then strove to put into practice what he had observed, and this was a great help to him. He was too preoccupied to bother with the feud.

Nevertheless, at school both Geraint and Betty Mai Shafto kept out of each other's way. In the school bus they could scarcely do this, and were often compelled to sit together when all other seats had been occupied. Betty Mai's elder brother, Maldwyn, travelled in the school bus, and he knew perfectly well what the situation was. From time to time he would trip Geraint by thrusting out a foot as Geraint made his way down the bus, or would knock Geraint over as they alighted. Maldwyn was sixteen, and big for his age; there was nothing Geraint could do about this petty persecution. To confide in his parents or a teacher was unthinkable.

Late spring became early summer; the yellow bells of the Welsh poppy bloomed amongst the riverside grasses, and mossy saxifrage dotted the screes of the upper slopes. On the surface of Llyn Padarn in the late evenings the rings made by rising trout welled out and faded and renewed themselves unendingly. The week-end climbers, who came all the year round, began to be supplemented by anglers and general holidaymakers. The cars and lay-bys filled; the hot-dog stands appeared; salmon began to run up from the sea into these late rivers; the first run of sea-trout came. All in all, with school and homework, violin practice and fishing, Geraint was very busy, and tolerably happy.

One afternoon, coming home from school, Geraint was sitting in the front seat of the bus with Billy Davies. Betty Mai Shafto sat in the opposite seat, and the three formed the nucleus of a small group of third-formers, who still found it exciting to travel near the front of the bus. Maldwyn Shafto, older and more sophisticated, sat amidships where the jolting of the vehicle was not so pronounced. Maldwyn desired above all else to play rugby football for Wales; he was mentally making a brilliant run from the Springboks' twenty-five-yard line to score a wonderful try, which he himself converted, and, having done so, was basking in the applause from a huge crowd at Arms Park, Cardiff. He ran through the game a few more times in his head, then composed some newspaper headlines: 'Brilliant new Welsh forward', 'Maldwyn Shafto—Wales strikes gold', and so forth. At intervals, when the light was favourable, he would study his reflection in the window of the bus. He liked it, for in the imperfect reflecting surface the pimples were hidden. These activities lasted him throughout the homeward journey, and when the bus stopped in Nant y Bont Maldwyn alighted and made his way dreamily home, signing imaginary autographs.

Geraint and Billy Davies, with Betty Mai and Olwen Morris, lingered in the street after the bus had turned round and gone. They were continuing an argument which had sprung up shortly before the bus had reached the village.

Olwen Morris, a pale, thin girl, said, 'It is true. I heard it on the television, and I saw a woman who could do it.'

Geraint said, 'Well, why didn't she do it on television, then?'

Betty Mai Shafto said, 'Silly, they wouldn't let her. If she could break glasses with her voice, and they had let her try on television, she might have broken millions of glasses everywhere in people's houses.'

Billy Davies said, 'I bet you could break a glass, Betty Mai. Have you ever tried?'

Geraint scuffed the sidewalk with his shoes.

' 'Course she hasn't,' he scoffed. 'She couldn't do it. Her voice is not loud enough.'

Betty Mai said, 'My voice is as loud as anybody's, let me tell you, Geraint Edwards. You haven't a voice, so who are you to talk?'

Olwen Morris said, 'I bet she could break a glass with her voice if she tried.'

Geraint said, 'Has anyone got a glass?'

No one had.

'Well,' said Geraint, 'have a go at Owen's shop window. That's glass, isn't it? Sing at that.'

Billy Davies said, 'That is plate glass. It is different. You could not break plate glass by singing at it.'

Geraint grunted.

Olwen Morris said, 'You could hear Betty Mai from the top of Moel Eifion if you stood down here at the top of the street, away from the traffic.'

Billy Davies said judiciously, 'No. No, that's too far. I do not believe that.'

'No more do I,' said Geraint.

'I bet you,' said Betty Mai.

Geraint said, 'I dare you to try.'

Betty Mai hesitated.

Geraint said triumphantly, 'You are afraid!'

'I am not afraid!'

'Yes, you are!'

Billy Davies said, 'Well, if you are not afraid, why not try?'

'All right,' said Betty Mai. 'I will. I am not afraid, I say.'

Geraint was incredulous.

'She would take a trumpet or something up there and blow that, and say it was her voice.'

Billy Davies said, 'Someone will have to go and see fair play.'

Olwen Morris said, 'Let Geraint go, Betty Mai. I will listen with Billy.'

Geraint thought of the summit of Moel Eifion. He had never been there, but he could imagine the twin ridges of Crib y Geifr and Crud y Gwynt springing down on each side of the sheer face above the quarry, and he felt a prickle of fear.

'It is too late,' he said.

Billy Davies waved aside the objection.

'Tomorrow is Saturday. What is wrong with tomorrow?'

Betty Mai said, 'I will go tomorrow, but not if it rains.'

Geraint said, desperately, 'I have to practise my violin tomorrow.'

'You cannot practise all day,' said Olwen Morris. 'Do that in the morning, and go up with Betty Mai in the afternoon—if you dare, that is.'

Geraint was trapped.

'Very well,' he said.

'We will all meet here at two o'clock,' said Billy Davies. 'And no one is to tell anybody else about this.'

Betty Mai said, 'I am not going if it rains.'

Geraint prayed for rain, fervently but vainly; the following morning dawned in a grey haze which promised a fine day. He practised his violin grimly for two hours in the parlour, while his grandfather sat by the window, listening and dozing as the increasing warmth of the sunlight made him sleepy; Geraint watched the sun on the old man's face and cursed.

After the midday meal he said, 'I am going fishing,' and gathered his tackle together, except for his rod, which he still kept hidden by Llyn Eifion. Then he made his way down to the village.

Betty Mai was waiting, and so were Billy Davies and Olwen Morris.

Billy Davies said, 'You will not get up there until five o'clock, say five-thirty to be on the safe side. Olwen and I will listen at five-thirty for half an hour.'

Betty Mai said, 'I have told my mam I am going for a picnic with Olwen. I have some sandwiches.'

Geraint had not thought of sandwiches. He said nothing.

'Are you ready, then?' asked Betty Mai.

'Yes.'

Geraint handed his creel and landing net to Billy to keep for him.

Betty Mai said to Olwen Morris, 'Now you take care my mam doesn't see you.'

She and Geraint walked up the street in silence, turning once to wave to the others.

At the end of the street Geraint said. 'We must not go past my house. Come on, up this way.'

Betty Mai followed as Geraint turned off the lane, heading towards Llyn Eifion, striking across country, and climbing the stone walls in his path. A lark trilled overhead. They walked through heather and bilberry bushes to the track; soon Betty Mai was red in the face and breathing hard, and the lark was singing below them. Geraint had thought that if he set a hot enough pace Betty Mai would give up long before they reached Llyn Eifion, let alone the summit of the mountain. But she hung on, panting and puffing, till they breasted the last rise before the lake, and saw its still surface extending before them. Geraint himself needed a rest then, and they sat down at the edge of the stream. Betty Mai Shafto turned so that she looked out over the expanse of Caernarvonshire and Anglesey; Geraint looked once, swallowed, and sat down facing the lake, saying that he wanted to see if there were any trout rising.

At length Betty Mai stood up. She was wearing slacks, a heavy fair-isle sweater, and was carrying a short blue rainproof jacket and a satchel containing her sandwiches. Geraint had on his heather-mixture sweater and a dark green fishing jacket.

Geraint said, 'It won't rain. I am too hot. I am going to leave my jacket here.'

'Well, I am going to leave my sweater and take the jacket. There may be a cold wind.'

Betty Mai removed her sweater and placed it next to Geraint's jacket; they put a heavy stone on each garment in case a strong wind sprang up and blew the clothes away. Then they skirted the right-hand shore of the lake and moved on to the flank of Crib y Geifr, climbing steadily. It was not a difficult ascent; on the grass below the rock turrets of the ridge they were able to use the sheep runs, which always led along the contours, and saved much effort. The grass began to peter out, and Geraint's hands were wet with sweat as he looked down to his left, where the lake lay far below. There was no wind; the air was still and warm. Then they were walking on a small plateau among jumbled rocks emerging from a tangle of blanket-peat and mat-grass, while the bare rock of the ridge soared away to their right, the summit nearer but still invisible. To Geraint's relief, there was no sense of height here; only when he looked over his left shoulder, past the apparent horizon two hundred yards away, could he see beyond it the tip of Elidir Fawr to tell him where he was.

They climbed farther, on to the confusion of rock detritus, making their way among boulders bigger than themselves, and finally they came to a small and undramatic hump of bare ground on which a cairn of stones had been built; having by-passed the upper sweep of the ridge, they were at the summit.

Betty Mai looked out over the peaks, over the misted blue valley and away south-westward to Cardigan Bay. Westward were the Hills of Wicklow, and in the far north, beyond Liverpool Bay, was the blue-grey shape of the Isle of Man. Geraint sat down and shut his eyes, then tentatively opened them again.

Over on Snowdon, just below the summit, was a long band of mist from which the two peaks emerged like the prow of a ship. Looking down the hog's back of Crib y Geifr, he could not see Llyn Padarn; there was only the blue haze below, and directly in front of them the ground fell away gently between the ridges in an innocuous-seeming incline. Geraint knew that this was deceptive; after three hundred and fifty feet, masked by the undulating ground, there was the sudden wall of the west face falling down to the cwm in which the quarry began.

'What time is it?' Geraint asked.

Betty Mai glanced at her watch.

'Ten to five.'

Geraint said, 'We have done well.'

'Yes.'

Betty Mai sat down, then stretched out on her back, gazing up into the sky.

'We have to wait until half past five,' she said, her eyes and nose wrinkled against the bright light.

Geraint stared doggedly out over the ranks of the mountains, thinking how fortunate it was that the view directly downwards was obscured. He could endure this.

Betty Mai said, 'I will show you whether I have a strong voice or not, Geraint Edwards.'

She yawned lazily, extending her arms behind her head. Geraint regarded her with disfavour.

'Lying about on this rock,' he said sternly. 'It is all very well for you. You are well enough upholstered.'

'Oh, be quiet,' said Betty Mai. She sat up, and fumbled in her satchel. 'Here. Have a sandwich.'

Surprised, Geraint took one, and inspected it carefully, as though seeking evidence of poison. Cheese and tomato.

'Thanks,' he said with his mouth full. 'I didn't bring anything to eat.'

'More fool you.'

They ate together grumpily. In a short while Geraint asked, 'What time is it?'

It was five o'clock. A few minutes later Geraint again asked the time.

Betty Mai said, 'Why can't you stop asking the time? I will tell you when it is half past five. You go on like an old woman.'

'Old woman yourself,' said Geraint. 'I am tired of being here, that's all.'

'Well, you will just have to wait.'

So they bickered, but their minds were not on the exchanges; they were merely keeping in practice and passing the time. They were waiting for half past five.

Geraint said, 'When you are waiting for something, why does it always seem so long?'

'Because you *are* waiting,' said Betty Mai. 'It stands to reason.

Geraint watched the band of mist on Snowdon.

'It is funny,' he said. 'After a while, things look nearer. When you look at them for a long time, I mean.'

Betty Mai said nothing. There was a long pause.

'What time is it?' asked Geraint.

Betty Mai said, 'I will count a hundred, and then I will look at my watch. I will not look at it until I have counted a hundred.'

'Well, count to yourself, not aloud,' said Geraint. 'I don't want to listen to you clacking away like a fat hen. Do it quietly.'

He pretended indifference. Betty Mai closed her eyes, and Geraint found himself watching her lips moving as she counted.

'Oh, come on,' he said eventually, certain that she must have reached a hundred.

She continued for what seemed to him another ten minutes, then opened her eyes.

'A hundred,' she said, and Geraint exhaled. Betty Mai looked at her watch, and leaped to her feet.

'It's twenty-eight minutes to six,' she said excitedly. 'Quick, we'll be late!'

'What do you mean, telling me to be quick?' Geraint said indignantly. 'You are the one who is supposed to be singing. Go on, then, sing!'

Betty Mai folded her hands demurely, as though about to sing in a drawing room.

With heavy sarcasm Geraint said, 'I ought not to bother telling you, but you are facing south-east. Or is your voice supposed to go right round the world first?'

Betty Mai said, 'Which way, then?'

The haze had thickened, but Geraint placed her so that she faced roughly north-west.

'There,' he said. 'Now get on with it, before they pack up and go home.'

'What shall I sing?'

She hesitated, self-conscious and uncertain.

Geraint raged at her.

'What does it matter what you sing? Who cares what you sing? They will never hear you, anyway. Sing anything at all.'

'I'll sing some scales, then.'

Betty Mai sang some scales, with growing assurance, then stopped.

'Old scales,' she said. 'I will sing something properly.'

She sang the *Indian Love Call*, in English.

Down in the quarry, Shafto stopped work suddenly, and said, 'Hush! What's that?'

After a moment he scratched his head and said, 'It is Betty Mai's voice. I do not understand this at all. It is Betty Mai's voice, and it is coming from up the mountain.'

Down in the village Billy Davies stood at the end of the street with Olwen Morris. They nudged each other significantly: faintly, ever so faintly, but clearly, they heard. Unseen behind them Mrs Shafto came out of the grocer's and halted, her head on one side.

'Dreaming,' she said. 'Dreaming, that is what I am doing.' Then she caught sight of Olwen Morris.

'Olwen Morris!'

Olwen turned, said 'Ssh!', and then recognized Betty Mai's mother.

'Oh dear,' she said hopelessly.

On the summit of Moel Eifion the last notes died away.

'Dear God,' said Geraint, moved to an oath. 'They must have heard that in Ireland. "When I'm calling you, hoo-hoo-hoo, *hoo-hoo-hoo*." Like a cross between an owl and a factory whistle you are, girl.'

Betty Mai looked pleased.

'Do you really think they heard me?'

Geraint said, 'We shall have to see. But I cannot see how anyone could have missed hearing you. I shall be deaf for a week.'

He turned away from her, looking out over a sea of mist. A gap suddenly opened up in it, and he gazed down to the elusively glimpsed lake. His fear of heights had gone. He made an effort to resurrect this fear, gazing over at the peaks when the gap in the mist closed, willing himself to be afraid, to experience again the draining sense of panic in his stomach, the wet hands, the desire to hurl himself on the ground with his eyes closed. But it was dead, quite dead. He felt no sense of triumph, but rather of anticlimax.

He swung round to Betty Mai, wanting against his judgement to tell her, knowing that she could have had nothing to do with it, but feeling simply a need to confide in someone, to blurt out his secret now that the necessity for keeping it a secret had gone. But she was staring past him.

'Look,' she whispered, her voice full of terror, and for the first time Geraint took in the significance of the mist rolling up towards them.

'Come on,' he said urgently. 'We must hurry.'

They hurried, and managed to leave behind them the summit detritus and the small plateau under the higher arch of Crib y Geifr, gaining the first patches of grass above the lake. Then they were engulfed in the mist.

8

THEY held hands to prevent becoming separated, and moved gingerly on the slippery, steep turf. Often they had to halt and keep perfectly still, unable to see their own feet. With the onset of the mist the temperature had dropped, and Geraint began to shiver. They found a sheep run at last, and moved gratefully along it, keeping the downward slope to their right. It took them two hours of groping, painful progress to arrive at the lake, and this arrival seemed to Geraint, when he looked back on it, to have been the merest accident, for when the grassy slopes petered out and they found themselves on rock again they wandered foolishly and at random downhill, in a danger which Geraint appreciated but of which Betty Mai was apparently unaware. Suddenly their feet were in water, cold, shallow water; Geraint almost wept with relief, sure that he now knew where they were.

He turned to Betty Mai, a sometimes disembodied presence beside him except for the hand gripping his, and said, 'Come on, we shall be all right now,' leading the way along the lake-shore. Betty Mai stumbled, and then followed. After some distance the ground became softer, and at Geraint's next step he began to sink over the ankles. He shouted in sudden panic, realizing that they had been going the wrong way, that they were heading into the bog at the upper end of the lake, then regained control and pulled his feet out of the ooze, staggering backwards into Betty Mai. They reeled together precariously and maintained their balance, but Betty Mai released Geraint's hand as they moved apart again, and she was gone in an instant. Geraint yelled at her; she screamed, and they blundered into each other, hugging each other tightly.

Geraint panted, 'Whatever you do you must not let go of my hand.'

Betty Mai was sobbing. Geraint calmed her, and they set off again, inching forward in the opposite direction. In half an hour they reached the stream at the lower end of the lake, and Geraint was faced with a decision.

Betty Mai tugged impatiently at his sleeve.

'Hurry up.'

Geraint said, 'Be quiet. I am thinking.'

In his mind he could visualize clearly the two hundred feet of small cascades which the stream made before the rate of its fall lessened. The path led by the stream in a series of zig-zags, crossing and recrossing it, sometimes leaving it altogether where the water fell over short but steep cliffs into a deep pool which formed in its turn the head of another cascade. In good light the path presented no difficulties, nor even in darkness, with a torch; Geraint had made the trip many times. Now, however, as he weighed the problem carefully, estimating his own ability, which had already proved less than he had thought—as witness his having led them the wrong way—estimating Betty Mai's, which was nil, he knew that it would be suicide to attempt the path. Geraint was at that moment of balance between childhood and adolescence, that strange point of stability before the onset of glandular disturbance, which for a little while can make a child of his age seem a small adult, far older and mature than he will be in a year's time.

Geraint said finally, 'If we try to go down in this mist all they will have to do is pick up the pieces at the bottom. We must stay up here.'

Betty Mai said, 'But it's so late. It is twenty to nine! They'll murder me when I get home.'

'And me,' said Geraint fatalistically. 'That is, *if* we get home.'

Betty Mai still protested, so Geraint said, 'All right, you go by yourself. Let go of my hand.'

He made as if to shake himself free, but Betty Mai hung on tightly.

'Well,' he said, 'please yourself.'

There was a sudden thin whistle from the direction of the lake.

Betty Mai said, 'There's someone there!'

'Only an otter,' said Geraint. 'Come on.'

They crossed the stream by the stepping-stones, and worked carefully up the other shore of the lake.

'Look,' said Geraint, picking up his jacket and Betty Mai's sweater. 'That was lucky.'

The sweater was damp and mist-bedewed, so Betty Mai put it on over her blue jacket, while Geraint slipped on his own jacket with gratitude.

'That is much better,' he said. 'I hope the mist will lift soon.'

They moved on, came to the ruined hut where Geraint kept his fishing rod, and sat hunched together in the angle formed by the three tumbledown walls.

'I'm hungry,' said Betty Mai. 'I still have two sandwiches. I thought I had eaten them all.' She reflected a moment, and added, 'I expect I would have done if you had not kept pestering me about the time. You had better have one.' She pulled up her satchel from the ground, opened it and offered Geraint a sandwich.

The sandwiches were messy and crumby, but Geraint and Betty Mai ate them quickly and silently.

'That was gone before I tasted it,' said Geraint with regret. 'You haven't any more?'

'You should be thankful I gave you that one.'

Geraint stared bitterly into the mist.

'It will do you good to go hungry,' he said. 'Get your weight down a bit. I am thin, and I need food.' He quoted his grandfather: 'I am so thin I could pull the skin of my belly over my head for an umbrella.'

He fidgeted for a while and then said, 'Excuse me,' and stood up.

'Where are you going? You will get lost.'

Geraint said prudishly, 'I am going to be excused, see?'

He vanished into the mist. There was silence for a moment, and then Betty Mai heard him whistling loudly and tactfully. Geraint returned.

'I could not get lost just here,' he said. 'I know every stone on this part of the lake-shore. Every stone. It is better to wait here till the mist lifts or someone comes to rescue us.'

Reassured, Betty Mai thought for a minute and said, 'It is like having a house of our own.'

She gazed dreamily around in the wreathing mist. Geraint snorted.

'You want some more walls and a roof,' he said. 'And a fire. I'm cold.'

Betty Mai said, 'I am quite warm.'

'And no wonder. You have enough fat on you to make up for three overcoats.'

Betty Mai burst into tears.

'Oh, shut up,' said Geraint callously, and turned his back to her. Her weeping subsided into a sniffing hiccup.

'Rude,' she said. 'I have never met anyone so rude as you, Geraint Edwards.'

'Aah, why don't you go and drown yourself? I bet I could get home by myself, instead of being stuck here with you.'

Betty Mai perked up and said, 'Well, go. I shall be all right. You go, and bring help.'

Geraint said, 'No, I didn't really mean that. Look. It is growing dark.'

The darkness came, impenetrably black. Geraint's teeth began to chatter. His eyelashes felt peculiar. He put up a hand to investigate, and pulled from them small, cold globules. Ice. His hair was frosted, and the surface of his jacket icy also.

'Betty Mai,' he said urgently. 'Get up!'

He forced the girl to her feet.

'We must keep moving,' he said. 'My dad once told me that if you sit down at night when you are lost in the mountains you die.'

Betty Mai said, 'I was just dozing off.'

Geraint said, 'You will freeze. Come on now, move! Dance, hop about, anything, but move!'

Startled into obedience by the ferocity of Geraint's tone, the girl rose and began to shuffle her feet and beat her arms together, following Geraint's example. In a while she said, 'I'm tired.'

Geraint said, 'It makes no difference how tired you are. Keep moving.'

She was crying again, but not in anger this time: a weary, quiet, despairing sobbing. Geraint began to feel desperate.

'Can't you stop that noise?' he asked, not knowing what to do.

'I'm tired,' she said. 'I cannot keep on any more.'

She stopped moving.

Geraint said, 'Why not sing or shout? Sing like you did on top.'

'All right,' she said.

Geraint heard her taking in air, and waited for the reciprocal blast of sound that would have every wineglass in Nant y Bont exploding into fragments. Instead he heard a faint note which cracked into a pitiful wheezing.

Betty Mai tried again, with a similar result.

'It's no use,' she said very hoarsely. 'I can't.'

Geraint said spitefully, 'Your voice will be breaking, I expect.'

Croaking, Betty Mai said, 'It must be the fog. Or nerves. Nerves, that's what it is. It happened like this the first time I sang at a party. Oh, Geraint, I'm scared.'

'Listen!'

Geraint stood still by the girl's side, the chill striking into them unheeded. They heard faint shouts.

'At last,' said Geraint.

The shouts grew louder, while Geraint answered them. Soon Geraint said, 'Hush!'

They paused, listening again.

'They are going away from us,' Geraint said. 'They must be thinking we are on Crib y Geifr, or still on top of the mountain. Stay here, Betty Mai. Do not go from this place on any account, and do not sit down or fall asleep if I don't come back. I must go after them or they will lose us.'

He felt his way out of the ruined building, shouting back at Betty Mai, 'I shall not be long, I hope. Jump about till I bring them.'

Geraint walked blindly forward till his feet were in water. Then he bent and moved on hands and feet, keeping his left hand and foot in the water, which was so cold that it seemed to burn. He yelled at intervals, heard a far-off answering hail, and then could hear nothing because of the rushing of the stream. He stood up and moved forward, found a stepping-stone, and leaped forward from it, finding the opposite bank, but turning his ankle in the gap between two stones. He howled with pain and sat down, rubbing his ankle, then standing again and testing it. He moved off in the blackness, limping and shouting.

'Geraint?' someone yelled.

'Come back. We are over here. Come back to the stream.'

'Stay where you are. Keep shouting.'

Shout and answer. Shout and answer. Then Shafto's voice.

'Over here somewhere. He is over here.'

The crunch of boots. Geraint felt something taut and icy hit his chest, sending him backward; he grabbed at it. A rope.

'Here,' he shouted. 'I am here, between you.'

He tugged at the rope. The searchers had been walking past, one on each side of him. He saw the dim halo of a light, then his father's face blurred above it.

'Thank God,' his father said.

Shafto reached them. He came up to Geraint and gripped the boy's shoulder so that it hurt, saying, 'Where is my girl? Where is she?'

His voice seemed as stretched and taut and icy as the rope had been.

Geraint felt suddenly weak and shaky.

'Come on,' he said, turned, and limped back, holding tightly to the rope.

'I told her to keep moving,' he said. 'You were going away from us.'

'Where is she?' Shafto said again.

Geraint did not answer. He felt too tired to talk. He walked, clinging to the rope until they came to the stream. They crossed by the stepping-stones, and Geraint found it easier this time, helped by the light of the two men's torches glowing dimly in the mist.

When they had moved some distance from the stream Geraint said, 'Shout now.'

Shafto shouted.

'I forgot. She can't yell now,' Geraint said.

They made their way to the ruin. Geraint could hear the small, regular sounds of Betty Mai still jigging up and down obediently. Shafty ran forward and disappeared; the rope jerked, and then Shafto came back to them, his arm round his daughter's shoulder.

Wil Edwards led down the path by the stream. He had placed the children in the middle of the rope, Geraint in front of Betty Mai, while Shafto brought up the rear. Both Geraint and Betty Mai moved like sleepwalkers, slipping and stumbling, to be brought up short by the rope. At the back of Geraint's mind was a small glow of satisfaction. He had been right. He and Betty Mai could never have got down by themselves. His ankle hurt, but he could walk.

Out of the frost hollow of the lake the mist was no longer so cold. Exhausted though they were, the children felt a little warmer, but they did not speak. Wil Edwards still kept them on the rope long after its use was necessary, until the mist thinned out and they reached the fields above the lane.

Unroping, he said, 'We heard Betty Mai singing just before we knocked off, and then we saw the mist. We went straight up from the quarry, up Crud y Gwynt and over the top, then down Crib y Geifr to the lake. We were going back up Crib y Geifr again, and it is a good thing that you heard us shouting, indeed, for by now there would be all four of us dead and frozen, as likely as not. I would not like to be on Crib y Geifr now, I am telling you.'

Shafto's van was standing outside Geraint's home.

Shafto said, 'The old woman is here. What is she doing here?'

They led the children into the cottage. Geraint's mother was sitting in the parlour in stony silence with Mrs Shafto, Billy Davies, and the minister.

'Hello, Billy,' said Geraint feebly. 'Could you hear her?'

Geraint's mother and Mrs Shafto had leaped up, first thanking God, then crying, then storming with anger. The minister calmed them eventually.

Shafto said to his wife, 'How did you get here?'

Mrs Shafto said, 'I saw Billy with Olwen Morris, and I heard Betty Mai on the mountain.' She turned for a brief moment to Betty Mai and said, 'I never heard of such a thing! Wait till I get you home, my girl.' Then she spoke to her husband again: 'When I saw the mist come down I went straight away to the telephone box. I rang the quarry, and the manager said you had gone up the mountain. We were just going to call in the Mountain Rescue people. I got the van from the quarry.'

'No need for that,' said Wil. 'We know what we are doing.'

Mrs Shafto burst out, 'Billy Davies has told me all about this, and I think it is a disgrace. Egging the girl on like that: it is all Billy Davies's and your Geraint's fault!'

The minister said, 'A youthful prank, no more. We must be thankful that all has ended well.'

Mrs Shafto looked at him darkly and said, 'Ah, but has it? That is what you are here to find out, and you are forgetting what I brought you here for.'

Mr Davies flushed and said, 'Geraint, you should be in a hot bath, or tucked up in bed. But I must ask you a few questions while your mother makes a nice hot meal. Come into the other room.'

Geraint followed Mr Davies obediently, while his mother bustled through to the kitchen. Mrs Shafto sat, her lips compressed, in the parlour with the others until the minister and Geraint returned; Geraint's face was flaming.

Mr Davies said, 'Er—nothing to worry about. No cause for alarm at all, I can assure you, Mrs Shafto. As far as I can make out, these two spent most of their time quarrelling.'

Geraint's father said, 'No cause for alarm? I should think not, indeed!'

Mrs Shafto said, 'Well, we'll see about that. I have a thing or two to say to this young miss when I get her home.'

'The sooner the better, then,' suggested the minister. 'They should be in their beds by now.'

Shafto said, 'The sooner I am out of this bloody house the better it will suit me, indeed. Sorry, Mr Davies, but that is how I feel.'

Shafto and his wife stood, while Mrs Shafto said, 'Come, Betty Mai,' and they went without another word.

Mr Davies hesitated, said to Wil, 'We had better be going too; come along, Billy.' He called good night to Geraint's mother, said, 'Good night, Mr Edwards; I shall be offering up a prayer of thanks for this deliverance,' patted Geraint's shoulder, and went.

Billy, following, said to Geraint glumly, 'We lost. You could hear her as clear as a bell,' and then ran after his father.

Geraint swayed in his chair; now that the tide of people had ebbed, he was aware of his grandfather sitting in a corner of the room.

'Taid . . .' he said, and was pitching forward when his father caught him and carried him to bed. In the morning, after a hot bath and a heavy breakfast, he was led up to the bedroom again, and his father purposefully unbuckled his belt. Geraint found it uncomfortable to sit down in chapel, but felt a sense of importance when Mr Davies offered up his prayer and whispers arose from the congregation around him. Betty Mai was not present.

·   ·   ·   ·   ·

On the Monday Geraint arrived early at the bus stop. When the bus came he kept the seat next to him for Betty Mai. They sat together, subdued and chastened.

'My dad leathered me yesterday,' said Geraint at length. 'They're mad. One minute they hop with joy because they have found you, and then the next minute they beat the stuffing out of you.'

'My dad leathered me, too,' said Betty Mai.

'Did he?'

Geraint looked at her with increased respect.

He said, 'Did they ask you questions?'

'My mam did. My dad just whacked me.'

Geraint said, 'Mr Davies asked me a lot of questions. I tell you, I did not know which way to look, with all those questions he asked.'

'I know. So did my mam.'

They reflected in silence, hurt and resentful.

'Do you know what?' said Geraint. 'I think grown-ups are a dirty-minded lot. That is what I think. They ought to be ashamed of themselves.'

'Yes,' said Betty Mai. 'After you saved my life, too.'

'Did I? Did I save your life?'

'Of course you did. If you had not made me keep moving I would have frozen to death.'

'Dear God,' said Geraint, feeling more cheerful. 'I suppose I did. Well, anyway, you saved mine, too—with that sandwich.'

His mood improved vastly.

'Do you know,' he said expansively, leaning back in his seat and folding his hands in front of him, 'I'm sorry I was rude. You know, saying you were fat and so on. I mean, my Uncle Tom says it is probably only puppy fat.'

He nodded sagely to himself, congratulating himself on his magnanimity, and was astonished when Betty Mai burst into tears.

On the homeward bus she sat with Olwen Morris, glancing

at Geraint from time to time, whispering to Olwen, and occasionally laughing loudly and falsely. Those mad Shaftos, thought Geraint, and then dismissed her from his mind. He had done his French homework during the lunch break, his algebra during a reading lesson, and he said to himself, 'If I can do this stupid history on the bus I shall be able to go fishing this evening,' and settled down to work. He would go to the lake, he decided, and call at Maitland's cottage. From the back seat of the bus Maldwyn Shafto watched him.

Geraint did not speak to anyone as he left the bus. He had read the short chapter in the history book which he had been required to prepare, and was rehearsing possible questions for the test tomorrow. Mr Rogerson, the history master, had a habit of awarding detention periods to those who did badly in tests, and though the punishment in itself was not very condign—half an hour after school—it meant that Geraint missed the school bus and had to wait till seven o'clock for another. He prepared very thoroughly for history tests in consequence.

'What was Offa's Dyke?' he said to himself. 'Describe the boundaries of Mercia. What was wergild?'

Maldwyn Shafto grabbed him by the arm and pulled him into the telephone call box. He hit Geraint twice in the stomach, once in the mouth, and once on the nose. Geraint sagged against the side of the box, gasping for breath and sobbing.

'If you were any bigger I would kill you,' said Maldwyn Shafto as he left the call box.

Geraint held on to the small platform on which stood the telephone. His movement dislodged the receiver, which purred and swung at the end of its flex. Geraint was sick on the floor. He stared down at it, drops of blood falling from his face, and then staggered into the open air.

'Geraint! What is the matter? What have you been doing?' said a woman passer-by.

Geraint wiped his nose and his split lip, and hurried home, dodging curious glances with a handkerchief to his face.

He went in through the kitchen door, and his mother said, 'What next? Up on the mountain one day, driving us all crazy with worry, nearly getting yourself killed, and now fighting, is it?'

And she clouted his ear, shouting, 'To the sink with you and wash yourself.'

Murderously Geraint went to the sink, stifling sudden tears. He washed and ate in sullen silence, then rose.

'I am going fishing,' he said.

'Indeed you are not. You will stay in, and then we shall see what your father has to say.'

Gerant started to speak, thought better of it, and hurried to the parlour, where he switched on the television set and watched the news, sneering at the incomprehensible gibberings of the news-reader. Grown-ups.

He heard his father come in at the back door, the sounds as his father washed, his mother's voice rising to a pitch of fury, his father's steps.

Geraint was ready, and jumped up; his father was a man, and would understand.

'Dad,' he said. 'Dad, Maldwyn Shafto beat me up. I was not fighting. He beat me up. Look.'

Geraint exhibited his face for his father's inspection.

'Look, Dad,' he said. 'Mam thinks I have been fighting. She wouldn't listen.'

His father said coldly, 'It is no more than you deserve, indeed, turned on his heel, and went back to the kitchen.

Geraint was hurt, baffled, and angry. There was no meaning to it, he felt. He wanted sympathy; what else were parents for? He had paid with a thrashing already for the escapade on the mountain, hadn't he? Maldwyn Shafto was a bully; just let him wait till Geraint had grown a bit more.

His grandfather came in.

'Taid,' said Geraint. 'Maldwyn Shafto beat me up, and he is much bigger than I am, and I couldn't do anything about it, and nobody cares.'

He sniffed, and his grandfather said, 'Switch that television off, will you, boy? You are not watching it, are you?'

Geraint switched off.

His grandfather said as he sat down, 'It is too late to lift your petticoat after you have piddled in it. You have got yourself in some bother these last few days, Geraint. Do not take it too much to heart. Your mam and your dad have been troubled, and when people are troubled they sometimes do things and say things which they do not mean. It is over and done with now, and it will all pass in time.'

He sighed, pulled his beard meditatively, and then cackled.

'It is a long time since I was up the mountain with a girl,' he said. 'Never mind, boy, there will be plenty more times. Now let me give you a bit of advice. If you go up the mountain always make sure there is a bit of a breeze. If there is a bit of a breeze it always keeps the mist away.'

He began nodding and chuckling to himself. For Geraint this was the last straw. He stood up in disgust and went into the dining room, where he did all his home-work for a second time. He took particular care over the algebra, working and reworking the equations which he had already solved perfectly. At least, he thought, you knew where you were with algebra.

9

ONE Friday evening in October Wil Edwards came home and flung his haversack violently into a corner of the kitchen, then sheepishly retrieved it and hung it on its nail behind the door.

'Why did you do that?' Geraint asked, looking up from his book. It was a story of a wartime escape from a prison camp, and Geraint found it thrilling. He had begun to read a great deal, preferring true adventure stories.

Wil Edwards said, 'I have a holiday.'

'A holiday?' said Geraint's mother.

'We are laid off next week. There is not enough work. We are to work two weeks in three.'

Gwen Edwards gasped.

Geraint's grandfather, sitting by the kitchen stove, raised his head and said, 'How is this, Wil? You have been blasting all the summer. What about all the blasting on Moonlight, too? And you have said there is a lot of slate.'

'There is slate enough,' said Wil. 'The trouble is that people don't seem to want to buy it. The management have told us that the demand has been falling off. They can either sack a third of us or go on to short-time working, and they have chosen short-time working. A mercy they have, too; I might have been among the third sacked, and what other work is there for a man like me to do here?'

Geraint said, 'Do you mean that you will be working for two weeks and then have a week off, Dad?'

'Yes.'

Geraint thought the matter over.

'I think it is a good idea,' he said. 'I should like to go to school for two weeks and then have a week off, and so on. It sounds fine.'

Wil said, 'It would, to you, but I have to pay the bills.'

Geraint's mother sighed.

'It will be hard,' she said.

Wil opened his jacket and yanked at his belt, pulling it in another hole.

'That is what we have to do, girl,' he said. 'Tighten our belts a bit. There is nothing else for it. And we may thank God it is no worse. The television is paid for, and we have no debts. Think of people like young Glyn Griffith. He is buying his own house on a mortgage, and a car and the television and a washing machine and the dear Lord knows what else on the hire purchase.'

Gwen Edwards sniffed.

'More fool Glyn Griffith,' she said. 'Living on the never-never.'

'What can you expect? Young people want to get ahead and enjoy the best they can. Glyn is a good boy and a hard worker, and, I tell you, I should not like to be working over on Y Senedd where he is. No, Gwen, you must be charitable.'

Geraint's grandfather said, 'Cheap tiles. Cheap tiles are at the bottom of all this. I remember a time when all the world's houses were roofed with slate from these mountains, slate from Dinorwic and Penrhyn and Bron Eifion, from Nantlle and Victoria and Alexandra, Gorseddau, Drws-y-Coed, and all the rest, to say nothing of those slate mines over Ffestiniog way. What has been happening? Victoria is closed, Hen Nantlle is closed; Drws-y-Coed is like a ghost village. And now the biggest quarries in the world are going on short-time. What is happening to the world? If you have slate over your head you are safe. Look at this house, Wil. I remember it when I was a boy. Look at the roof. My dad had the landlord fix twelve new slates and renew the ridge slates and fillets while he was alive. When he died and just after you were born I looked at the roof, and I called in the landlord's agent, and he had one new slate and a ridge slate fitted. I never had to touch the roof after that; year after year, rain, gales, time: that roof stood. When you bought the house, Wil, how many slates did you have to replace?'

'Not one,' said Wil. 'Not a single slate. That roof is sound.'

Geraint's grandfather said, 'It is the same with the coal, indeed: the demand has been falling off. But you hear a lot about the coal and about the miners, how hard the job is and everything. It is cold and dark under the ground, indeed, and it is dangerous; but if you put a miner on the south end of Monkey Brand, or the south end of Y Senedd, he would mess his trousers. You know I was on the south end of Monkey Brand when I lost my sight, long before they opened Patagonia. Monkey Brand was the highest gallery then.'

'Yes, we know,' said Wil impatiently.

Geraint said, 'Tell us again, Taid.'

'Very well,' said the old man indulgently, while Wil made an impatient gesture. 'I was working right above the Slabs, a terrible place it was, and a mad game we played. There was black powder enough for the charges, but some bright spark in the management had the idea that we should use nitro-glycerine for a fuse trail. Some people would never believe that, but as God is my witness it is true. Nitro-glycerine! You had to drip a trail of the stuff from a bottle. It was mad and criminal; you only had to give the bottle a little shake and up she went. You would have thought the village had been in a war or something, with the people that were going about with a leg or an arm or a hand missing. Well, I had set up a charge and I was laying the fuse trail from the little bottle when I slipped. I dropped the bottle, and I heard it blow up like a gong of doom when it hit the Slabs. But I fell forward and my head hit the fuse trail, slap-bang in the middle, and there was a flash that seemed right inside my head. I did not feel a thing then; and the next thing I knew was the whole world falling away as the charge blew, and I have never known to this day how it missed killing me; they said there was rocks and slates and stones flying all round me. When the rock stopped falling I was dangling at the end of my rope like an old spider and it was then that my eyes began to hurt, and when they pulled me up they pulled up a blind man. They stopped using that nitro-glycerine soon afterwards, and a good job too, or there would not have been an able-bodied man for miles around, I am telling you.'

Wil Edwards said brusquely, 'Yes, we have heard it all before, Dad.'

Geraint said, 'Taid, what is it like, being blind?'

The old man sighed and said, 'It will be different for different people, isn't it? But for me, well, it is a great comfort when a man grows old. The world is changing all the time, but the time in my head stays the same, and the world for me is just the same as it was the day I was blinded. Perhaps that is why I have lived so long.'

Geraint looked doubtful.

'Well,' he asserted, 'when I leave school I am not going to that old quarry.'

His mother kissed his head.

'Indeed you are not.'

Geraint knew what he was going to be. He was going to be a great violinist, as great as Paganini. Geraint could see himself, all dressed up in tails, nodding casually to the conductor of the London Symphony Orchestra, or it might be the New York Philharmonic, as a signal that he was ready. The Beethoven Concerto. He would wait all through the extended introduction, then play. . . . At the end he would take the hand of the first violin, magnanimously. . . . Or the Bach Double Concerto, with Isaac Stern. Stern, though, might be past it by then. He would see.

In the winter the quarry went on ostensible full-time work for a while; often the weather limited production to the short-time level. Geraint's thirteenth birthday came. Ever since November, when Billy Davies had received a bicycle for his birthday, Geraint had been nagging his parents to buy him one. Wil bought a second-hand machine for two pounds, laboriously repainted it, and taped the rusty handlebars. He fitted new wheels, and presented the machine to Geraint, who was over-joyed. This time Maitland was invited to tea by Geraint's father. He did not come, but sent a note to say that he was in London, and asked Wil to call and see him the following week. Wil came home with a sheaf of sheet music for the violin, which Maitland had asked him to give to Geraint if Wil thought fit.

'He is a gentleman,' said Wil, his earlier misgivings forgotten. 'A real gentleman.'

Geraint went to Maitland's cottage perhaps once a month now, played occasionally, and hoped each time that Maitland would be a little more enthusiastic about his playing. But Maitland would merely content himself with a grudging nod if the recital had been satisfactory, or scald Geraint with sarcasm if it did not come up to expectation. Two years ago Geraint would have remained unmoved by this, but now he found himself deeply wounded. Once he let two months pass without approaching Maitland.

Geraint was beginning to drift on the choppy seas of adoles-cence. With some of its problems he came to terms matter-of-factly, but others defeated him. He grew clumsy as he grew taller. In half-terms and longer holidays he evinced a great talent for annoying his father; short-time had been reintro-duced in the spring, and Wil Edwards was much about the house, fretful and quick-tempered. Geraint blundered about, all hands and feet, touchy and stubborn, arguing with his father at every opportunity, attacking him on the subjects of politics, religion, art, competing with him and sulking for hours after each inevitable defeat.

He began to blush easily and for no apparent cause. In the school bus he was tormented by a hopeless passion for a young conductress; he would engage in transparent subterfuges in order to stand next to her, inarticulate and red-eared. She was transferred to another route and he tormented himself with the thought that he would never see her again, that he did not even know her name.

During the summer Geraint began to pay great attention to Maitland's dog, Hennessey. He increased the frequency of his visits to Maitland's cottage, and either played or listened perfunctorily, then asked if he might take the dog for a walk.

'If you like,' said Maitland. 'But keep him on the lead. There is no common land at all in this bloody country, as far as I can make out. I don't want some ape of a farmer coming here frothing at the mouth and accusing Hennessey of eating his mangel-wurzels or something.'

Geraint found a quality in the company of the dog which he had missed in that of human beings. Hennessey was a perfect companion for him in his present state. Geraint and his friends had recently found themselves arguing constantly about what they should do, and time went by in bickering at the street corner while they sat on their bicycles; they had scarcely finished their argument when it was time to go home, with nothing accomplished. The dog did not argue; if Geraint wanted to go to Llyn Eifion, Hennessey was agreeable; if he wanted to go to the river, Hennessey went along too, grinning, panting, indefatigable.

'One thing I am bound to say,' Maitland remarked. 'You seem to be doing Hennessey some good. He was becoming obese, but the fat has been melting from his bones since you started taking him out with you.'

'I like Hennessey,' said Geraint.

He was not allowed to approach Uncle Tom at the river, though. Uncle Tom had no time for dogs, and hated to see a dog near the water.

'Well, he's on a lead,' Geraint had protested.

'Makes no difference,' his uncle had said. 'That black spawn of darkness once took the seat out of my pants, he did. Not that I hold it against him any more. But dogs and fishing just do not mix. You clear off, and take that thing with you. If you want to come fishing with me leave the dog where it belongs—with that English nob.'

Geraint renewed his acquaintance with Mr Griffiths. He was putting out tendrils into his environment, testing, palpitating tendrils, some of them establishing relationships, others causing tensions, risking rebuffs, ridicule, but hoping all the while for approbation. Mr Griffiths asked him to tea, and Billy Davies too; the youths sat tongue-tied and admired his beard.

In July Mr Griffiths took Geraint and Billy on a fishing trip to Llyn Llydaw. They left their bicycles some distance up the old copper-miners' track from Beddgelert and made their way up to the lake. Mr Griffiths caught twelve trout, Geraint four, and Billy none at all, which made him gloomy and withdrawn for a time, while Geraint became boastful. Then they ate sandwiches by the lake-shore, looking across to the ruined mine buildings and the towering summit of Snowdon.

'See the pass?' said Mr Griffiths, pointing slightly to the left, high up. 'There, above the black cliffs you can see. That is the Bwlch y Saethau, the Pass of the Arrows. Have you read any Tennyson yet at the grammar school? *Morte d'Arthur*?'

'Oh, yes,' said Billy Davies. 'I like it.'

Mr Griffiths quoted sonorously in English:

' "So all day long the noise of battle rolled
    Among the mountains by the winter sea,
    Till all King Arthur's table, man by man,
    Had fall'n about their lord, King Arthur. . . ." '

Geraint said, 'Yes, we know that,' feeling bored and wanting to talk about fishing.

'But did you know that is where Arthur fell, up there in the Pass of the Arrows?'

Geraint's boredom vanished.

'Up there? No, I had no idea.'

'They brought him down here to Llyn Llydaw, and over these cold waters he sailed away. Now then, in 1856, when they lowered the water level to make the miners' road, they found an ancient canoe: a dug-out made from solid oak, preserved in the mud. Arthur's barge—a good deal less magnificent than Tennyson's version, but a good deal more tangible. And up there by Lliwedd, the brave knights sleep standing in a cave, leaning on their shields, waiting for Arthur to come again, waiting till the trumpets sound and waiting to drive the Saxon into the sea. And here, on the bottom of the lake, lying in the green depths on the stones, is the sword Excalibur. . . .'

He looked at the water and said quietly, ' "And on the mere the wailing died away",' and Geraint thought with surprise that he could see tears in the man's eyes.

Mr Griffiths said with sudden intensity, 'Never forget this. England was conquered in 1066, but it took another two hundred years to subjugate Wales. Here in these mountains, if anywhere, the spirit of Arthur lives on.'

After that day a new world began to open up for Geraint. He began to live with history, now vitalized for him, and saw the mountains and the country with new eyes. He would look down from Llyn Eifion to Anglesey, where smoke rose from burning gorse; in his mind he was a white-robed druid watching the fires lighted by Paulinus in the bloody year of 61, when the druid strongholds were destroyed before Paulinus had to hurry east to face Boadicea. He would watch the summer traffic on the Caernarvon road, and see the legions pulling out from Segontium after three hundred years of precarious occupation; clad in sheepskins, he would loose in imagination a final derisive arrow into the throat of a marching Falernian, and see the legion tramp on uncaring while the thrashing in the blood-dabbled hawkweed and fern at the roadside ceased, and the crows and buzzards began to feed. He would wait by the Lake of Dogs on the heights above Idwal, hearing the horn of Llywelyn the Great grow louder, the thunder of hoofs, the sudden uproar of baying hounds as they were unleashed after the stag. He would slip ghostlike through the mist, picking off stragglers from a great Norman army which floundered and died among the quagmires of the Carneddau without ever having seen a Welshman, which heard nothing of the enemy save, ever and again, the *fftok!* of the sudden deadly arrow from the mist.

10

DURING the Easter holiday, after Geraint's fourteenth birthday, nine people were killed in the Snowdon mountains, and Elliott and Harvard were among them. They died on the Eifion Slabs in the cold and the darkness.

Every year someone dies in Snowdonia through lack of experience: a youth out from Birmingham on a motor-bike decides to climb the Milestone Buttress on Tryfan in city shoes; a middle-aged rambler tries to take a short cut over Crib Goch; a foolhardy youth-club leader sets an initiative test at a Shropshire club which sends two teenagers to climb Snowdon in March, wearing gumboots and raincoats. Every year the Mountain Rescue and R.A.F. rescue teams, the University College Climbing Club, the police, and sometimes the quarrymen, have their lives put in hazard by the ignorance of the inexperienced or the negligence of the experienced.

Elliott and Harvard had cut their climbing teeth on Great Gable; they had climbed in Skye, in Switzerland, in the Dolomites, and in Snowdonia once, a long time ago. Too long. When they looked down at the Eifion Slabs from Crud y Gwynt it must have seemed a very petty climb. Perhaps they remembered looking down at Cortina from the immense pinnacles of the Pomagagnón, and smiled gently to each other. Nobody knows; but at nine-thirty that April evening, when Geraint was sitting with his parents watching television and waiting to be sent off to bed, a knock came at the door.

Geraint's mother answered the knock, and ushered in three men. Wil Edwards stood up.

'Shafto is outside,' his wife said. 'He will not come in.'

Wil Edwards said, 'An accident?'

The three men were dressed in climbing outfits: anoraks, warm sweaters, breeches, thick stockings, tricouni-nailed boots.

Wil said to one of them, a tall, thin man with a sandy moustache, 'I think I remember you. Mr Williams from the police.'

'That's right,' Williams said. 'We are sorry to bother you, Mr Edwards.'

Wil said, 'Five years, it must be. On Crib y Geifr, when we went up after that poor lad. I remember distinctly now. You gave me a sausage to eat, of all things.'

Williams smiled slightly.

One of the other men said heavily, 'May we sit down? We are a little tired.'

Geraint's mother said, 'Sit down? Of course. I will make tea while you talk.' She went to the door and shouted, 'Mr Shafto! I am making tea, and you are welcome to a cup if you will not be pig-headed.'

She came back and said, 'That fool is sitting there in the cold. He will not come in.'

'Leave him,' said Wil as his wife went to the kitchen. 'Now then, what has happened?'

'An accident on the Eifion Slabs,' said Williams. 'We rang the quarry manager at his house and he said that you and Mr Shafto might be able to help us. Two men fell. Some students from the College were climbing above on Crud y Gwynt, and tried to get down to the men, but failed. One of them was still alive at six; we think the other was dead.'

'One still alive?' said Wil. He shouted, 'Hurry up with that tea, girl,' and asked Williams, 'Where are they?'

Williams said, 'They are about thirty feet apart; the first is lying perhaps three hundred feet from the top of the Slabs. It is a hellish position.'

Wil said to Geraint, 'You make yourself scarce. It is long past your bedtime.'

Geraint gave his father an appealing glance, realized it would be useless to protest, and went into the kitchen. His mother was pouring boiling water into the teapot.

He said, 'Mam, will Dad go with them?'

Geraint's mother said, 'Who am I to say? I am only your dad's wife, that is all. Who am I to prevent him from killing himself on the mountains? He has been climbing since before he was your age, and he is not dead yet, but every time he goes out it is the same for me: I am the one who is left behind to wonder and wait.'

She took tea in to the men, returned and placed before Geraint a cup of tea and some biscuits.

'Be quick,' she said. 'Then wash, and upstairs with you.'

Geraint went to his room after the hasty supper. His grandfather had been in bed since half past eight, and was fast asleep. Geraint undressed, listening to the murmur of the men's voices. He heard the front door close; he peeped out of the bedroom window and saw his father, with the three men, get into a Land Rover, while the sudden flare of a match showed him Shafto's big nose and beetle brows as Shafto lighted a cigarette. The Land Rover roared away, and Geraint stole downstairs. Snores were coming from his grandfather's bedroom. I hope Shafto gets killed, Geraint thought.

Geraint opened the kitchen door and looked in. His mother was sitting at the kitchen table, a teacup clasped with both of her hands. She had been crying, he knew, for her eyes were red and her face mottled. He went over to her and stood by her, while she set the cup in its saucer and placed an arm round him.

'Never mind, Mam,' he said. 'Never mind, then. Dad will be all right. You'll see.'

'Yes,' she said flatly. 'We will see. One way or the other, we will see.'

In the Land Rover Shafto said to Williams, 'Do you mean to tell me that you clods tried to get down to these men from Crud y Gwynt?'

Williams said stiffly, 'There is no need to be rude. We only had the word of those students to go by. Roberts and Taplin here went down *en rappel* as far as they could, but they had to give up. They were kicking down loose rocks, and if one of the men was alive he might have been killed by the loose stuff.'

Shafto said, '*En rappel?*'

'Double-roping down, he means,' said Wil to Shafto. And to Williams, 'From what you tell me I would say that we should go into the quarry. We might be able to get to them from Monkey Brand, or even from Y Senedd.'

'Good idea,' said Williams. 'We never thought of that.'

Shafto spat on the floor of the Land Rover.

'You wouldn't.'

They took the bottom road into the quarry, which was deserted, thrust ropes and gear through the fence, and then climbed the gates, moving among the silent sheds. They walked to the foot of the truck incline, and Williams looked speculatively at his two colleagues.

He said to Wil and Shafto, 'These two men are clapped out. Look, this is what we'd better do. They can take the Land Rover back and arrange for an ambulance from the town, and report back to headquarters and Mountain Rescue, then come here and wait. I had thought there would be somebody on duty in the quarry, so that we could telephone.'

Wil said, 'Get two ambulances while you are about it: one here, and one at Pen-y-Llyn by the level-crossing. If anything happens on the Slabs tonight it is down by the lake that the ambulance will be needed, not in the quarry. We will try from Y Senedd.'

Shafto nodded. Williams' men turned and went, with no noticeable disappointment; they walked with the mechanical steps of exhausted men, a little drunkenly.

Williams, Shafto and Wil Edwards climbed the steps by the truck incline, up to the right-hand end of The Haymarket, and then up to the left-hand end of Y Senedd, over the dump. They turned right, along the roadway of Y Senedd. Above them, the cliffs of slate on Moonlight ceased abruptly; the rock, harsh in the glowing night sky, reared above. Y Senedd cut its way into a fault in the Slabs where there was good black slate. The roadway finally petered out in an anti-climactic way, first becoming a track, and then ending in a small heap of rubble. But, looking down, Wil saw the Shoulder, a slightly humped formation two-thirds of the way down the Slabs, and beyond that, shivering on the water, the reflected lights of houses and car headlamps on the Llanberis road. He could not see, below the Shoulder, the hundred and fifty feet of the lower Slabs, nor, below that, the overhanging face of unscalable smooth rock that was the Big Cliff, nor the lake surface below it; but he knew that if they fell from this position they might well hit the lake with no more than a couple of bounces.

Williams said, 'Ready, then?'

Shafto said, 'Wil had better lead, and you had better go Number Two, Mr Williams.'

Roped, they moved off on the Slabs. The first pitch was an easy traverse with an ample foothold of at least three inches on a small ledge. Wil moved, Williams belayed, Shafto anchored, while Williams paid out rope. Williams moved, Wil belayed, Shafto belayed behind himself and paid out rope round his body and over another belay. Then Wil Edwards and Williams belayed while Shafto moved up to them, and Williams took in the slack, keeping the rope taut. Again and again they repeated the sequence, to the end of the pitch.

'See anything?' Williams called.

'No,' said Wil.

Williams said, 'You'll have to give me a little while to get my bearings; I don't quite know where we are. We had better listen for half a minute: perhaps we may hear something.'

They listened. Nothing. Wil now began to climb upward, feeling for holds, on a pitch that by daylight would have presented few problems to a skilled rock-climber, but which in darkness was very severe. The holds were small to begin with, then seemed to cease; Wil's groping fingers encountered only a hair crack. He hammered in a piton as high as he could reach, snapped on the ring, and pulled his rope through it.

As he fixed the rope he called down to Williams, 'This bit is not so good. You and Shafto haul away when I tell you.... Got it? Right!'

As Williams and Shafto hauled, Wil was pulled up to the piton, gaining seven feet. He anchored himself with the spare rope, reached up into the darkness, and hammered in another piton. In two and a half hours of work—work which would have been hair-raising to an untrained climber, but was merely dull and laborious to Wil, savouring too much of his daily job— they surmounted the pitch and found themselves on a deep ledge. When Williams shone his torch round they saw that they were sharing the ledge with someone, or something. It had no head, and when they made to lift it from the blood-spattered rock on which it lay, it bent in the wrong places.

They laid it down again.

'Jesus,' said Williams softly.

A rope led upwards from the body. The three men climbed a slanting fissure to the next ledge, and there they found the second man. He was sitting with his back to the rock. His face was a network of blood, and from it his open and undamaged eyes stared out over the lake to the lights of Llanberis.

'Poor devil,' said Williams. 'This is the one who was alive.'

He made a brief examination of the body.

'Poor devil,' he said again. 'Both arms broken.'

Shafto rolled a cigarette and smoked.

'Anything to drink?' he asked Williams.

Williams shook his head.

'Pity. I need a drink.'

Williams said, 'How did they come to fall? That is what beats me. I know of these men. One was called Harvard and the other Elliott. They were not novices, they were good climbers.'

'Not good enough,' said Shafto.

Wil said, 'There is nothing exceptionally difficult above here in daylight, though it would be impossible in the dark because of the loose rock. I can see that you could not have got to them from Crud y Gwynt, but why did you not go down from Monkey Brand?'

Williams said, 'I have told you. We do not know the quarry, and we didn't know exactly where these men were until my chaps roped down from Crud y Gwynt and spotted them.'

'It is a pity indeed. You might have saved this man.' Wil shook his head and then said, 'I know why they fell. If you get on the top pitches of the Slabs, where the face is all broken up, it is easy enough except for the loose rock. You have to test every belay very carefully, and then you are all right. But these men cannot have belayed at all. They were too clever. How else could they have fallen?'

Williams said, 'They may have belayed to bad rock.'

'No,' said Wil. 'If they were experienced, and belayed at all, they would not make that mistake; they would make good belays or none. They thought they were so good they did not need to belay at all on the Eifion Slabs.'

Shafto said, 'We can't carry them down from here now. What should we do: shove them over and collect what's left at the lake?'

Williams was horrified.

'We cannot do that, man! What are you thinking of? No, they can remain here till daylight; Mountain Rescue can fetch them then. How can you be so callous, man?'

Shafto said, 'I've seen plenty dead fellers in my time. Well, we'll go home, then. It is two o'clock in the morning, and we have a day's work to do. Not that we shall be in much shape to do it after all this, eh? People going and getting themselves killed all over the bloody mountains, they never spare a thought for us poor mugs losing pay and risking our lives on account of their stupidity.'

'Don't talk silly,' said Wil Edwards sharply. He turned to Williams. 'You must not mind what he says, Mr Williams. A man should be proud to help. It is no more than is right and proper. And now we will be going down.' He added simply, as they turned, 'I will pray for the souls of these poor people.'

And on the road home in the Land Rover he said, 'One thing I know: I will teach my boy Geraint to climb properly next year.'

The Land Rover stopped outside Wil's cottage.

'Coming in for a cup of tea?'

'No thank you,' said Williams. 'We still have a lot to do. I am very grateful for your help. The Mountain Rescue and R.A.F. have been out all day on Tryfan and Pen yr Oleu Wen, and there were no men to spare. There have been three killed today in the Nant Ffrancon alone. It is a sad business.'

He clicked his tongue and said again, 'A sad business. Well, good night now, Mr Edwards.'

'Good night to you all,' said Wil, and walked up to the house, hearing the Land Rover move off and turning to see the lights of the ambulance pass it. His wife was still waiting in the kitchen; she was sitting by the dying fire.

'I'm back, then.'

They held each other wordlessly for a long time, and then Wil said, 'There's a fussy old thing you are, waiting up for me.'

'I'll make you a cup of tea.'

Wil said, 'I do not want that.'

His eyes held hers, and she said, 'What do you want, then?'

'I want to go to bed. Come on, Gwen,' he said urgently.

She tapped his cheek.

'Tell me about what you did on the mountain. What happened?'

'Tomorrow,' he said. 'Come on now.'

Gwen Edwards said, smiling, 'I will make a pot of tea first, you old cucumber.'

Wil said, 'Bring it upstairs then,' and went.

She pouted a kiss at him, then, humming to herself, she made a pot of tea, tiptoeing upstairs with the tray of tea-things. Wil was in bed, the light was on, and he was fast asleep. She shook her head wryly and undressed, switching off the light and slipping into bed beside him, listening to his breathing and finding that he was still aroused though deep in exhausted sleep.

Men, she thought. Babies, grabbing for the breast even when the milk was bubbling out of their ears. Working on a mountain all day, and climbing it all night. Dead beat, and still they wouldn't lie down, still one last muscle flexed and ready to affirm life in the face of sleep and death. Sighing, and moving stealthily so as not to wake her husband, she drank her tea and then snuggled down beside him.

11

IN THE bus on the following morning Geraint made certain of a seat next to Betty Mai Shafto. He no longer had to shove her to make room for himself, he found; she had grown much slimmer as well as taller, and though he had recognized in one sense that this process had been under way, he had never fully taken account of it before.

'Hello, Betty Mai,' he said, and was about to add something about her metamorphosis, but suddenly became embarrassed.

Betty Mai said coolly, 'What do you want?'

She was neat and slim-waisted, clean and fresh, her hair impeccable. Even in a school uniform she looked a woman, and Geraint saw past her to his own reflection in the window: the tousled black hair and the raw bony features. He looked at Betty Mai again with a sense of outrage. What had been going on? She was two months younger than he was; how had she shot past him in this mysterious way? It wasn't fair. He glanced down at his hands, red and none too clean, at his stained school blazer and creaseless dirty grey flannel pants; his shoes, cleaned that morning but showing no sign of it, Geraint having kicked a pebble from the cottage all the way to the bus stop.

He said eagerly, 'Did you hear about last night? I expect you had gone to bed. There were two men killed on Moel Eifion. My dad and yours helped to find them.'

He plucked at the black fuzz on his upper lip. Next Saturday he would buy a razor. If you shaved, the hair soon began to grow all thick and bristly, and in no time he would be able to grow whiskers like Mr Griffiths. One thing Betty Mai Shafto would never be able to do, at any rate.

'Tell me something I don't know,' said Betty Mai.

'Do you know what? I think they're heroes. Do you think they will get a medal?'

Betty Mai said, 'Yes, a putty medal with a plaster rim.'

Fascinated, Geraint had been watching her speak. He had never noticed before how red and full her mouth was, how the small white teeth glistened wetly and deliciously as she talked.

He said desperately, 'How is Maldwyn getting on?'

Geraint had not the slightest interest in Maldwyn Shafto, who had left school the previous summer and joined a firm of engineers in Birmingham; but he knew that if anything could make Betty Mai keep talking it was Maldwyn.

She said, 'He is doing very well. He is going to specialize in heavy electrical plant. The company have a scheme for training their student apprentices, and he has to go to the College of Technology on a sandwich course. Are you listening?'

Nodding, hypnotized, Geraint said, 'Sandwiches, of course.'

Those lips, he was thinking, gazing at her. That mouth. Those lovely teeth.

'I think you're a nit,' she said impatiently. 'It is a waste of time talking to a steaming nit like you. Go away and play your silly old fiddle.'

She opened a women's magazine, and began to read. In a hopeless attempt to reassert himself, Geraint said, 'Don't tell me you read that tripe! Here, let me see.'

He snatched the magazine.

'Give me that!'

' "Painless childbirth",' he read. ' "Easy exercises for the mother-to-be." Whee!'

'Read it,' Betty Mai advised sweetly. 'You might find it useful.'

Geraint flung the magazine back at her and sulked for the remainder of the journey, but when the bus stopped he followed Betty Mai into school, trailing after her and goggling at her legs.

The girls were not permitted to wear stockings sheerer than thirty-denier, but to Geraint's abruptly awakened gaze they clothed Betty Mai's legs in ineffable beauty.

During succeeding days Geraint neglected to practise his violin. He ceased to take Hennessey for walks, and mooned about the village with his friends, morose and dreamy. Whenever he could he haunted Betty Mai, stung by her sarcasms, but coming back each time for more. She made much of Billy Davies, who had begun to plaster his hair with oil. Moved to emulation, Geraint bought a bottle of hair oil and applied so much that it ran down the back of his neck, while his hair assumed the likeness of a surface of black iron, smooth at the front and sticking out at the back in jagged shards.

'You look terrible,' said Betty Mai. 'Whatever is that stuff on your hair, train-oil?'

In the quarry Shafto said to Wil Edwards, 'Keep that kid of yours away from Betty Mai, will you? He traipses around after her like a bloody lost dog.'

Wil said with dignity, 'I did not know that. I will attend to it.'

'See that you do. I don't want any kid of yours sniffing round Betty Mai, not after that business up the mountain that time. He very near had her killed in the mist.'

'I am not going to argue about that any more,' Wil said. 'I have told you that I will attend to the matter, and that is enough. The less I hear of your voice the better I am pleased.'

They were on top of Patagonia, and Wil had been drilling; blasting was to take place at four-thirty.

He turned his back on Shafto and went down his rope, fixed the charge and the fuse, and then adjourned to the big cabin for tea. At four o'clock he left the cabin with Persimmon Hughes, Madog Parry, and Shafto. Wil and Shafto, unspeaking, made their way up to the top of Patagonia again. Shafto waited until Wil was safely down the rope, then disappeared. The warning whistles blew. Wil stripped the fuse and fitted it into the square of *papur poeth*, lighted it, and began to haul himself up the face of slate. There was a roar below him, and the mountain seemed to fall away as he lost consciousness.

He swam up out of white, rushing water, opened his eyes and blinked. Above him the faces of Shafto and Madog Parry and Persimmon Hughes wavered through the water. Then the water was gone, and the faces in normal focus. Wil tried to raise himself, but there was no strength in his body.

'Wil, can you hear me?'

The voice seemed to come from a great distance. It was Persimmon Hughes, who bent over Wil.

'A bad fuse,' said Persimmon. 'You might have been blown to bits.'

'It is a mercy the rope held,' said Madog Parry. 'And the bar.'

Wil nodded weakly.

'I used a half-charge. If I had used a full charge I should not be here at all.'

Madog Parry said, 'Can you stand up now?'

They helped Wil to his feet and supported him down to the big cabin. Wil sat dazed while the overseer asked him questions and the doctor came to look him over.

Afterwards the doctor said, 'You are a lucky man. You have a punctured left eardrum and some bruised ribs where the rope tightened round your chest; nothing else. Come and see me in three days, and take a week off work.'

Wil said, 'It is Friday, and we are not working next week.'

'Good,' said the doctor. 'Come and see me on Monday just the same, though; I may want to put you in for X-ray. You'll find it will hurt when you laugh, but that is to be expected.'

Wil said dourly, 'After this it is not to be expected that I will be doing much laughing.'

The overseer finished making out the accident report, and stood up as the inspector came into the cabin.

The inspector's name was Iolo Jones. He was a short, tubby man with a florid complexion, a small button nose and aggressive black eyes.

He said to Wil, 'All right now, are you?'

The doctor said, 'He's all right,' and left.

Shafto said to the inspector, 'Have you seen that crack up on top of Patagonia?'

'Crack? What crack?'

'I am telling you, isn't it?' said Shafto. 'There is a crack on top of Patagonia.'

Jones sighed.

'How can there be? Every morning at half past seven I make my rounds, a damn' sight before you ever think of starting work, and I have seen no crack. That rock is like iron.'

Shafto said, 'I am bloody telling you there is a crack up there. It isn't a wide one, but it is a hell of a long one, and I want you to come and see it.'

Jones said, 'Oh, damn, what a day! I will come with you, but you are wasting my time.' He said to Wil, 'Go home now, man, to your bed with you.'

Shafto said, 'I give him a lift in my van, not for the pleasure of his company, but because he and the others help to pay my petrol bills. He had better wait.'

Madog Parry brought Wil a mug of tea and said, 'I will wait here with him while you and Persimmon go up with Mr Jones.'

'All right, that is settled,' said the inspector. 'Now hurry up; I have to see the manager, and he will be hopping mad if I take too long up here.'

Wil drank his tea and leaned back against the trestle, then straightened up swiftly as his sore ribs came into contact with the wood. He whistled with pain.

'Hurts, does it?' asked Madog Parry.

Wil grunted.

Then he said, 'My dad has told me time and again how he came to be blinded. You know the story, Madog?'

Madog Parry said, 'Everybody who knows your dad knows that story. If he had a pound for every time he has told it he would be a millionaire.'

He rolled a cigarette and offered his tobacco tin to Wil, who shook his head.

Wil said, 'If I would be getting the missis to push me about in a wheelchair, with no legs on me after that bad fuse up there, I think I would be telling the story of it. Yes, I think I would be telling it to anybody who would listen. I know now what happened to my dad.'

He shook his head meditatively and went on, 'It takes a long time for a man to understand his father, and when he does it is as near too late as can be. There is a sin upon me that I did not know until now. *Honour thy father and thy mother.* Well, my mam is dead since years and years, but my dad is still alive.'

Madog Parry said, 'What are you driving at? You have given the old man a home with you. You look after him, don't you? What more can you do?'

'Given him a home? Yes, I have given him a home, in the house he was born in, and I bought it over his head when I was a big, strong man home from the war. He must have been shamed, but he said nothing. Every time he has told that story about losing his sight I have tried to choke him off, but that is only a part of it. He is a blind old man, and he has been shoved in a corner like a piece of old furniture or something. Why, it must be two days since I have talked to him.'

He paused, and then said, 'I will buy him a rocking-chair for himself, and he shall sit in it and tell his old story a hundred times a day, and I will listen every time.'

The inspector came into the cabin in a little while, followed by Shafto and Persimmon Hughes.

'Well?' said Madog Parry.

Shafto said sullenly, 'Some people will not believe their own eyes. That crack is two hundred feet long, and as thick as a pencil.'

The inspector snorted.

'It is only a surface crack, I say. It is quite safe.' He turned to Wil Edwards. 'How are you feeling?'

'I shall be all right, thank you.'

Persimmon Hughes said, 'It is past time to knock off. We had better be going.'

'And isn't that what I have been saying?' Iolo Jones demanded with some asperity. 'It will take me half an hour to get down to the bottom again, and the manager will be waiting and cursing me, because I know he wants to go to Port Dinorwic to take out that boat of his for the week-end. You do nothing but waste time, you men, and I do not mind that because you are on piecework, and anyway it is none of my business, but when it comes to wasting my time as well, I mind a lot.'

He hurried out of the cabin, slamming the door.

Persimmon Hughes said, 'Well, I do not know what to think. It is a long crack indeed.'

'I know what to think,' said Shafto. 'It is downright bloody dangerous, that crack.'

Wil said, 'I have never liked all that blasting down on Moonlight. They have been undercutting.'

Madog Parry said, 'I am hungry, and I want to go home. Are you going to the Prince tonight, eh, Shafto?'

'Too true I am,' said Shafto emphatically. 'I'll be there before eight.'

Wil climbed wearily up the steps home. Gwen Edwards was waiting with Geraint and the old man in the kitchen. Geraint was reading Keats abstractedly.

'Wil,' said the woman. 'You are late.'

'Aye. I had a bit of a fall. Nothing to worry about. How are you, Dad? What have you been doing today?'

Surprised, the old man said, 'Nothing much. I have sat in the window-seat where I get a bit of the sunshine. It is beginning to get some warmth with it.'

123

Gwen Edwards said, 'Do you mean you have had an accident, Wil?'

Geraint looked up from his book and asked, 'What happened, Dad?'

Wil said impatiently, 'It was nothing at all. I just slipped and the rope brought me up a bit short, bruised a couple of ribs. Nothing to worry about, but you must not tell me any funny stories because I am not allowed to laugh.'

He lighted a cigarette, coughed, winced, and stubbed out the the cigarette quickly.

'Nor cough, either,' he said with a grimace. 'But it was nothing. Not like when you had your accident, eh, Dad?'

The old man said, 'Yes, that was a real accident, that was. . . .'

Wil listened, and at the end of the story he said, 'Well now, that is what I would call an accident.' He turned to Geraint and said suddenly, 'What is this I hear about you and Betty Mai Shafto?'

Geraint flushed.

'Me and Betty Mai? What do you mean, Dad?'

'You are not to have anything to do with her, do you hear? That Shafto is no good, except as a worker. Outside the work I have nothing to do with him, and you must have nothing to do with that girl of his.'

'You climb with him,' Geraint said stubbornly.

Wil seldom raised his voice in speaking to Geraint, but this time he shouted, 'Do not tell me what I do!' He recollected himself and said, 'Shafto is a good man on rock, though where he gets it from I do not know, since he is from the south. But I never climb with him for fun, do I? It is to save life. And, anyway, it is only once in a while. Now no more arguments. You are to have nothing to do with that Betty Mai Shafto, do you understand?'

Geraint said carefully, weighing his words, 'But I do not have anything to do with her, as you call it. She has nothing to do with me, anyhow; put it that way if you like. I don't care.'

Wil said sternly, 'You will do as I say. You are going to be busy, young man. As soon as I am better, you and I will be building a conservatory porch at the front of the house.' He said to the old man, 'I have seen you in that window-seat, stretching your neck like an old tortoise to catch the sun where it comes slanting in. Well, I will make a conservatory porch, and then you can sit under glass like a tomato, and have the sun round you from morning to night when it will be shining. Geraint will have a fine time mixing mortar and doing the sawing.'

Wil ate his supper slowly, stopping from time to time to massage his ribs. When he had finished he turned once more to Geraint, who had been seething quietly, and asked, 'What is this violin examination you are supposed to be going in for?'

'Associated Board of the Royal Schools of Music, Grade Six,' said Geraint formally.

'Well, from now on you practise for an hour every day. You have been doing nothing lately.'

Geraint slammed his book down murderously on the table.

'You won't mind if I *breathe* now and then?' he asked with heavy irony. 'I suppose it will be all right to do a bit of *breathing*?'

Gwen Edwards said hastily, 'Now then, Geraint, you are not to upset your father. I want you to take this cheese-and-onion pie down to your Uncle Tom. Go along with you now.'

Geraint walked towards his uncle's cottage, talking to himself.

'Won't even let you *breathe*. Do this. Do that. Mix mortar, saw wood. Practise, practise, practise. Take this pie. Cah!'

He sat on the wall at the bottom of the lane. Trout would be rising now down on Llyn Padarn, but he didn't care. He was an Arthurian knight, not an authentic fifth-century guerilla leader, but a fourteenth-century knight by television out of Malory, the version he now preferred. He cradled the pie-dish in his lap, breaking off bits of the crust and nibbling at them while King Arthur said to him in English, 'Sir Geraint, wit ye well there is a fair damosel hight the lady Betty—er, shut up in Dolbadarn Castle by a dolorous knight that hath smote even Sir Launcelot, and all to-brast his helm, so that he lieth in peril of his life.' 'Nay, sire,' said Sir Geraint, 'that wot I not of, but sweet Jesu my help, then will I fare forth to-morn and strive with this dolorous knight.' King Arthur said, 'Jolly good show. May God send you great honour and worship, for ye are the best and courteoust of all my knights, saving only Sir Launcelot.' So Sir Geraint fared forth and met the dolorous knight and said to him, 'Sir knight, I would strive with thee for the fair lady that thou hast in this castle,' and the dolorous knight said, 'Thou shalt die therefor,' and smote Sir Geraint with a grim weapon. They contended there all that day, and at the last was Sir Geraint smitten to the ground with his helm all to-brast, just like Sir Launcelot only a sight worse, and Betty Mai came and said, 'Alas, Sir Geraint, this is little amend for the love I bear thee,' and as he was dying she bent down and kissed him and said, 'Look, yon traitor knight is slain by thy last blow,' and she wept as Geraint died, his head in her lap like the pie-dish in his.

Geraint had been moved by all this, and it came as something of a surprise to him when he found that all the pie-crust had disappeared. He wandered down to his uncle's and knocked at the door, then walked in.

His uncle was sitting in the kitchen, tying trout flies.

'Hello,' said Geraint.

His uncle did not look up; he was too busy tying in a seal's fur dubbing to the body of the fly.

He said, 'Oh, it is you, Geraint. I am going on the lake tonight with the otter board and the long line with two hundred flies. Do you think your dad would let you come along? I will have the boat full of fish, and I shall be wanting a hand with them. Ten shillings, you can have.'

Geraint said shortly, 'Dad wouldn't let me. Anyway, I do not want to go.'

'Please yourself. I do not know what has got into you lately, boy. I was talking to the Reverend Davies the other day, about my council house, and he said, "That Geraint Edwards is behaving most peculiarly, Mr Edwards." It sounds a bit confusing, put like that, but you know what he means. That is what he said: "That boy is behaving most peculiarly," see?'

'He has no room to talk,' said Geraint, aggrieved. 'He went to a meeting in Caernarvon last Tuesday morning. At least, he was suppose to go to the meeting, but he stopped outside and turned right round to light his pipe, because of the wind. When he had lighted his pipe he marched off and came straight back here and asked Mrs Davies if his tea was ready, at ten o'clock in the morning! How can you be more peculiar than that?'

He watched his uncle's busy fingers and then said, 'Mam sent me with a cheese-and-onion pie for you.'

'Keep quiet a minute now, while I finish this fly.'

Geraint's uncle tied in the hackle with a whip-finish and applied a dab of spirit varnish to the head of the fly, his breath labouring.

'There.' He looked at the pie for the first time and said, 'Man, devil, what has been happening with that pie?'

Geraint said, 'Oh, yes. . . . Well, I just had a little bite out of it on the way.'

Uncle Tom said, 'Mr Davies was right.' Then he chuckled. 'You had better stay and finish it with me.'

'No,' said Geraint. 'I—I must be getting back now. Good night, Uncle Tom.'

He walked slowly through the village towards the chip shop, where a knot of youngsters had gathered, Billy Davies among them.

'Hey there, Billy,' Geraint greeted him. 'Have they whipped your old man off to Denbigh yet, to the lunatic asylum?'

He spoke in English, affecting the sort of mid-Atlantic accent of the English pop-singer. Billy replied in Welsh.

'Betty Mai has gone home. Bryn Ffoulkes bought her a bag of chips and then took her round the back of the bakery.' He giggled. 'You ask Bryn what happened. He is not feeling too well, that one.'

With a sick sensation in his stomach, Geraint pushed his way into the chattering knot of teenagers. Bryn Ffoulkes was

127

seventeen, a burly, broad-shouldered youth who had already been working for two years at the quarry. Geraint clapped a hand on the leather-jacketed shoulder, and Bryn Ffoulkes spun round, then grinned down at Geraint.

'Well, well, it is Mary's little lamb,' he said.

'What have you been doing with Betty Mai Shafto?'

'You ask a silly question, you get a silly answer,' said Bryn Ffoulkes, dabbing with a handkerchief at a long scratch which ran from the corner of his left eye down to his neck. 'No, honest, I just asked her to come for a ride on my motor-bike. Asked her nicely, I did, back of the bakery. A teaser, that one is, just a teaser. "Dad won't let me go out with boys," so I just started to give her a kiss and a cuddle to cheer her up, and look at me!'

The dolorous knight, thought Geraint.

He said, 'You big fool, she is only fourteen. You keep away from her or it will be the worse for you.'

Bryn Ffoulkes took hold of Geraint's lapels in the approved style and said in English, 'Wise guy, huh? And what d'you think you're going to do about it?'

Geraint said, 'If I tell my dad what has happened he will tell old Shafto, just because he doesn't like him, and then you will have to say your prayers, Bryn Ffoulkes.'

The older youth loosed his grip on Geraint and said palely, 'You would never do that? Old Shafto would kill me.'

'I know he would. You keep away from Betty Mai or I swear I will tell.'

'Tell-tale!' said Bryn Ffoulkes.

Geraint said, 'You can say what you like. I am not a tell-tale, but this is different. You go near Betty Mai Shafto once more and I will see that her dad gets to know about it, and then I will be dancing the twist on your coffin.'

Bryn Ffoulkes said, 'Aw, what's the odds? I was only having a bit of a joke. I ain't a cradle-snatcher. She may look about twenty, but she's only a silly kid like you. I'm going to the Prince for a pint.'

Geraint said, 'See you, Billy,' and walked down the street, turning into the row of terraced houses where Shafto lived. At the house he heard music from the parlour window; Betty Mai was demurely singing, accompanying herself at the piano. The fair damosel was looking remarkably self-possessed. Geraint tapped on the window, and she turned, her eyes wide; then she came over and raised the sash.

'What are you doing here? Go away, quick!'

Geraint said lamely, 'I just came to see if you were all right.'

'All right? Why should I not be all right?'

'Well, you know, I heard about Bryn Ffoulkes.'

Betty Mai laughed.

'Bryn Ffoulkes! Don't you worry about him. I gave him something to remember me by, and it wasn't what he wanted, either. You go away; you are an old nuisance, and I want to do my practice.'

She slammed the window down, narrowly missing Geraint's fingers, and he walked gloomily away. In his versions of the story the fair damosel never insisted on remaining in her tower. And as for himself, he ought to have been lying outside the chip shop, dying.

12

GERAINT mixed mortar, carted bricks, sawed wood, did his homework, practised the violin, and kissed Olwen Morris a few times, pursuing experimental and inconclusive explorations in the almost non-existent leisure time while the conservatory porch was being built. Geraint and his father finished it just before Whitsuntide. Wil Edwards bought a rocking-chair for the old man, who sat contented in the porch in the spring sunshine.

In late June, Maitland came to see Geraint's father and said, 'Yehudi Menuhin is playing at a concert in Liverpool.'

'Who?' asked Wil Edwards.

Maitland said, 'Good Lord, have you never heard of Yehudi Menuhin?'

'Have you ever heard of Ifan y Gorlan?' asked Wil.

'Don't be silly,' said Maitland severely. 'That is different. Nobody has heard of your Ivan whatsisname outside this godforsaken principality in which some crazy masochistic streak in me makes me reside. Exist, I should have said. No, my dear good chap, Yehudi Menuhin is one of the greatest violinists in the world—one of the greatest of all time—and I am offering your half-licked cub the honour and the privilege of clapping eyes on him and hearing him play. It will be an occasion which he will remember with pride for the rest of his life, I promise you.'

Wil said dubiously, 'Well, I don't know. . . . Oh, all right, he can go, but I will be paying for him. You will be letting me know what it costs, and I will pay.'

'Right,' said Maitland. 'That's settled, then. I will book seats for next Thursday.' He looked at Geraint and said, 'My God, the boy looks like a scarecrow. What is that black dung he has taken to putting on his hair?'

Wil said, 'I know, it is terrible, Mr Maitland. I have been telling him and telling him, but you might as well talk to a block of wood.'

Maitland said decisively, 'Well, the block of wood will wash that indescribable filth out of its hair before next Thursday, and have a haircut into the bargain. I might actually meet someone I know while we are in Liverpool, and, anyway, if by some remote chance Menuhin happened to catch sight of that hair while he was playing, he would break every string on the fiddle, I swear to God.'

For the opportunity of hearing Menuhin in the flesh, Geraint would have shaved his head and varnished it. He washed his hair three times, had a haircut, shaved quite unnecessarily every day instead of once a fortnight, and polished his best shoes for hours. He scrubbed his fingernails morning and evening, washed his neck until it was sore. His parents watched with amazement.

Gwen Edwards said, 'Well, never say that no good has come out of that boy's learning the violin, Wil Edwards. It is all worth it just for this, just for seeing him wash.'

They went to Liverpool in Maitland's car, a three-litre Rover, Geraint sitting in his best suit importantly in the front, straining upwards so that he could show off his safety harness to any by-standers. There was little need for the harness: Maitland never exceeded forty miles an hour. Geraint enjoyed the trip just the same; they passed through the Mersey Tunnel from Birken-head to Liverpool, and the lights and roar of traffic all enchanted Geraint.

They emerged at the city exit of the tunnel, and Maitland drove to a side street near the concert hall to park the car.

Before they entered the hall he stopped Geraint and looked at him.

'Well,' he said, 'you look almost human, I must confess. An extraordinary transformation. You may not be able to make a silk purse out of a sow's ear, but you can botch up a passable pigskin wallet.'

They took their seats in the dress circle. The audience was buzzing; Geraint was delighted and a little overawed by the great size of the auditorium. Soon the orchestra came to their places, then there was a roar of applause for the guest conductor, Sir John Barbirolli. The orchestra tuned their instruments, and the discordant sounds filled Geraint with excitement. A tap from Barbirolli, and a hush fell. Overture: *The Magic Flute*.

Then Menuhin. Bruch's G Minor Concerto. Geraint passed into a sort of catalepsy, and when, during the Adagio, Maitland whispered, 'Listen, here comes Gershwin's "Love is the sweetest thing",' Geraint made an angry, impatient motion. At the beginning of the last movement Maitland said, 'Now, watch this double-stopping,' but Geraint needed no telling; his eyes were fixed as though they would burn the varnish off the soloist's violin. At the end he leaped to his feet and clapped until the palms of his hands were sore, bellowing 'Encore!' and oblivious of the curious heads turned in his direction. Menuhin took four bows, but there was no encore.

Geraint sat tolerantly through the rest of the programme, living through Brahms' First Symphony, nodding casual agreement when Maitland pointed out what he took to be certain derivative features in the string passage in the finale; Maitland had a passion for finding derivations. 'D'you hear? Beethoven's Ninth.'

They had supper in the sort of restaurant which promises much but performs little. Maitland badgered the waiter, and Geraint, whose head was filled with music, coped with an array of cutlery which in normal circumstances would have daunted him; as it was, he followed Maitland's lead and ate the indifferent food in silence.

On the way home Maitland passed from an uncritical admiration of Menuhin into a carping mood. He stopped on
the road out of Birkenhead. Geraint saw a large building in
imitation half-timbering. It was floodlit, and a notice read
Holly Tree Country Club'.

Maitland said, 'I'm a member here. Want me to bring you a
drink, boy? Lemonade or some such sewage, I mean, not a real
drink.'

Geraint said, 'No, thank you, Mr Maitland. I don't really want
anything.'

'Right. Won't be a moment. Wait here.'

Maitland returned after half an hour, smelling strongly of
whisky. He drove slowly and with extreme caution, taking the
coast road for Bangor and then turning up towards Bethesda,
then branching right and arriving at his cottage from the Nant
Ffrancon side.

He stopped the car and said, 'Better run you home now, I
suppose.'

Geraint said, 'I would like to go to the lavatory first, please.
I don't think I can wait any longer.'

'All right. Come in.'

When Geraint returned from the lavatory Maitland was sitting with a bottle of whisky and a glass at his side, and a violin
on his knees. He drained the glass and refilled it.

'Yehudi Menuhin,' he said contemptuously.

He emptied the glass and refilled it again, took a drink and
set down the glass.

'Yehudi Menuhin,' he said again. 'Competent, of course.
Highly competent, I would be the last to deny it, but lacking
that extra essential fire, that extra essential fire in the belly.'

Geraint was patting Hennessey, who was fussing round him,
wagging his whole hind quarters rather than just his tail.

'Fire in your belly!' Maitland shouted. 'That's what a man
needs to play the fiddle.'

Geraint looked up and said, 'Is that clock right? It is almost
one in the morning. I had better go home.'

Maitland said boastfully, 'Not before I show you how to play a fiddle with fire in your belly. Listen, boy, you think you are going to be great, don't you? You poor little slob, you will never make the grade. A good third-rater, that's all you'll ever be; but if you get some fire in your belly you might become a fair second-rater. Now listen to this.'

He began to play the solo part of the Bruch last movement. Geraint, hurt and angry though he was, had been frightened by Maitland's outburst, and listened sullenly, watching.

Maitland was good for an amateur, and Geraint had to admit this to himself, but to compare him with Menuhin was ridiculous. Maitland's playing was as far below Menuhin's as Geraint's was below Maitland's. Maitland's execution was flamboyant, his bowing uncertain, even allowing for the whisky. He was making it all sound like a Spanish dance or something, thought Geraint.

Maitland played on. Turning a little, he met Geraint's eyes. The notes faltered and stopped. There was a long silence.

Then Maitland said slowly, 'Terrible. Terrible. I——'

He broke off and laid the violin on the floor, went to the cupboard and brought three more violins, laying them by the first. He picked up the whisky bottle and drank from it long and deliberately, then placed it carefully on the table and, without speaking a word, jumped up and down on the violins, stamping them, grinding the broken mess with his heels, his breath snoring and panting, his eyes fixed and staring in the purple face. His feet caught in the tangled strings, and he fell heavily.

Geraint laughed, a sudden devastating reaction for which he was to reproach himself all his life. The smashing of the violins had contained some quality of frightful ceremonial, had held him horror-struck. And then Maitland had fallen, the idol toppled, and Geraint's horse-laugh pealed out, paying for all the insults and sarcasms and humiliations.

Maitland rolled into a sitting position, rid his feet of the strings and bits of broken wood, and stood up.

He said, 'The biter bit. I took you to that concert to show you how far you still have to go. I have been guilty of *hubris*, and God has said to His angel, "Look, that fellow Maitland's getting a bit above himself; just cut along and kick him up the arse, will you?" But why, why, you bloody Welsh yob, did He have to lay on your presence at my moment of truth?'

He spoke quietly, almost calmly except for a shaking under-tone in his voice.

He said, 'I had a son once, and the poor little bugger died in Korea, and he was a better man than you'll ever be. Now get out, and never come back.'

Geraint said, 'I'm sorry. I didn't——'

'I don't care what you didn't,' said Maitland. 'Just bog off and leave me alone. Albatross yourself off my neck, that's all. Clear out. You can walk home.'

Geraint stood for a moment, then made a helpless gesture and went.

Geraint's grandfather was waiting up for him in the kitchen, sitting in his new rocking-chair.

He said, 'Geraint? You are late, boy. Your supper is on the table, and a glass of milk. Your mam and dad have gone to bed long ago.'

'You should not have waited up for me, Taid,' said Geraint.

'I have been sleeping here. It makes no difference when you are as old as I am: sleep in a bed, sleep in a chair, it is all the same. I like this chair your dad bought me, anyway. When a man gets to my age he likes to sleep a little and then wake a little. Did you enjoy the concert?'

'Oh, yes,' said Geraint. He felt very guilty about the scene at Maitland's cottage, and decided to tell no one about its details. One thing worried him apart from this. He sat at the table and uncovered a plate of sandwiches, took a sip of milk, and began to eat. In a little while he looked up.

'Taid?' he said indistinctly.

'Well, boy?'

Geraint thought a moment and then said, 'Taid, if you want to be really great at something, and then you find out that you will never be really great, is it worth going on?'

The old man said, 'Has that happened to you tonight?'

Geraint said simply, 'Yes. Yes, it has. I have heard Yehudi Menuhin. I shall never be able to play like that.'

'Listen, boy,' said Geraint's grandfather. 'When I was about twenty, and fancying myself with the harp, I went to hear Elis Rowland play. The music of the spheres, no less, music that froze my face into a lump of marble with the tears running down it like the rain. I went home afterwards and played, and the strings of the harp felt like brambles under my fingers, and I very nearly put my foot through the harp.'

'But you didn't?' said Geraint intently.

The old man smiled and said, 'A harp costs money. No, that is a thing that can happen to any musician. There is always someone greater, someone better than people like you and your old Taid. But we are the lucky ones, boy.'

'Lucky? How do you mean?'

'Look. You become the best player in the world, and what happens? You are perfect, and there is only one thing that can take place: one day, you fall from that perfection. It is the price you have to pay for it. Now don't mistake me, Geraint. I am not saying that a man should strive to be something less than the best, that it is good to do that. That is sinful. But if you try, and still you are less than the best, then you have hope. It doesn't matter how long you live, you can still strive and hope that one day you are going to add a cubit to your stature. Sometimes it happens; more often it does not, but the chance is there, even when your hands feel like a bunch of sausages and all the ears in the audience are stuffed with fingers.'

Geraint said, 'Yes, I suppose you are right, and he was wrong. I should not have laughed, though.'

'Eh? What did you say?'

'Oh, nothing,' said Geraint.

The old man's eyes closed, and Geraint thought he had gone

to sleep. He stood up to take the dishes to the sink, and his grandfather said, 'Geraint?' without opening his eyes.

'Yes?'

'Geraint, when will you be going fishing again? There is hunger on me for trout. You have not been fishing as you used to.'

Geraint's heart was warm toward his grandfather.

'I'll go tomorrow night,' he said, 'and you shall have trout for breakfast on Saturday.'

13

DURING that summer Geraint spent much time fishing with his Uncle Tom. When the heavy rain came in August they went on bicycles to the river in the next valley, where the white water leaped and roared amongst great boulders. Uncle Tom fished legitimately for once, and initiated Geraint into the art of fishing a bunch of worms for salmon in high water. Leaning over the bridge, he scrutinized the river for what seemed to Geraint an excessive period of time, then turned, the rain streaming from his sou'wester.

'There are eleven fish in this pool,' he said. 'Can you see them?'

Geraint strained his eyes, and at length saw two grey, shadowy shapes side by side in the middle of the pool, where the bridge shielded a patch of smooth water from the pockmarks of the rain.

He said excitedly, 'I can see two.'

'Come along, then. You had better be having a salmon for yourself.'

They crossed a ladder stile and slithered down the steep wet path. A dipper flitted downstream from a boulder at their approach. Shouting above the roar of the river, Geraint's uncle showed Geraint how to bait the hook.

'Cast straight across,' he advised. 'Drop the worms in at the edge of the rough water, then the current will bring them down on the bottom through the middle of the pool. If you get a knock from a fish wait a bit before you tighten on him. Then swing your rod point downstream, not up, or you will pull the bait right out of his mouth. And, whatever you do, you must hold him. He will run downstream, and if he gets below the tail of the pool he will be gone.'

Geraint cast, retrieved, cast again, retrieved, cast again, retrieved.

'Nothing,' he said, disappointed. 'I didn't feel a thing.'

His uncle said, 'You are fishing for the salmons now, boy, not for your old trout. Keep on fishing. You will not scare them. Sooner or later one will take. Look at it this way: these fish are coming up from the sea through the heavy water, and by the time they get up as far as this, they are tired. This pool is like a waiting-room. The fish come into the pool and say, "Ah, just the job; now for a bit of a rest." Think of your salmon as a man who just wants to settle down for an hour's nap in the waiting-room, when a bluebottle keeps buzzing round his head. He opens his eyes, shuts them again, can't go to sleep for that old buzzing, so he takes a whack at the bluebottle. He gets murder in his heart, boy, I can tell you. Well now, here's your salmon, kipping down on the bottom in the waiting-room, having a rest before he runs farther upstream. Your worms trundle past him, once, again, again. "Man, devil!" he says. "Is there no peace to be had in this pool?" He doesn't want to eat those worms: he just gets annoyed with them, and sooner or later you rattle him into wanting to kill them. Then he's yours. Now try again.'

Geraint cast, and his uncle watched keenly.

'Over his head. Cast just a little upstream as well as across, then your bait will have time to sink to the bottom before the current takes hold of it.'

Geraint obeyed; the worms hit the water, sank, and then the line began to move through an arc with the current, faster and faster. The line stopped, moved slightly, stopped again, two-thirds of the way through the arc.

'Now!'

Geraint swung the rod point downstream and then in towards the bank. The rod bent and the reel screamed briefly before Geraint braked it, staggering backwards and yelling incoherently. Balked of its downstream rush, the salmon zigzagged at the tail of the pool, safely above the white water. Then when it began to run up Geraint applied side strain and turned the fish, making it run down, assuming control and mastery. He forced it up and then down again; then up once more. The fish rolled, its back gleaming in the surface water. Uncle Tom moved softly into the stream, gaffed the fish and brought it to the bank, killing it swiftly and painlessly by letting the blood from the main artery.

'No sense bashing the head off the fish like a fellow coshing some old woman,' he said. 'Well, Geraint, there is your salmon for you. He might make ten and a half pounds; not too bad for a beginning.'

Geraint gazed at the bright silver fish, pride in his heart.

'The nobs say you should always get below your fish to play it,' said his uncle. 'Not in this water, lad: that is the quickest way to lose them. You did well.'

They moved upstream to the next holding pool, where Uncle Tom caught a seventeen-pounder. The rain stopped, so they sat on the bank and ate their sandwiches. Geraint got up repeatedly to look at his fish.

Uncle Tom began to wheeze and cough.

'Hell, devil,' he said. 'This wet does not suit me at all.'

He chewed and coughed, and then said, 'I have not told you the news. I am on the list for a council house, one of those tiny little bungalows with one bedroom. I am right at the bottom of the list, but still it is a start.'

He ate for a while longer, and threw a crust into the river.

'Why do you poach fish?' asked Geraint. 'You can catch fish without poaching them.'

'I know, but it is a matter of principle,' said his uncle seriously. 'It needs a good deal of thought. I have always poached fish and game because it is the only way I can feel free. Look at this country. In the time of your Taid's Taid the land was nearly all common land, and the fishing was free. Then the big landlords started to enclose the common land and take over the fishing rights, and they swindled the smallholders out of their freeholds, making them no better than serfs, indeed. It went on for years and years, and now there is hardly any common land except for what is called common grazing on some of the mountain tops; but I ask you, where can a man go with a rod and catch a fish, or with a gun and shoot a bird, without somebody telling him, "This is our fishing", or, "This is our shooting"? I will tell you. No bloody where at all. Yet our people were here before these others. You have read your history. We were here before the Romans or the Irish or the Saxons or the Normans—why the hell should I pay English landlords or their lickspittles for *my* fish, for *my* game? Eh?'

Geraint was doubtful, though he could see his uncle's point.

'But what about the association? You could join that. The association fees are not high.'

'It doesn't matter,' said Uncle Tom. 'They are fees, and I will not pay a penny to buy what is mine by right.'

Geraint thought about this, and some days later, when the salmon had been eaten and enjoyed amid a chorus of praise from his family, he put the matter to his father.

Wil Edwards said, 'Tom is pig-headed. When there was no organization at all people could take what they liked. Back in the stone age, that would be. But now people own the land, and the River Board stock the waters. All the poacher does is get his living at other people's expense. Tom is just pig-headed.'

Gwen Edwards said, 'Well, we do not turn up our noses when Tom brings us a salmon or a sewin he has poached. Ask no questions, that is my motto.'

Pig-headed? wondered Geraint. It seemed to him that all grown-ups were pig-headed in one way or another. His father, for example, or Shafto, or Maitland. Why did his father still forbid him to see Betty Mai when there was no need to continue a rivalry which did not really have any basis? Betty Mai sang; he played the violin, yet his father and Shafto were still scarcely on speaking terms. There had been that business on the mountain, of course, and Shafto and Geraint's father had had that fight, which was beginning to pass into the mythological annals of the village. But it was pride, Geraint decided. Grown-ups took up an attitude, and then froze in it. Pride did not necessarily lead to a fall, but it certainly led to pig-headedness. In Maitland's case too. Maitland might have been able to delude himself into thinking he was as brilliant a violinist as Yehudi Menuhin, but the bubble of his pride had been pricked in Geraint's presence. So he had destroyed those violins. What was that if not pig-headedness? Geraint considered the matter further, and concluded that he had every reason to continue to see Betty Mai if he wanted to, as he did. And if he detected a trace of pig-headedness in his decision he decided that he had plenty of grown-up example to follow.

Later in the month the local fair was to be held. Maldwyn Shafto came home for a fortnight's holiday, accompanied by a friend, and roared into the village in the friend's sports car in British racing green. Maldwyn was transformed, and Geraint gawped with Billy Davies as the two men stopped outside the Prince of Gwynedd and alighted from the sports car. Maldwyn now had two cauliflower ears instead of just one, for he had continued to play rugby football for his company's team in the Midlands; he was now six feet four, and he was dressed in a way which made Geraint acutely conscious of his baggy and thread-bare school uniform. Maldwyn wore narrow biscuit-coloured slacks, suède shoes, a green corduroy jacket without lapels, and a plum-coloured shirt with a yellow cravat. The driver of the car wore black slacks, suède shoes similar to Maldwyn's, and an enormous hairy fawn sweater.

'Phew!' said Billy Davies. 'Look at those brothel-creepers they are wearing.' He called, 'Hi, Maldwyn!'

Maldwyn turned, looked through Billy and Geraint without recognition, and steered his companion into the inn. Geraint and Billy drifted across the street and looked critically at the sports car, discussing it with great attention to the finer technical points. The car was dusty, and they were debating whether to risk writing *Clean me* in the dust on a door panel when they noticed Shafto himself coming along the street, and so they faded away before him and went into the grounds of the minister's house.

'I am fed up,' said Billy Davies. 'Nothing to do.'

'You wait,' Geraint advised. 'There is the fair next week. We will have a good time at the fair, I bet. You will all be entertained.' He hunted for a phrase, and then went on in English, 'The local populace will be astonished.'

'Why?' said Billy.

'Just you wait, that's all.'

Two days later Geraint met Betty Mai in the village.

'Hello, Betty Mai,' he said.

She was carrying a basket of groceries. Geraint walked along with her, without offering to carry the basket. He slouched along beside her with his hands in his pockets.

'Why don't you stand up straight when you walk?' said Betty Mai.

Geraint grunted and said, 'Who is that character who has come home with your Maldwyn?'

Betty Mai simpered.

'Nice, isn't he?'

'Nice?' said Geraint, aghast. 'Like a wandering hearthrug he seemed to me, in that sweater. I thought it was an old English sheepdog or something.'

Betty Mai said, 'His name is Peter, and I think he is nice. He's twenty, and his dad gave him that car for his birthday: think of that!'

'For his birthday? I don't believe it. No one has as much money as that.'

'Peter's dad has. Maldwyn says they have three cars at home—a great big house it is, with servants and all.'

Geraint whistled, much impressed. Then he recalled his attention to the matter in hand.

'Listen, Betty Mai,' he said. 'How about coming with me to the fair?'

Betty Mai said, 'Why, don't be silly! You know as well as I do that Maldwyn would murder you if he saw you with me.'

Geraint said, 'He won't, I promise. Come with me, and I swear there will be no bother. No bother over you and me, I mean.'

They arrived at the house, and Betty Mai said quickly and rather breathlessly, 'Would you like to come in?'

Geraint said, 'But——'

'Oh, it's all right. Peter has taken everybody off to the sea, and they are going to have lunch out. If I know my dad, Peter will be paying, too. Peter wanted to take me with Maldwyn, but Dad said he wanted to go with Mam. You should have seen them, squashed up on that tiny back seat! I think Peter was quite disappointed I didn't go.' She added demurely, 'I think he suggested the trip in the first place because he wanted to go with me.'

Geraint ground his teeth and said, 'Oh, you do?'

'Well?' said Betty Mai. 'Are you coming in?'

Geraint slunk into the house behind Betty Mai. He had seen plenty of movies and television plays, and his course was charted by them. As soon as the door closed he grabbed Betty Mai by the shoulders, spun her round to face him, and kissed her clumsily. She pushed him away, though not fiercely.

'Now then,' she said. 'Who do you think I am—Olwen Morris?'

Taken aback, Geraint released her, and she wagged a finger at him.

She smiled innocently up into his eyes.

'Kiss and tell,' she said 'Olwen Morris kisses and tells. Talk about laugh!'

Geraint turned his head, staring in embarrassed rage at an aspidistra in a stand on a level with his eyes.

'Come upstairs,' Betty Mai commanded suddenly.

Geraint said, 'But——'

She turned on her heel and went up the narrow stairs, Geraint following like a prisoner going to execution. She opened a door.

'This is my bedroom,' she said.

Geraint blundered forward. Betty Mai shut the door hastily.

'Not in there,' she said. 'I haven't made the bed yet.' She turned to another door. 'In here.'

The beds were not made in that room either. Geraint went in with Betty Mai and stood helplessly, his knees weak, his mouth dry. What would happen now?

'Maldwyn and Peter sleep here,' said Betty Mai. 'It is a mess, isn't it?'

She moved over to a chest of drawers and rummaged.

'Look,' she said. 'Here is that sweater of Peter's.'

Betty Mai held it up.

'Put it on,' she said. 'Go on.'

Obediently Geraint thrust his head into the hairy folds of the sweater. It hung about him, and the sleeves were too long. He pulled them up and looked at Betty Mai in a sort of dumb supplication. She came over to him, her eyes glistening, and put her arms round him, then buried her face in the chest of the sweater. Numbly Geraint held her. He bent his head, and her hair tickled his nose while he breathed the scent of it. He kissed the top of her head.

They stood together awkwardly, and Geraint began to feel his shyness being overmastered by a variety of sensations. Then Betty Mai released him abruptly and stood back, regarding him objectively and sadly.

'It's no good,' she said. 'Take it off.'

Geraint removed the sweater, which had been making him feel very hot, and Betty Mai replaced it in the drawer, folding it with what seemed to Geraint excessive care.

'Come on,' she said with sudden haste. 'They'll kill me if anyone finds us here.'

She took his hand and dragged him out of the bedroom and downstairs, opening the street door and pushing him outside.

'Here,' said Geraint. 'What's all this hurry all of a sudden? What's the idea?'

Betty Mai said, 'Er, I just remembered the rent man will be coming. Go now, quickly.'

Geraint said, 'Well, what about the fair?'

She shrugged indifferently.

'Oh, all right, I'll come to the old fair with you if you like, and if you're sure there will be no trouble. About seven, at the end of the street next Tuesday?'

Geraint walked slowly away in a fog compounded of equal parts of puzzlement and joy. He had kissed Betty Mai Shafto in a bedroom; that fact was indubitable. That would make Billy Davies blink. But why had she wanted to make him wear that sweater? Perhaps she thought it suited him. She had said it was no good; well, anyone could see that it was miles too big. He shook his head and went home to his own bedroom, where he considered his own wardrobe, and had to admit that it could not be called extensive or up-to-date.

He possessed a school uniform, a best suit of prickly grey worsted, a pair of blue jeans which he seldom wore, having once caught himself in the zipper of the fly and having conceived a dislike for them in consequence. He had two pairs of khaki shorts, now a tight fit, a raincoat of school regulation navy blue, a navy-blue overcoat, and two fishing jackets, one of which was much too small to be worn. He had plenty of shirts, mostly of regulation cream-coloured flannel. There was one bright check shirt.

'Great God,' he said to himself. 'I shall just have to have clothes for all my birthdays and for Christmas for the next ninety years.'

He would just have to wear the blue jeans with the check shirt, he decided. He would watch out for those jeans, though.

He moped downstairs and sat gloomily in the kitchen. He

could hear his grandfather even at that distance, snoring in the conservatory porch, and clicked his tongue with irritation.

'What is it with you?' his mother asked sharply.

'Taid,' said Geraint. 'Ought to have him fitted with a silencer or something. Rattling away there.'

'Tut now,' his mother said. 'What are you doing tonight, fishing again?'

Geraint said, 'Think I'll go round to old Billy's. We want to ask his old man if he will let us give that jalopy of his a decoke.'

'What language!' his mother sighed. 'Sometimes I can scarcely understand you at all. A decoke?'

Geraint said patiently, 'The car has not been pulling at all well because it is all coked up, see? I think Billy and I will be able to get the cylinder head off, and all I hope is that we'll be able to put it back again afterwards.'

Gwen Edwards said, 'Well, whatever it is that you are doing, I'll be bound it is something that will make you with dirt up to your eyebrows.'

'Brrmm!' said Geraint. 'When we've finished with it that car will go like a bomb. Mr Davies the Flying Baptist, that's what he will be.'

'As long as it doesn't blow up like a bomb,' his mother said.

'Mam?'

'Well?'

'Mam, could you knit me one of those real thick sweaters for Christmas? You know, a great thick hairy one: I don't know what they are called.'

'Mohair, I expect. Why do you want one of those?'

Geraint said, 'Er—well, it might be a hard winter, mightn't it?'

On the evening of the fair Geraint dressed carefully in blue jeans and check shirt. His hair was cut short, and without oil. It was a warm, oppressive evening. He took out the larger of his two fishing jackets, holding it up and considering; then he replaced it. If it rained he would just have to shelter. He went downstairs.

'Where are you going?' his father asked.

Geraint said, 'Why, to the fair. Didn't you know?'

Wil Edwards said, 'And how much money have you?'

'Not much. I'm only taking about five shillings.'

'I should think so too. Five shillings is a lot of money. Try not to spend it all, and don't be late. I want you home by half past nine, do you hear? And keep away from those Shaftos.'

Geraint stood registering unutterable weariness.

His mother said, 'He looks tired, Wil. Outgrowing his strength, that is what he is doing. Why, the boy is not fifteen yet, and look at him: he is going to be taller than you.'

'I am not tired,' Geraint said irritably. 'Have you both finished going on at me? That is what makes me feel tired. I feel fine when you stop.'

He turned quickly and left the house before his parents could find a rejoinder.

'Gwen,' said Wil Edwards. 'That boy is getting above himself. I cannot make him out.'

'He is growing fast,' his wife said. 'You must make allowances.'

'But why does he always have to argue and put on that stupid expression? Half the time he moons about the house like a dying duck, and half the time he is getting under my feet and wilfully annoying me. I cannot understand it.'

'He will grow out of it,' said Gwen Edwards. 'A fine big lad he is getting.'

Wil said, 'It is time I taught him to climb.'

'Next year, Wil. Leave it till next year, please,' said Gwen Edwards. 'He will have more of his strength then.'

Geraint felt quite strong as it was. And nervous, too, as he waited at the farther end of the village street, imagining that the eyes of every passer-by were upon him—as indeed they were. Mrs Owen the butcher's wife passed with Mrs Evans the bakery.

Geraint said, reconstructing their conversation to his liking,

'Who is that Geraint Edwards waiting for?' 'I don't know; I bet he's up to no good.' 'Has your husband locked the shop? You want to be careful: he is a proper daredevil.' 'Yes, but a handsome young man. I wish it was a hundred years ago and I was his age. Isn't he good-looking?'

Geraint grinned at his image in a shop window. Where was Betty Mai?

Betty Mai appeared unhurriedly at twenty past seven, wearing tight slacks and an imitation-sheepskin jacket.

'Hello,' she said. 'Am I very late?'

'Oh, no,' said Geraint, 'it is only about midnight. Come on.'

They walked down the street, leaving the village behind.

'Is Maldwyn coming to the fair?' asked Geraint.

Betty Mai sniffed.

'I have been waiting and waiting,' she said. 'I thought Peter might take us in his car. If he had given me a lift I would have asked him to stop and pick you up. But Maldwyn is taking him to some pub, and they are coming to the fair later.'

'I hope it won't be too late,' said Geraint earnestly.

'Why? I thought you didn't like Maldwyn. He doesn't like you, anyway.'

'Oh,' said Geraint evasively. 'All that was a long time ago. I—er—I think Maldwyn is quite okay, really. You tell him that when you get a chance.'

Betty Mai looked surprised.

'I certainly will,' she said.

The fair was a small and dilapidated collection of stalls and sideshows, with a rickety roundabout which clattered round to the music of an asthmatic steam organ. It was held in one of Prydderch's fields—the one which had held kale, and a pheasant, just before Geraint's twelfth birthday. That had been two and a half years ago. It seemed an incredible distance of time to Geraint. Why, he thought, as they walked past a coconut-shy, people were throwing at coconuts just about on the spot where he and Uncle Tom had caught the pheasant. And he had hated Betty Mai then.

'This used to be a field of kale a long time ago,' he said excitedly. 'Do you remember?'

'Goodness, no. Why should I?'

'My Uncle Tom had a pheasant out of it. I remember that all right.' He grinned and said, 'It was the summer after that when we got lost in the mist, remember?'

'Now that is something I shall never forget, indeed,' said Betty Mai. 'How about having a shot at the coconuts?'

Geraint said, 'Very well.'

He paid for six balls, threw them hard and with some accuracy, but failed to win a prize.

'Those coconuts are riveted on to the stands,' he said. 'It was funny up the mountain that time, wasn't it?'

'Not so funny when we got back.'

'. . . Betty Mai?'

'What?'

'How about coming for a walk next week sometime—up the mountain?'

Betty Mai said, 'You keep your mind on this fair, Geraint Edwards. You win me one of those big furry pandas.'

'Well, if I do will you come for a walk with me?'

'I might,' said Betty Mai. 'I might. Here, let's have a go at throwing those darts. I'll pay this time.'

Geraint stood next to Betty Mai, holding his darts and watching her as she threw, her eyes shining, her tongue protruding between her lips as she concentrated.

'No good,' she said as she threw the final dart. 'Why, you haven't thrown yours yet!'

'No . . .' said Geraint.

She said impatiently, 'Go on, then, what are you waiting for?'

Geraint threw his darts, one after the other, without taking aim properly.

'You weren't even trying,' Betty Mai accused him.

'I wish it would get dark,' Geraint said miserably. 'I have to be home by half past nine. Why, it won't be anywhere near dark by then.'

They moved on to the rifle-range.

'All these rifles have crooked barrels,' Geraint grumbled, as he selected one and took aim at a row of clay pipes. He smashed them all, and stood back in wonderment. The stallkeeper glowered at him, and wordlessly handed over a blue and white plush rabbit two feet high.

Geraint said indignantly, 'Here, what am I supposed to do with this? I don't want a rabbit. Give me that box of chocolates.'

The stallkeeper was English. He said, 'Them chocolates is for show only. You take that rabbit and be thankful. Many a kid would give his bleeding left hand for a rabbit like that, straight up he would. You take it and sling your bleeding hook.'

Geraint pulled Betty Mai to a safe distance and said, 'Did you hear that? I very nearly punched him on the nose. I would have done if it hadn't been for you.'

Betty Mai said, 'I think it is a lovely rabbit.'

'Here,' said Geraint ungraciously. 'Have it. I don't want the thing. Why wouldn't he give us those chocolates?'

'Oh, stop grousing,' said Betty Mai, hugging the toy rabbit. 'He's a beautiful old bun, aren't you, bunny? I'll take him to bed with me tonight and cuddle him. Peter Rabbit.'

'You can't call a rabbit Peter.'

'Peter Rabbit is called Peter, isn't he? I can't call him Geraint, now can I? Geraint doesn't fit a rabbit at all. Geraint is a silly name. It doesn't fit anything.'

Geraint said, 'Shut up. Here comes Bryn Ffoulkes. I don't want to see him just now.'

But there was no avoiding him in the narrow path between the stalls. He lurched towards them with two of his cronies, clad in shiny black P.V.C. jackets.

'Hey, look who's here,' said Bryn Ffoulkes. 'Mary Mary quite contrary and her little lamb, no less.'

Betty Mai tossed her head in contempt and turned away. Geraint stood quietly, waiting.

One of Bryn Ffoulkes's friends said, 'What's up with him?'

'Who, him?' said Bryn Ffoulkes. 'I don't know. What is it, babby, did he go and lose his mammy?'

He eyed the rabbit which Betty Mai was holding. He leaned forward and grabbed it swiftly.

'What's this?' he demanded.

'Give me that.'

Betty Mai leaped for the rabbit as Bryn Ffoulkes held it aloft. Geraint jumped too, getting a whiff of the beer from Bryn Ffoulkes's breath. Bryn Ffoulkes threw the rabbit to one of his friends, who passed it to the other, who tossed it to Bryn Ffoulkes again, while Geraint and Betty Mai stood helpless. Then Bryn Ffoulkes dropped the rabbit on the muddy, foot-churned surface of the ground and spurned it with his foot.

'That for your rabbit,' he said. 'And that for you as well.'

His friends laughed.

Bryn Ffoulkes said with sly menace, 'We may meet you two later, on the way home. Two of us to hold the little lamb while I have a good time with Mary, isn't it?'

They moved off. Betty Mai was crying quietly.

Geraint bent, picked up the rabbit, and gave it to her.

'Never mind,' he said. 'It will clean up when the mud dries. It will all brush off.'

Betty Mai said, 'I hate that Bryn Ffoulkes. Do you think . . .? I mean, will they really do anything on the way home?'

'They have it coming to them,' Geraint said. 'At least, I hope so.'

They went on the roundabout. Geraint sat on a big cockerel, while Betty Mai chose a bear. They held hands disconsolately, the unsynchronized motions of their steeds stretching first Geraint's and then Betty Mai's arm up and down like a pump-handle. Round and round they went, the music wheezing about them. Halfway through the course of the roundabout Geraint caught a glimpse through the crowd of Betty Mai's brother and his friend Peter. When the roundabout jerked to a halt Geraint leaped off, handed down Betty Mai and then dropped her hand.

'Wait here,' he said. 'I'll be back in a minute.'

He pushed his way through the crowd and looked round for Maldwyn Shafto. Maldwyn and Peter were at the rifle-range, and Geraint walked purposefully towards them, then waited while they finished shooting. The stallkeeper noted Geraint's arrival with a dyspeptic eye.

He said, 'I thought I bleeding well told you to sling your hook.'

Maldwyn and Peter laid down their rifles, shrugged.

'Crooked barrels, that's what they have,' said Peter.

Geraint said, 'Maldwyn.'

Maldwyn turned, his cauliflower-eared, broken-nosed face in strong contrast to Peter's fair and unmarked features.

He said, 'My God, it's young Edwards. What the hell do you want? I don't want to talk to you.'

Geraint said, 'No, but you will want to listen to what I have to say.'

'Who's this?' Peter demanded. 'Friend of yours, Mal?'

Both men smelled of whisky, and the reek recalled to Geraint's mind a sudden memory of Maitland.

'God no,' said Maldwyn. 'A local kid, that's all. Clear off.'

'Just what I been telling him,' the stallkeeper said.

Geraint said, 'Maldwyn, Betty Mai and I had a rabbit from this stall, and Bryn Ffoulkes took it and stamped it in the mud.'

'Kid stuff. Why don't you fight your own battles? I thought I once showed you what would happen if you didn't stay away from Betty Mai.'

Maldwyn took a step forward, his open hand raised. Geraint stood firm.

He said darkly, 'Last Whitsun Bryn Ffoulkes took Betty Mai round the back of the bakery one night.'

Maldwyn's hand fell.

'What?'

'Ask anybody, they will tell you. Ask Billy Davies. Bryn Ffoulkes said he would take care of you if you wanted to start anything.'

Maldwyn breathed slowly out.

'He said that?'

He turned to Peter.

'Come on. We have an appointment.'

Geraint said, as an extra spur, 'Bryn Ffoulkes said he was going to catch us on the way home and have a good time with Betty Mai.'

He followed Maldwyn and Peter, signalling to Betty Mai, who joined him, running up to him and holding his hand tightly, while Maldwyn stalked unnoticing through the fairground.

Bryn Ffoulkes was at the bob-apple barrel, his head over the water, his big mouth with its bad teeth gaping wide, while his two cronies grinned and shouted encouragingly. He bit into the apple.

'A gift from heaven,' said Maldwyn Shafto softly. 'It is a gift from heaven.'

He strode forward, picked up Bryn Ffoulkes by the ankles, and up-ended him into the barrel. A quantity of displaced water splashed out, drenching down the side of the barrel. Someone shouted gleefully.

Bryn Ffoulkes's legs waved a moment, then began to thrash about; water poured over the feet of Bryn Ffoulkes's companions, and Bryn Ffoulkes heaved out of the barrel, the apple still in his mouth. He spat it out, gasping, dripping.

'Who did that?'

'Why, I did,' said Maldwyn Shafto. 'Who else?'

'Take him, fellers!' Bryn Ffoulkes roared, and hurled himself at Maldwyn; the other two rushed forward also. Peter thrust his foot between the legs of the nearer, who fell heavily. Peter jumped with both feet on his victim's head, then staggered forward, recovered himself like a cat, and dropped Bryn Ffoulkes's other friend with three fast, boxer's punches—left to the solar plexus, right to the throat, left to the point of the chin. Then he stood back and watched.

Bryn Ffoulkes swung a right at Maldwyn, who countered it

with his left forearm as he went in and drove his head at Bryn Ffoulkes's jaw. Bryn Ffoulkes dodged sideways and uppercut; Maldwyn's nose began to bleed. A left from Maldwyn, delivered with all his force at the point of the jaw, landed high, into Bryn Ffoulkes's mouth; he spat teeth.

Geraint squeezed Betty Mai's hand, smiling seraphically.

Bryn Ffoulkes banged his head into Maldwyn's already damaged nose. Maldwyn reeled back into the crowd which had collected, and which was yelling excitedly. He came forward again, becoming calm but breathing heavily through his mouth.

The second friend of Bryn Ffoulkes got dizzily to his feet.

Peter went over to him, said, 'Haven't you forgotten something, old man?' and hit him crisply under the right side of the jaw; he went down and stayed there. The one whose head had been jumped on had not stirred.

Bryn Ffoulkes was tiring. He was younger than Maldwyn, and, though probably stronger, had not the rugby player's stamina; also, he had drunk a lot more. His guard began to drop, and Maldwyn pierced it again and again. Bryn Ffoulkes's cheek was cut, and a puffy lump appeared under the right eye, which began to close.

Somebody shouted, 'Police!' and the crowd melted, dematerialized. Bryn Ffoulkes said thickly, 'Copperth. It'th the copperth. That'th enough,' through the gaps in his teeth.

Maldwyn said adenoidally, 'Go od, thed. Ad just you stay away frob Betty Bai.'

Bryn Ffoulkes shambled off, leaving his friends where they lay.

Maldwyn said, 'Cub od, Peter, that bastard's bust by dose. We'll have to rud for it to the car.'

Betty Mai said, 'Oh, Peter, I think you were wonderful!' and ran off with them, grasping Peter's arm and leaving Geraint standing flabbergasted by the two unconscious men.

The policeman, Mr Pritchard, arrived.

'Geraint Edwards,' he said sternly. 'Did you do this? Have you been fighting?'

Geraint said to himself, 'That sweater. That was why she wanted me to wear that sweater. Why, the——' He turned to the policeman and said, 'Fighting? No, I have not been fighting. I was just standing here.'

The man upon whose head Peter had jumped sat up.

He said, 'Oh Christ.'

Mr Pritchard said, 'What has been going on here, then?'

The second man rolled over and stood up groggily.

'What has been going on?' Mr Pritchard demanded again.

The first man said, 'Well now, you see . . .' and thought for a moment, then went on, 'We were running. I was running to catch my bus, and he was running the other way, with our heads down like, isn't it? We never saw each other.'

He got painfully to his feet, rubbing his neck. Mr Pritchard was a kind, scholarly man, but observation was not his strongest point.

'Head on,' said the second man. 'A head-on crash we had.'

Mr Pritchard sighed.

'That is your story,' he said. 'No fighting?'

'Fighting?' said the first man. 'Never in a million years. We're friends, we are.'

'Are you sure you saw no fighting?' Mr Pritchard asked Geraint.

Geraint said, 'I saw nothing at all. I heard a lot of people shouting, and the next I knew these two were lying on the ground.'

Mr Pritchard said, 'Oh, it is a frustrating life in the extreme. This village is a hot-bed of illicit activities, but can you pin anything down? No. Fighting, boozing, poaching; the Mosaic Law shattered into a veritable jigsaw puzzle; but can you get a case? No. Nine long years I have been here, and two cases, both holiday visitors and both parking on the bus stop where the lettering on the road has been worn away. Both cases dismissed in the interests of the tourist trade.'

He sighed again and said, 'Well, my troubles are no concern of yours, Geraint.' To the other two he said severely, 'Now just make yourselves scarce, because I tell you it is growing on me to have you both for conduct likely to cause a breach of the peace.'

Geraint walked home as a shaft of sunlight touched the summit of Moel Eifion above his head; the sun was setting and the valley was growing darker already. Overlaying his triumph over Bryn Ffoulkes and Maldwyn—the long-standing scores settled at last—was the pain of his parting with Betty Mai. Peter, he thought. It had been Peter all the time. Damn Betty Mai. He would never speak to her again.

When he arrived home his father and mother were in the parlour with the old man. There was a strange feeling of something wrong. The television set was not switched on; Wil Edwards and the old man were sitting with set faces, Wil leaning forward with his hands clasped. Geraint's mother had been crying.

Geraint said, 'Why, what is the matter, Mam?'

Wil Edwards rose and placed a hand on Geraint's shoulder.

'Geraint,' he said. 'It is your Uncle Tom. He is dead.'

14

GERAINT attended his uncle's funeral like an un-
interested and uninvolved spectator, curious about
the burial service but unable to connect the wooden
coffin, as it was lowered into the grave, with his uncle at all. He
felt no sense of loss. His abiding impression on that occasion was
the black, enormous-seeming depth of the grave in relation to
its width. He heard the grown-ups sobbing and sniffing as a
background to the minister's prayers, but Geraint was staring
down into the grave, a pitch-black lift shaft straight down to the
bowels of the earth. They went back after the service to the
cottage, accompanied by seldom-seen cousins and aunts and the
minister.

Everybody talked about Uncle Tom as though he had been a
saint. Well, of course, Geraint thought he had been a good man,
but not in a grown-ups' way. He had been a lifelong poacher,
none too clean in his habits, had no respect for the law at all,
used the minister as a lever to try to obtain a council house but
scarcely ever had gone near the chapel, had been from all
accounts the randiest bachelor for miles around in his younger
days—and here they all were, talking about him as though he
had been hoisted up to heaven after a personal appearance of
the Archangel Gabriel. Geraint shook his head. If the grown-
ups were right, then something was wrong.

Gwen Edwards fed her family and guests on cold ham and
pickles, followed by biscuits and sweet pastries, and the tearful
elegies abruptly ceased as they got down to the job in hand.

Geraint ate as busily as anyone, for he found himself very hungry.

Geraint's grandfather had said nothing so far, but suddenly spoke.

'He was a good boy, Tom was. When he was a baby we used to wonder whether we should be able to rear him, he was so thin and weakly. But he was always a good boy in his way. And now he is the first to go after his mam.'

Wil Edwards said, 'It is a pity he never got his council house before he died. He had set his heart on that.'

No one else said anything, the grown-ups because they presumably felt that they had already done their bit, and Geraint because his mouth was full. But he thought that his grandfather had said the best that should have been said about Uncle Tom.

In the months that followed Geraint realized that his Uncle Tom was really dead, that he would never poach a salmon or catch a pheasant again, and Geraint felt desolate when his first numbness had passed. He missed his uncle keenly then. It had not been the silicosis which had killed him, but a heart condition aggravated by his bronchitis.

The quarry was on full-time working, and Wil Edwards brought home a pay-packet every week, which made things easier. In due course Uncle Tom's will was proved. He left his gold watch to Geraint, together with his fly-tying equipment and various items of fishing tackle; the rest of his estate, about a hundred and seventy pounds, came to Wil, went into the bank, and there it stayed on deposit. Wil was a careful man.

Geraint's fifteenth birthday arrived, and he was given a new bicycle, having grown out of the old one, which Wil sold for two pounds: as much as he had paid for it in the first place. In the spring Wil took Geraint into the hills and began to teach him to climb.

Geraint had passed his Grade VI music examination, and was to take his General Certificate of Education in the summer. His father had said, 'Enough is enough, boy: you are working too hard over your books. We will go out and you shall learn how to be safe on a mountain.'

They spent the first day on the slopes of Elidir Fawr, while Wil taught Geraint the knots to use on the rope, and how to move while roped. The following week-end they went over to the rock-faces above Marchlyn Mawr, and there Geraint learnt how to belay the rope. They did a practice climb up a very easy pitch, and Wil expressed his satisfaction.

Munching a tomato sandwich and looking down at the almost circular lake, Geraint said, 'Dad, do you know I was once afraid of the mountains? I never told you, but I was scared stiff. I used to think it was caused when we saw that man fall into the lake—remember?—but I don't think that was the reason. I suddenly found I wasn't frightened any more, and it has always puzzled me. I think now I was afraid because I knew how good you were, and I thought you would suddenly start making me climb very difficult pitches, and laugh at me or something. I don't know, though; it is a mystery.'

His father said, 'When did you find your fear had gone?'

'When I went up to the top of Moel Eifion with Betty Mai that time.'

'Hm,' said his father. 'The less said about that the better. But it was the first time you had been to the top of a mountain?'

'Yes.'

'There you are,' said his father. 'A fear faced is a fear overcome. But fear leads to respect. Respect the mountains; that way, you have a better chance of staying alive.'

Under his father's tuition Geraint developed into a sound climber on dry rock. His father had bought boots for him and nailed them with tricouni nails; Geraint delighted in the security of foothold which these afforded. He delighted, too, in a new-found freedom of relationship with his father. Wil Edwards seemed now to treat Geraint less as a baby and more as an equal. On one occasion his father was leading on a traverse when he slipped. Geraint had been paying out the rope, keeping it taut. He had belayed in front of him, round his body, and behind him. His father uttered no cry as he fell, swung for a moment until his scrabbling feet found a hold, and then regained his place. He simply turned round to Geraint and said, panting a little, 'You belayed well. Come up to me now, and you can lead on the next pitch.' Geraint had never loved his father so much as in that instant: he looked up at the man, his big, powerful frame looming above, the wind ruffling the thinning hair over the broad, swarthy, rather flat face, and adored him.

June approached, and they had to restrict their climbing because of the onset of Geraint's examinations. Day after day Geraint sat with his classmates in the school hall, scribbling furiously. Betty Mai, Olwen Morris, Billy Davies, and the others —all were similarly scribbling, pausing for thought, biting their pens, scribbling again, while the late June sun sent its burning shafts through the tall windows, lighting here a head of soft haloed hair, there a dazzling white script, the only sounds the quiet footfalls of the invigilators and the interminable scratching of pens like the stridulation of some alien species of grasshopper in the dry grass of summer outside.

Madog Parry bent over a half-ton block of slate and moved it, casually and easily. He had the quarryman's understanding of the way stone behaves, the place where power must be applied to move weights far beyond mere brutish strength, an appreciation of the way in which to use the strength of the body in conjunction with the readiness of the stone to move in a certain direction—a sort of judo against an immeasurably stronger opponent. There is experience in it, there is knack, and there is something else: an affinity with the nature of the rock.

He mopped his brow, left the block of slate, and went up to the top of Patagonia. Wil Edwards was sitting with Persimmon Hughes, their backs to the cliff, looking out over the galleries, over the tiny figures busy below, to the slopes of Moel Eilio, blue and purple in the heat. The sound of a drill came to them faintly from The Haymarket like a bluebottle buzzing in a window pane.

'You have some sense, then,' Madog Parry said, as he seated himself next to Wil. 'There is a touch of breeze up here, but it is like an oven down on the roadway. I thought of making a start with that big block, but then I came up to see what you were doing. It is the best thing to sit down and take a breather.'

Persimmon Hughes said, 'We were having a look at that crack, see?'

Madog Parry stood up and inspected the crack.

'It hasn't changed in a year,' he said. 'I reckon Iolo Jones knows his job all right. He said the crack was safe.'

He sat down again.

Persimmon Hughes said, 'Iolo Jones knows his job well enough, none better in the whole of the Bron Eifion. The trouble is he does not know himself. He is a man for letting his temper rule his good judgement, is Iolo. Shafto still thinks the crack is dangerous.'

Wil Edwards said, 'Shafto is just being awkward. You tell him the moon is not made of green cheese and he will argue that it is. Iolo is the same, too.'

'Well,' said Madog Parry, 'it is as may be. One thing: if this mountain suddenly took it into its head to fall down we should know about it, right enough, for we are sitting on it.'

Persimmon Hughes chuckled and said, 'You would not see our backsides for dust, indeed.'

Wil Edwards got up and went to the edge. Persimmon Hughes followed him; Wil pointed down to the top of Jim Crow, where the curve of the gallery was interrupted by a sudden scar, and below it lay a fan-shaped jumble of rock.

He said, 'That rock fell on the day I was born. Two thousand tons or more. It might have killed fifty men, but it fell half an hour after knocking-off time. I often think about it, for my old man was working on Jim Crow in those days.'

Persimmon Hughes said, 'It is a funny thing. When there is a big fall it always happens at night, or at the week-end, or when there is a holiday. A funny thing indeed.'

Wil said seriously, 'It is the hand of God, Persimmon. If He takes account of the fall of a sparrow you can bet He will choose His time for letting a couple of thousand tons of rock fall down.'

'Well,' said Persimmon Hughes, 'as long as I am not underneath or on top when He blows the fuse, that is all. I have always been happiest on the touchline watching the game. A natural spectator I am.'

Wil suddenly burst out, 'I would be happier if that Shafto would go back to his coal. He has not come today, and we have had to walk to work and get here late, and why? Madog says he has a hangover.' He turned to Madog Parry and shouted, 'Why cannot you see that Shafto drinks less? If you must drink you could at least see that Shafto is going to be fit for work next morning. Or push him into the river and have done. I am tired of this. He keeps missing work and throwing us sim-sam because he does not turn up, and then when he is here he needles Iolo Jones every time they meet.'

Madog Parry said, 'Take it easy, Wil. I like a drink, you know that. We are not all like you. You can sweat all day and make it up on tea, but I have to have my beer. So does Shafto. He just gets carried away, that's all: just carried away from time to time. Celebrating, you know.'

'Celebrating? What has he got to celebrate?'

Madog Parry said, 'Well, you might call it celebrating in advance. He was going on about Betty Mai last night—you know —how she was going to win first prize at the eisteddfod and so on.'

Blackly, Wil said, 'We have hung about here long enough. And now we will go and work.'

Geraint finished his examinations; the results would be known in August. He could not relax completely, because he had entered the solo violin competition in his age group at the eisteddfod, which was to be held in August also. He practised for four hours a day at the beginning of the school vacation, and then stepped this up to five hours. From time to time, driven by his need for fresh air and exercise, he went fishing or rambling; proper climbing was temporarily abandoned for fear of damage to his hands. He had scarcely exchanged a word with Betty Mai for a year, since the fair.

Maldwyn Shafto came home on holiday, broader but no taller; Peter came with him; and Geraint saw them one evening roaring out of the village with Betty Mai in the back of the sports car. He grimaced and cycled down the street, intending to fish the river pools at the head of the lake.

He was about to by-pass the usual knot of young people outside the chip shop, but suddenly stopped and leaned his bicycle against the kerb. Then he went into the shop and bought four pennyworth of chips, joining Billy Davies on the sidewalk and eating busily, sucking in cold air as the hot vinegary chips stung his mouth.

'Hi,' said Billy Davies. 'Going fishing?'

Geraint said, 'No, playing golf: can't you see my golf rod?' He nudged Billy Davies and said, 'Hey, who's that?'

There was a plump, dark-haired girl standing with Olwen Morris. A very pretty girl indeed, thought Geraint with interest.

Billy said lugubriously, 'Nansi Williams, her name is. Too old for us. She's about eighteen.'

Geraint said, 'Yes, but when did she come here? Is she on holiday or what?'

'They have just arrived this week. Her dad is the new manager at the Co-op. She is going to work there too, in the office. A smasher, I think she is.'

Geraint grunted noncommittally, said, 'See you, Billy,' and went to his bicycle, walking round past Olwen Morris and her companion. 'Hello, Olwen,' he said, but looked into the other girl's deep dark eyes as he did so. She gave a half-smile, which stayed with Geraint a long time and made him miss a good sea-trout when at last he started fishing.

The village ran a coach to the eisteddfod, which took place in a town two hours' drive away. Geraint and his father sat next to each other in their best suits; Geraint's violin reposed in the rack above his head. His mother sat with Mrs Davies, and Billy with his father, in the two pairs of seats ahead. The Shafto contingent—Betty Mai, her father, then Mrs Shafto and an aunt, then Maldwyn and Peter—sat at the back of the bus. Geraint was surprised to see Nansi Williams and her father right up at the front, talking with Mr Pritchard the police and Mr and Mrs Owen the butcher. Mr Griffiths sat next to Mr Pritchard. The rest of the coach was filled with other chattering contestants, their parents, relatives, and friends.

The girls' vocal events and the junior instrumental solos were held amongst the rag-tag and bobtail, as it was a regional occasion and not the great National Eisteddfod. The spectators were accommodated in a large marquee, and the events took place on a rostrum of boards and trestles, the muted light glowing through the fawn canvas of the marquee. When the time came Geraint went and waited with other performers in the competitors' tent, sitting on a folding chair with his feet on brown, worn turf, breathing the musty smell of the canvas and glancing round at the opposition: a fat, pimply youth, a tall and adenoidal youth who was so fair he looked almost albino, and a small, mouselike youth with glasses and short trousers.

A steward entered and said, 'First, please. Alun Bowen?'

The tall youth stood up and shambled out. The others listened. After a while the opening notes of the set piece came to their ears. Saint-Saëns: Introduction and Rondo Capriccioso, op. 28. It was accompanied by a piano, not an orchestra. Geraint sighed.

The fat youth said, 'I wish I had an ice-cream for every time I have played that thing. I hate it.'

The mouselike youth said, 'Me too. It is too difficult; too high a standard, I think. They ought to set easier pieces. My dad says I sound like a tomcat on the tiles when I play it.'

Geraint said, 'Did you hear that? I think he has broken a string.'

The sound of piano and violin had ceased.

The fat youth said, 'Lucky devil. I hope I break a string as well. They are always sympathetic when that happens, especially if you look all put out and embarrassed: that's the way to pick up an extra mark or two.'

He thought for a moment and said, 'I think I'll just give my A string a little nick.'

He opened his violin case and took a penknife from his pocket.

'Just a little nick to help things along,' he said.

'Hey, that's cheating,' the mouselike youth protested.

The fat youth said, 'You tell anyone and I will cut your liver out with this knife, I swear I will.'

Geraint said, 'Oh, cut your fiddle in half while you are about it, if you like. We don't care.'

The music resumed, and they listened morosely.

The tall youth came back.

'I broke a string,' he said.

'So shall I,' said the fat youth.

The steward poked his head round the flap of the tent and said, 'Huw Edwards?'

It was the turn of the mouselike youth. Geraint and the other competitors listened in silence. He was good, thought Geraint judiciously. Geraint's music master had said to him on the last day of term, 'The Saint-Saëns is a virtuoso piece. You won't be expected to play it like Campoli. Just watch your bowing, and don't do anything too stupid, that's all; you will be allowed mistakes.'

The mouselike youth returned, and the steward said, 'Hywel Edwards.'

Geraint said, 'Three Edwardses. My name is Edwards as well.'

166

'Don't let it worry you,' said the fat youth. To the steward he said loudly and virtuously, 'Well, I hope I do not break a string or anything like that,' and left the tent with the steward.

The mouselike youth said, 'I hope that one breaks his neck going up the steps, never mind a string.'

'He won't,' said Geraint. 'That sort never does. He will probably win.'

They listened. All went well for a time, then there were several excruciating discords; the performer picked up briefly, but soon the discords came again.

'What is he playing at?' asked the tall youth.

Eventually the fat youth came back, furious.

'I tried and tried to break that string,' he said. 'It just wouldn't break. Did you hear those false notes? That was me trying to break the string.'

Geraint said, 'Crime does not pay,' and stood up resignedly as the steward called his name. He followed the steward to the competition marquee. He heard his name called, walked forward with his violin up the steps to the rostrum, bobbed his head to the adjudicating committee, tuned his violin, nodded to the accompanist and began to play, staring out unseeing across the drooping floral decorations of the rostrum to the far end of the marquee.

He won the first prize.

After his parents' congratulations and lunch, a cheque for two guineas crisp in his pocket, Geraint took his seat in the marquee by his parents' side and listened to the girls' vocal contests. Betty Mai's turn came just after three o'clock. The soprano set piece was the Welsh song *Cwcw Bach*, and when he had heard it five times Geraint began to weary of it. Still, he had to admit that Betty Mai was very good. She seemed certain to win the first prize, for the girl who followed her stumbled badly on a high note. Then, to Geraint's amazement, Nansi Williams mounted the rostrum.

Well, he thought, she couldn't be eighteen yet, because eighteen was the upper age limit for this section. Any further conclusions were cut short when Geraint heard Nansi Williams sing. He gasped.

Poor old Betty Mai, he thought. Mr Griffiths leaned forward from the seat behind Geraint and tapped him on the shoulder excitedly.

'Wonderful,' he whispered to Geraint. 'She is wonderful. What a voice!'

Nansi Williams won first prize, and Betty Mai Shafto was second. Geraint looked from smiling Nansi to glum Betty Mai while the prizes were being distributed, and then craned his neck to look at Shafto in the audience. Shafto wore the expression of a man in pain, and Geraint grinned. His father was clapping his knees with his fists and making a noise like a soda siphon.

After tea the coach departed for home. The Shaftos sat gloomily in the back, trying not to listen to Wil and Gwen Edwards talking loudly about Nansi Williams. Mr Williams had placed her next to Geraint—'First-prize winners together, eh?' —and he was sitting behind them with Mr Griffiths, who kept leaning forward to talk to Geraint and Nansi, interrupting Geraint, who had been trying hard to break the ice with Nansi and was thinking how little Nansi had to say for herself, nodding, smiling her secret smile, and speaking in monosyllables.

Mr Griffiths said to Nansi's father, 'Does your daughter's work occupy her full-time? I am sure Mr Rhys would be glad of some part-time help with the singing at the school. He was talking about it only the other day. It would be just a matter of an hour a day, first thing in the mornings.'

'Well, indeed,' said Mr Williams, 'I shall have to think about it. She is working in the office, you know. I could ask permission. What do you think of the idea, Nansi?'

'It would be nice.'

Mr Griffiths began discussing the prospect with Nansi's father.

Geraint said to her, 'You are shy, aren't you? How do you ever bring yourself to get up on the platform and sing?'

'I don't know,' she said, smiling into his eyes.

When the coach stopped in the village Geraint alighted with Nansi and stood waiting for his parents. Nansi stood with him. Her father came down the steps of the coach with his wife and Mr Griffiths.

Mr Williams said, 'Mr Griffiths will be coming to supper. You will not be long, Nansi?'

'Not very,' she said. 'Do not wait.'

Her parents and Mr Griffiths moved away as Geraint's parents came down, followed by the policeman and the Owens.

'Are you coming home now, Geraint?' asked his mother.

Geraint said, 'Well——'

He was interrupted by Nansi, who said, 'Just having a talk about the eisteddfod, we are. We have some plans.'

Geraint looked at Nansi with his mouth open.

'Why, look at your father!' Gwen Edwards said.

His father had crossed the road and was entering the Prince of Gwynedd with Mr Pritchard.

'The first time in twenty years,' Gwen Edwards said wonderingly. 'Well, this is a day and no mistake. I am going home to put my feet up. Do not be late now, Geraint.'

Betty Mai got off the coach.

'Hard luck, Betty Mai,' Geraint said.

Betty Mai said, 'Hmff,' and shot a corrosive stare at Nansi, who smiled sweetly. Betty Mai pushed past, followed by the Shaftos. Mrs Shafto went home with Betty Mai; Shafto, Maldwyn, and Peter went into the Prince of Gwynedd. Geraint saw them enter the bar, where his father had preceded them. Then they shot out into the street hastily and went into the next entrance, the lounge.

Geraint grinned. The Shaftos were in no mood to confront his father.

The coach, now empty of passengers, turned and left the village.

'Er—well . . .' said Geraint, lingering uncertainly.

Nansi said, 'It is getting twilight.'

'Yes,' said Geraint.

She said, 'My legs are a bit stiff after the journey. I will walk a little to stretch my legs. You can come with me if you like.'

Geraint's heart beat faster.

'Good idea,' he said.

'Come, then.'

They walked together out of the village, not speaking until they were on the mountain path.

Geraint asked, 'What was that you said about having plans? Violin and voice, you mean?'

Nansi said, 'No.'

They walked on in the gathering dusk, and eventually sat down on Geraint's raincoat in a field of bracken, looking down to the rolling shadowy slopes of grass and scrub-oak below.

In a little while Nansi said, 'This is what I mean.'

It was ten-fifteen when Geraint entered the cottage. He walked with deliberate steps, picking up his feet and putting them down as if he were consciously directing them, his eyes fixed and wondering.

Gwen Edwards said, 'Have you seen your father?'

Geraint said, 'What? No. No, I have not seen him.'

His grandfather was sitting by the kitchen window.

'Geraint,' he said. 'So you won first prize!'

'Yes.'

His mother said, 'I wonder what is keeping your father. He is late. I will just go and look in the lane; perhaps he is out there talking.'

She left the kitchen.

'Well,' said Geraint's grandfather, 'this is a day to remember.'

'It is,' said Geraint with emphasis.

He washed and went to bed without supper, lying in the darkness with his eyes open, staring and seeing the closed eyes beneath him, the secret smile in the glimmering dusk.

Long afterwards he heard his father come home singing and

shouting, royally drunk. He heard his mother's voice raised in anger, his grandfather's placatory tones. Wil Edwards stumbled upstairs to bed; then Geraint heard his grandfather's steps; and finally his mother's. The house became quiet, and Geraint slept.

At breakfast next morning Wil Edwards was red-eyed and subdued.

Geraint said, 'My word, you did make a noise last night, Dad.'

'Hush!' said his mother.

Wil Edwards looked up.

'I was drunk. It is the first time I have touched drink since my twenty-first birthday, when I was pouring beer into a piano and just about ruined it, so that I gave up for shame. The first time since then, and the last.'

Gwen Edwards said, 'You ought to be ashamed of yourself. What Mr Davies will say . . .'

'He will say what I say. There is no excuse. I wanted to flaunt my triumph in Shafto's face, and I degraded myself to his level in order to do it. I did not even succeed, for he scuttled into the lounge as soon as he saw I was in the bar. Well, I have learned my lesson, and I have got a little man with a hammer and chisel in my head to make sure I remember it, so now we will have quiet, woman.'

15

THAT summer Geraint passed in eight subjects in the examinations for the General Certificate of Education, and so did Betty Mai. That seemed about all they had in common; somehow or other Betty Mai had come to hear of Geraint's walk on the mountain with Nansi Williams, and she treated him with cold disdain. This would not have troubled Geraint in the slightest at that time had he not found Nansi extremely elusive. He never succeeded in persuading her to take any more walks with him, and he spent a fretful autumn climbing with his father and fishing. Nansi was teaching singing at the primary school for an hour every other day, moving easily in an adult world which was still alien to Geraint. He was now in the lower sixth form at the grammar school, and began to feel that he had been there for ever; his school cap sat ridiculously on his head, seeming to him to be a badge of a kind of permanent infancy: he detested it.

Once at school he was made to accompany Betty Mai while she sang. Afterwards he went up to her impulsively and said, 'Betty Mai?'

'What do you want?' she asked coldly.

'It's just . . . Betty Mai, I think your voice is as good as Nansi's any day.'

Betty Mai said, 'Don't try that soft soap on me. It won't wash,' and turned away so that Geraint could not see her face.

.   .   .   .   .

In January, just before Geraint's sixteenth birthday, his father came home from the quarry with a long face.

He said, 'That crack on top of Patagonia, it has grown wider. The frost has got into it and opened it up. I do not like it at all. It is about a foot wide.'

'What does the inspector say?' asked Gwen Edwards.

'He says it is safe. Shafto says it is dangerous. For once I am inclined to agree with Shafto, though it goes against the grain, I can tell you.'

'I should think it must be serious if it can make you agree with Shafto,' his wife said.

'We have asked if we can put in the wedges.'

'Wedges?' said Geraint.

'You drop in the wedges at intervals in the crack, see? Then you measure how far down each wedge has fallen, and keep on taking measurements. If the crack is opening up, the wedges slip farther and farther down, isn't it? The measurements tell you the rate at which the crack is opening up.'

The wedges were inserted, and sank three feet in the first week. Just after Geraint's sixteenth birthday they stopped sinking, and no further movement was recorded in February. Geraint forgot about the crack on Patagonia, and set himself to break down Betty Mai's reserves, but had no success whatever.

One Saturday he went for a long walk, and ate a sandwich lunch at the summit of Mynydd Perfedd, standing on a hard snow crust and gazing round at the higher peaks. He walked down past Llyn y Mynydd and was interested to see, far off, a group of men in the lane by Maitland's cottage. He heard the report of a shotgun, and then saw the men drift away to a van and drive off.

It took Geraint fifteen minutes to reach Maitland's lane. Maitland was standing in the freezing air without his jacket, which lay covering something on the ground.

Geraint said, 'Mr Maitland, what is it?'

Maitland looked much older. He was shivering in the cold.

He seemed not to have heard Geraint at first, but then he looked up.

'Hennessey,' he said. 'They have shot Hennessey.'

'No,' said Geraint. 'Oh, no!'

Maitland said, 'They caught him running sheep with two other dogs. There was blood on his mouth.'

He made a vague, hopeless gesture with one hand.

Geraint said, 'Come inside. You will freeze,' and took Maitland's unresisting arm, leading him into the cottage. He seated Maitland in a chair and stood, not knowing what to do. Then he put coal on the fire.

Maitland said at last, 'Hennessey was a good dog. I don't understand.'

Geraint said, 'Yes, he was a good dog. My Uncle Tom once said that a dog never just starts off running sheep by himself; he has to be taught by another. Then he comes to enjoy it.'

'They caught him in the act,' said Maitland. He paused and then said dully, 'My God, you've grown. Do you still play the violin?'

'Yes. I still play.'

Maitland said, 'I should never have broken my violins like that. I have often thought about it. I have never played since then.'

He shook his head slowly.

'I should have given them to you,' he said.

Geraint said, 'I was a silly little fool, laughing that time. I shall never forgive myself, Mr. Maitland, never.'

Maitland looked up at him.

'You're growing up. Forgive yourself? Not being able to forgive yourself is part of growing up. Whether I shall ever forgive you I don't know.'

Geraint said, 'You have the right not to.'

Maitland said, 'Oh, what's the use? Hennessey is dead, and we are talking abstractions. I suppose I had better go and bury him.'

'But you can't,' said Geraint. 'The ground is frozen too hard. I will take him into the back garden and cover him with stones against the crows and buzzards, and then when the thaw comes you can bury him.'

He went into the lane and removed Maitland's jacket from the carcass of the dog, averting his eyes from the frightful head wound. He carried the carcass into the back garden and took stones from the wall, covering the body. Then he took Maitland's bloodstained jacket into the cottage. After some thought he hung the jacket behind the front door.

Maitland was still sitting as Geraint had left him.

He said, 'Thank you. Do you know—if you ever have a son and lose him, don't try to find him in somebody else's. Nor even in a dog. I shall sell this filthy place and go to live in Cheltenham or Buxton or somewhere like that. I don't fit in here. Somewhere in the retired-major belt I might. I just might.'

Maitland's face suddenly contorted, and tears ran down his cheeks. He was crying. An old man. Geraint had not known that old men could cry.

He said, 'I should not have stopped taking Hennessey for walks. If I had kept on taking him out perhaps he would not have gone by himself.'

Maitland recovered himself a little and said in a thick voice, 'No, don't blame yourself. He was my dog.'

He stood and straightened himself.

'My God,' he said, 'you're taller than I am. You'll be all right, boy. Forget all those things I said to you. I didn't mean them. Shake hands.'

Why, Maitland was still putting on an act, thought Geraint with amazement. He shook hands impassively and left the cottage. He mourned for Hennessey in succeeding weeks, but the memory of the dog faded then; and Maitland he scarcely understood at all. Maitland sold his cottage and went away— to Bournemouth, Geraint heard. Maitland said no farewell to Geraint, or to anyone else for that matter.

In the spring Mr Griffiths and Nansi Williams announced

their engagement, and the smoke from the village went up on a gabble of gossip and speculation and giggles like a fire in bracken, every flame a woman's tongue. But Mr Davies preached on the text 'The laughter of fools is as the crackling of thorns under a pot', and quenched it, making both Mr Griffiths and Nansi Williams tortured with embarrassment in the process.

Though the flames died down, there was still a good deal of smoke.

'What can the man be thinking of?' said Gwen Edwards. 'Old enough to be her father. He must be forty at least.'

Wil Edwards said, 'Mr Griffiths is a well-set-up man, make no mistake about that. I think the girl has shown some sense choosing him instead of some half-baked boy.'

Geraint reddened and sank his head in a newspaper.

Gwen Edwards sighed.

'I remember when Geraint must have been about eleven— in his last year at the little school he was—Mr Griffiths came here with Geraint after they had been fishing. I remember thinking then what a catch Mr Griffiths himself would be, never mind those old trout. Truth to tell, I have had a soft spot for Mr Griffiths ever since.'

Wil said, 'Oho, have you? No need for me to worry; he will be fully occupied now. I am thinking it is just as well he is getting married instead of turning the heads of other people's womenfolk.'

He patted his wife's hand and added, 'Now you will just have to put up with me, girl.' He turned to Geraint and said, 'Did you hear your mam, boy? Pining away for Mr Griffiths, she is.'

Gwen Edwards bridled.

'Old fool,' she said, but Geraint could tell that she was both pleased and, in a way, sad. At least in this by-play neither his father nor his mother had noticed his own embarrassment.

He was quite nonplussed by the turn of events. Though Nansi's father had tried to insist on a long engagement, the couple were married in chapel by Mr Davies on Whit Monday.

All the village went to the wedding, Geraint included; but afterwards he stood aside and did not join in the shouts and good wishes as the couple drove away to the reception. That night he lay awake for a long time, thinking of Mr Griffiths, but rather more of Nansi. The couple spent the rest of that week in London and then set up house in the village, which watched Nansi's figure with absorbed intensity. But the months passed by, and as they passed the village had to admit that Nansi Griffiths was making a very good wife. She had given up singing and no longer taught at the school, but she still worked in the Co-op office to supplement her husband's salary.

One day Geraint was sent to the butcher to buy steak, and found himself standing behind Nansi. She waited for him, and after he had been served and had paid for the meat, she walked with him into the street.

She said, 'Well, Geraint, how are you? We never seem to see much of you.' And then she smiled that slow, secret smile and added, swiftly and quietly, 'How are things up the mountain these days?' and clicked her tongue twice, *tuk-tuk*.

She walked away, and Geraint shivered as though a glass of ice-water had been poured down his back.

Three weeks later Mr Griffiths asked Geraint and Billy Davies to tea. Geraint was apprehensive about this visit, and in a subdued frame of mind when he called for Billy at the minister's house.

Billy said, 'Wonder what we'll have to eat? I hope they don't treat us like a pair of kids. You know what I mean. Old Griffiths and people like that, when they taught you when you were small, they seem to think you're still just a kid. Anyway, Nansi isn't much older than we are. It is funny, isn't it? I mean, Nansi being a married woman and everything.'

Geraint found it impossible to attain Billy's objectivity. He ate thin slices of bread-and-butter with raspberry jam, munched sticky cakes and drank sweet tea, while Nansi queened it at the tea-table and Mr Griffiths talked amiably.

'You are very quiet this afternoon, Geraint,' he said.

Geraint mumbled something, while Nansi said, 'Well, still waters run deep, Mervyn.'

Geraint reddened and said nothing, feeling oafish and foolish. She would be telling her husband about that time on the mountain next.

'How old are you, Geraint?' asked Mr Griffiths.

'Seventeen next January.'

Billy Davies said, 'I am older than Geraint. I am seventeen in November. The fifth of November. My father wanted to call me Guy, but Mam wouldn't let him.'

'What do you want to do for a living? Are you going to follow your father and be a minister?'

Billy said, 'Not on your life. You have to have a call, and I haven't had one yet. My father keeps on praying for me to have a call to join the ministry, and I keep on praying not to have one. So far I am winning. I want to go to England and be an engineer like Maldwyn Shafto. He is doing fine.'

'And what about you, Geraint? Are you going to take the world by storm as a concert violinist?'

Geraint said, 'I doubt it. I am going to study music, though, somehow or other. I may try for a scholarship at the Royal Institute of Music in Liverpool. I should like to be the best violinist in the world, but I do not think I am going to be. I started learning a few years too late for that: I should be satisfied to end up as first violin in a good orchestra.'

Mr Griffiths said to Nansi, 'Geraint has a realistic appraisal of his abilities.'

Nansi said, 'I am sure he has plenty of ability. I remember thinking that after the eisteddfod.'

Geraint decided that he was going to steer clear of quiet, smiling women for the rest of his life. Their company might have its advantages, but it was too dangerous for subsequent comfort. Soon he and Billy rose and said they must be going. They thanked Nansi for the tea, shook hands with Mr Griffiths, and started to leave the room.

'I'll see you to the door,' said Nansi.

She caught Geraint's arm in the porch as Billy went on ahead, and said, 'Silly boy! I was only teasing you. Now just you forget about that old mountain, and I will, too.' She smiled, and said pensively, 'Well, not quite, perhaps: just a scrap of it somewhere at the back of our minds, eh?' She squeezed his arm and added, 'Anyway, don't worry. Mervyn knows all about it. I told him. Good-bye now—come again.'

Geraint tottered down the steps and joined Billy Davies, who was awaiting him.

Billy said, 'Mervyn! I never knew that. . . . What is the matter with you, man?'

Geraint burst out, 'I wish to God I was fifty and married to Betty Mai Shafto, with ten kids. A man would feel safe then. Mr Griffiths is a saint, that is what he is, a saint, and I am not worthy to lick his boots.'

16

IN THE late autumn Geraint and Betty Mai both sat the examination for scholarships at the Royal Institute of Music at Liverpool. They travelled on the same train, but sat in separate compartments, not greeting nor speaking to each other after Geraint's first wave to her on the platform while waiting for the train had been met by a decisively turned back from Betty Mai. The examination for Geraint consisted of an interview, a theory paper, a sight-reading test, and a set piece. Geraint did not feel that he had done too badly, but the result would not be known until the following spring.

After his Uncle Tom's death Geraint had acquired the fly-tying materials which his uncle had used, and had taught himself to tie flies. It was Thursday, 28th December, a little less than a month before Geraint's seventeenth birthday. His school was still on Christmas vacation, and his father was at home as well. There had been a violent snowstorm on Boxing Day, and the snow had drifted halfway up the front door of the cottage. Wil and Geraint had cleared the doorway and shovelled a path to the lane, but they had been cut off from the village by a very deep drift in the lane below the cottage. The snow-plough had come through early that morning, disappointing Geraint, who had enjoyed the experience of being marooned. There would be no work at the Bron Eifion quarry until the snowfall had thawed.

Geraint fixed the bare hook by its point in the fly vice and wound on a body of yellow silk. He tied in a partridge hackle and made an invisible whip finish with the silk, then he dabbed spirit varnish on the head of the fly and put it aside to dry.

'Neat fingers you have, Geraint,' his father said, looking up from a week-old newspaper.

Geraint said, 'It saves me about sixpence a fly if I make my own. It is something to do in the winter, too.'

'Is your mother getting up?'

'She said she was when I took her tea,' Geraint said. 'There is not much to get up for on a morning like this, is there?'

His father said, 'Well, I am getting hungry, sitting about with this old newspaper that I have read twenty times already. Nearly eight o'clock.' He went to the foot of the stairs and shouted, 'Gwen!' then came back and sat down again.

'Your Taid will be up before your mam at this rate,' he said. And then: 'Did you hear the thunder in the night?'

Geraint said with surprise, 'Thunder? No.'

'You would sleep through the last trumpet, indeed. It was thundering away like an artillery bombardment. I was dreaming I was under fire in the desert until it woke me.'

Geraint said, 'Well, I never heard anything. Are you sure? I didn't know it could thunder in winter.'

'Well, it did last night.'

Gwen Edwards appeared, still in her dressing-gown and rubbing her eyes.

'It is cold,' she said. 'I hope you two have made a good fire in the kitchen. Oh dear, I am late. I did not get off to sleep till nearly four o'clock after that old thunder woke me up.'

She went into the kitchen, and soon Geraint heard and smelt bacon frying. He tied another Partridge and Yellow.

His grandfather came in quietly.

'Who is here?' he said. 'Oh, Wil and Geraint. Good morning. Did you hear that thunder in the night? It sounded like the blasting in the old days, only bigger. I was dreaming I was blasting out the bottom of the whole Bron Eifion; I had filled the Twll Mawr with a million cart-loads of black powder.'

He walked accurately to his chair and sat down.

Exasperated, Geraint said, 'It is not fair. Everyone heard that thunder except me. I didn't hear anything and I didn't dream anything. I wish I had heard it; it must be something out of the ordinary to have thunder like that after a snowstorm. Anyway, I saw the snow-plough come through early on. I suppose that is something.'

'Good,' said Wil. 'Then the road is clear.'

They chattered quietly, and then moved into the kitchen when Gwen Edwards called them to breakfast.

His mouth full of bacon and fried bread, Geraint said, 'I wish I had a pair of skis. I bet you could ski right down from the top road to Pen-y-Llyn. That would be fun.'

They finished breakfast, and Wil said, 'Well, I am going to make a proper roarer of a fire in the parlour, and then I am going to put my feet up and have a really lazy day.' He paused, and then said, 'Listen.'

Geraint and his mother turned from the sink where Geraint was helping with the washing-up.

Geraint's grandfather said, 'A car or a van.'

'It will have chains on the wheels,' Geraint said.

Gwen Edwards said, 'It has stopped.'

There was a knock at the door, and Wil Edwards went to answer it. In a moment he returned, his face grave.

'So much for my lazy day,' he said. 'You had better bring a cup of tea into the parlour, Gwen. It is Mr Williams from the police.'

Mr Williams was sitting in the parlour. He turned as Geraint and his father entered.

'My word, your boy has grown, Mr Edwards,' he said. 'Well now, this is the situation. At about five o'clock this morning an A.A. motor-cycle patrolman saw something crawling in the snow at the side of the main road. The ploughs were through there yesterday, you understand. It was a man, and I can tell you he was in a bad way. He had head injuries, and frostbite on his feet and nose. The A.A. man threw all his kit out of the sidecar and brought him in to hospital. Real quick thinking, that. They were putting the man to bed when he told them he had come from a crashed aircraft.'

Gwen Edwards brought tea, and Williams sipped it grate-fully.

'Of course, the hospital rang us at once, and I went round to see this man. He is a civilian test pilot working for the R.A.F. He was on a proving flight with some very important people. He says that all engines cut out on him without warning, and they crashed on the summit of a mountain. He didn't know how long he had taken coming down from the wreck. He was in a bad way, and that is all we got out of him. He might have been crawling round in circles.'

'Where did they crash?' asked Wil.

'That is just the point. He doesn't know. He tried to turn and make for the sea, losing height gradually, but the plane wouldn't play.'

Wil said, 'Well, have you had no reports of aircraft crashing?'

'Not a thing. The plane must have crashed during the thunderstorm, and anyhow the snow would blanket a lot of the noise of the crash. The R.A.F. have made an aerial search, but the cloud base is too low for them to see anything. Now listen, we are wasting time. Will you help?'

'You do not need to ask,' said Wil.

'Good. We have to allow for the fact that when the plane crashed it was probably off course. Man, it is a hell of a job, and we are going to be stretched by tonight, I can tell you. This is the set-up. The police are starting from Aber, and they are to search the following summits: Foel Fras, Foel Grach, Craig y Dulyn, Carnedd Llywelyn.' He paused and said grimly, 'There is an old wrecked aircraft up on Carnedd Llywelyn from the last war; perhaps it has company now.' Then he went on, 'The R.A.F. Rescue people are to search Carnedd Dafydd, Y Garn, some of the minor summits, and Glyder Fawr. Ogwen Cottage Mountain Rescue and a couple of volunteers from the Idwal Cottage Youth Hostel are taking Glyder Fach, Tryfan, and Pen yr Oleu Wen—oh, and Moel Siabod; the Gwydir Mountain Training School are going there; it is a long shot, but we can-not afford to neglect anything. Four Bethesda quarrymen are working along the north-east slopes to the tops of Carnedd y Filiast, Foel Goch, and Mynydd Perfedd. The Pen y Gwryd people are going to work over all the Snowdon ridges just in case. Now then, we want you to cover Moel Eifion, Elidir Fach, Elidir Fawr, and then rendezvous on Y Garn with the R.A.F.'

'Right,' said Wil. 'You have been to see Shafto?'

'I called on the way. He is fitting chains to his van and then coming up here.'

Wil called his wife and said, 'We are going out after a wrecked aircraft, Gwen. Get a big flask of coffee ready, and sandwiches. Make a lot. Geraint is coming, and you know how hungry the boy gets.'

Gwen Edwards bit her lip.

Then she said, 'So it has come to this. I knew it would one day. Oh, Geraint——'

Wil said, 'Off with you and do as I say.'

She shook her head numbly and rushed into the kitchen.

Geraint's face had lighted up, but he did not speak.

'Is the lad safe?' asked Mr Williams.

'Man, devil,' said Wil. 'We are not going to do any climbing today. Just a long walk, that is all. I hope we find these poor people.'

Mr Williams stood up.

He said heavily, 'I was at Conway in the winter of 'forty-two when an airman crawled into Glan Conwy. That one had been crawling for fourteen hours. A hero he was, trying to get help for the rest of the crew. But he thought he had crashed on Snowdon, poor devil. We sent search parties there, and there was nothing. By the time we found the plane—it was on Craig y Dulyn—they were all dead.' He pursed his lips and said, 'It is a pity the University College is on vacation. We could have used some more help. Well, thank you for the tea. I will be going now, over to Aber to see if there is any news.'

Geraint heard Williams drive away.

He said, 'Oh, Dad, thank you for letting me come. I did not dare ask you. Will Mam . . . ?'

His father said, 'Your mam will do as I say, and in the end she will see that I am right. Come now, and change. You will need three pairs of socks, and put on two thin sweaters and a thick one on top: that big fawn one. Gloves and a scarf, too. We must hurry.'

Geraint changed as quickly as he could, but Wil was ready before him and tapping impatiently with his feet in the hall as Shafto hooted outside. Geraint ran downstairs, his father inspected him briefly, then nodded and gave him the haversack to carry.

'Take this,' he said. 'No use keeping a dog and barking myself.'

Gwen Edwards hugged Geraint and kissed him.

She pecked Wil's cheek coldly and said, 'I hope you know what you are doing, taking him with you, that is all. If anything happens to Geraint you will sleep by yourself for the rest of your life.'

'Oh, toot,' said Wil.

Geraint followed his father to the van.

Shafto said to Wil, 'I thought you were going to be all day.' He looked at Geraint and said, 'Who told you to come? We don't want kids holding us back.'

Wil said, 'Get in, Geraint,' and folded the front passenger seat forward while Geraint squeezed past it into the back of the van.

Wil said to Shafto, 'We will have no argument. Geraint will be all right, and three are better than two on this sort of job.'

Shafto grunted and moved off, the chains clinking on the smooth white surface left by the snow-plough.

'We will go up the top road and leave the van near the top powder store,' he said.

Wil said, 'That's it. Then we can cut up to the lake and go round by the back of Crib y Geifr to the top, then over the ridge to Cwm Edwy and on to Elidir Fach. That will save time.'

Shafto said, 'We will beat the bloody lot of them to this aeroplane, I bet you.'

They turned off the lane on to the unploughed top road.

Shafto soon had to stop the van; before them lay a drift from wall to wall.

'All change,' he said.

Geraint handed out the ropes, and slipped one of the heavy coils over his shoulders.

The three moved in silence on to the snow crust and started to walk uphill across country. Wil led, setting a steady, all-day pace, with Shafto behind him and Geraint bringing up the rear. He thought how slowly his father was walking.

'Can't you go any faster, Dad?' he asked.

Shafto said, 'Save your breath to cool your bloody porridge. You'll find this fast enough by tea-time.'

Geraint's father said nothing, and Geraint felt rather wounded. He plodded on behind Shafto's broad back, walking in the others' footsteps. Then he found himself breaking through the snow crust and slipping into the powder snow below it up to his thighs. This broke his rhythm and he began to pant with exertion, but then he took an independent line and found he could walk more easily on the crust.

They breasted the last rise before the lake, and turning before they reached the frozen glacier of the stream, met a north-east wind. The lake itself was frozen in ragged waves of ice.

The snow was badly drifted below Crib y Geifr, and they floundered through the drifts until they reached steeper ground where the snow had blown away and exposed the icy rock.

Wil Edwards said, 'Rope now.'

They roped up and moved away immediately. Geraint began to feel he needed a rest, but Wil continued up and along the weather side of the ridge at that implacable pace. It was hard going among the jumbled detritus of the little high saddle, and this tired Geraint rather more than the upward climb. They left the saddle behind, and came on to the summit.

It was ten-fifteen.

'Not a thing,' said Shafto. 'Come on. Wherever that plane is, we'll get there before the R.A.F.'

Geraint said, 'Aren't we going to have a rest?'

Wil laughed.

'A rest?' he said. 'Why, we haven't started yet. Come now!'

He led along a gentle ridge which stretched north-east into the wind. Then the ridge curved west. The slope was downhill, and Wil moved quickly and easily on the ice covering the rock, ignoring the steep drop to his right where there was a small horseshoe-shaped valley. He fairly galloped over the last quarter-mile, then paused.

'You wanted to go faster, Geraint,' he said. 'How was that?'

Geraint grinned sadly.

'I preferred the slower pace, indeed,' he said.

'Right. Remember we know what we are doing. Now then, Shafto, you had better lead now.'

They changed positions, and Shafto led them north along the two-thousand-foot contour, the ground falling away to their left. After perhaps twenty minutes they turned south-east and began to ascend the easy slope for the next five hundred or so feet to the summit of Elidir Fach. They stood on the broad, flattish expanse from which the wind had whipped all save a thin covering of frozen snow. It was eleven-twenty-five.

Geraint said, 'I must sit down just for a minute.'

Shafto rolled a cigarette, snapped his lighter. It worked at the third attempt; he stood smoking. Wil gave Geraint half a cup of scalding coffee.

After five minutes Wil said, 'There are men dying somewhere in these mountains, if indeed they are not already dead. Come, Geraint.'

Shafto still leading, they descended a few hundred feet in a south-easterly direction. The ground was quite steep, and they had to exercise great care, kicking footholds in the snow crust with the heels of their boots. Then they climbed upwards, north-easterly, up the long easy pull to the summit of Elidir Fawr, which they reached at one o'clock. The summit was bare.

Geraint was very disappointed. He was really tired now.

'Nothing,' said Wil. 'Well, we had better have something to eat. Give me the haversack, Geraint.'

Wil and Geraint sat on the frozen snow, still roped, eating their sandwiches and drinking coffee. Shafto drank tea supplemented by a small tot from a hip flask of whisky, and ate three cold sausages and a thick slice of bread and dripping.

They rested for half an hour all told, then Wil said, 'Y Garn is our last hope.'

Shafto said, 'We can cut down into the valley and cross the Dudodyn, then up and over. It will save time.'

'Not if we break our necks doing it,' said Wil. 'Think, man, it is too steep.'

Shafto grumbled, but allowed himself to be persuaded, and instead of risking the precipitous descent into the valley of the Dudodyn they moved first in an easterly direction, skirting the rocks above Marchlyn Mawr on which Geraint had first learned to belay a rope. They went down to two thousand feet, and again followed the contour as best they could until they were on the western slopes of Nant Ffrancon's Foel Goch, where they turned south and then south-east under Y Garn. It was a long, hard slog. Geraint had never felt so weary in his life. The first feeling of tiredness had passed; his second wind had come and gone, and as they began to work their way up the north-western side of Y Garn he found that he was losing all sensation in his legs. His head bent, he saw his feet moving as though they belonged to someone else, but he still kept the rhythm which he had maintained ever since the summit of Elidir Fawr. He refused to give up.

The pitch of the slope increased. Geraint's breath rasped in his throat, and his mouth was dry. In front of him he could see Shafto's legs moving like pistons, never faltering, never halting. Geraint bent his head once more and forced himself to keep going, losing all sense of time. He did not notice that his father and Shafto had stopped until he walked into Shafto's broad back. Shafto cursed him, and he looked up.

The aircraft was before them, a great broken-backed bird lying just below the sharp summit cone of Y Garn. Behind it the snow was gashed and scarred, exposing rock and earth and grass.

The nose of the fuselage was crushed against an outcrop of rock; one wing was torn off and lay fifty feet to the south of the wreck. Men were moving about it.

Shafto said bitterly, 'They have beaten us to it.'

They went closer, and Shafto said, 'The R.A. bloody F. it is, by damn.'

They unroped, Geraint feeling a sense of anticlimax. He coiled the rope and slung the heavy coil over his shoulder, following his father and Shafto to the four men who stood by the wreck.

Wil Edwards greeted the men in Welsh and said, 'I see you found it first.'

One of the men said, 'We're English, mate. Flight-Sergeant Andrews, me.'

'Oh, yes, of course,' said Wil in English. 'Sorry. Is there anything we can do?'

'Not for those bods inside,' said Andrews. 'Five are just in bits and pieces, a proper butcher's shop. There may be more than five, you can't hardly tell. One bloke hasn't a mark on him that you can see, but he's a deader just the same. Fancy that, eh?— not a mark on him!'

Smouldering, Shafto said, 'Johnny on the bloody spot you are, isn't it?'

Andrews looked surprised and said, 'What's the matter with you, mate?'

'Take no notice,' Wil said.

Geraint walked round the wreck while his father talked with Andrews. He knew very little about aircraft, but could tell that this was a piston-engined plane. The starboard motors were intact except for the twisted and buckled propeller blades, and petrol was leaking in a tiny trickle from the nacelle of the starboard outer motor. Geraint did not dare peer in at a door in the fuselage which stood open. He went back and stood for a moment with his father, then sat down and put his head on his knees. It was growing dusk.

'Four o'clock,' said Andrews. 'You chaps want a bite to eat?'

Wil said, 'We have food, thank you.'

'Get some of it inside you, then,' Andrews advised, and went to supervise the work of the three other men.

Geraint drank some coffee, but could not bring himself to eat: the R.A.F. Rescue men were fetching the bodies out of the wreck and arranging them as best they could on the ground ready for the stretcher party.

'Dear God,' said Wil. 'A terrible business.' He had sat down next to Geraint, but now stood and said, 'I will go and help.'

Shafto said, 'Ah, leave them. They found them first, didn't they?'

He followed Wil nevertheless, while Geraint sat, too exhausted to move until compelled by the freezing air. As the darkness fell, concealing the gruesome array on the snow, he felt that he dared approach a little more closely. Shafto was standing watching Wil and the others. Geraint heard voices to his right, and looked over to where lights were flickering and wavering.

'That'll be the stretcher party,' said Andrews.

The Nant Ffrancon face of Y Garn consists of very steep grass slopes interspersed by rock cliffs. The eight men of the stretcher party had had a stiff pull up from the rescue post. One was a policeman, and the others were from Idwal Cottage; they explained that the Ogwen Cottage parties were still out on the opposite side of the valley.

'Right on the doorstep, and we never heard it!' said one of them. 'The plane must have hit at the same moment as a thunder-clap.'

Another said to Shafto, 'Hey, you, lend a hand getting these fellows on to the stretchers, will you?'

Shafto said, 'Do it yourself,' his face harsh and obdurate in the glimmering light.

The man said incredulously, 'Well, you dirty dog!'

Shafto said, 'Ah, jump off the mountain, will you?'

Andrews came up and asked, 'Now then, what's going on here?'

The stretcher-bearer said, 'This bastard won't help. What is he doing here, anyway—a sightseer or something, is he?'

'Watch it,' said Shafto. 'Watch it, or you'll get filled in good and proper, you will, I'm telling you.'

Andrews said to the stretcher-bearer, 'From what his pal tells me he is all cross because the nasty R.A.F. got here first, did-dums.' He turned to Shafto and said, 'Never mind, then, he shall have his fluffy bloody teddy-bear when Mummy tucks him up in beddy-byes tonight.'

Shafto snarled, and rolled a cigarette. He snapped his lighter several times; it sparked but did not ignite.

'Out of petrol,' he said.

Andrews watched him keenly and held a torch beam on him as he stalked to the stream of petrol still escaping from the starboard outer engine. He unscrewed the bottom plug of the lighter and held it under the flow. Then he replaced the plug and came back, snapping the lighter into flame.

'Right,' said Andrews. 'I've got you now, I have, by God.' He called over to the policeman, 'Sergeant Pugh! Come here a minute, will you, please?'

The policeman came over and Andrews said, 'I am giving this man in charge. Stealing government property: to wit, a quantity of aviation spirit.'

Shafto said, 'Hey, you can't do that.'

'Can't I?' said Andrews. 'I've done it, you prize sod.'

The policeman laid a hand on Shafto's arm and said, 'Come along, then.'

Shafto hit him on the nose. The policeman roared, and Shafto was overwhelmed by struggling men.

Geraint waited in the Mountain Rescue post with his father. Warm drinks and a hot stove combined to make him drowsy, and he would have dropped into sleep despite the bustle of activity and the voices raised around him, except that he was too excited.

Williams came from Aber in his Land Rover and took them home, dropping them at the cottage and then driving away at once.

Wil and Geraint went into the kitchen, where Geraint's mother and grandfather awaited them.

'Well, we're back,' said Wil. 'There was nothing we could do; we were too late. Have you a cup of tea, girl?'

Geraint gabbled, 'That old Shafto got himself arrested for stealing petrol from the plane and hitting a policeman. He was like a bear with a sore head because the R.A.F. were first at the wreck. Mam, we went right over Moel Eifion and Elidir Fach and Elidir Fawr and right up to the top of Y Garn, and I didn't hold Dad back at all, did I, Dad?'

His mother came to him and put her arms round him.

She said to her husband, 'He will have no time for his old mam, I suppose, now you have made a man of him, Wil.'

She hugged Geraint briefly and then said, 'Well, I will be seeing about that tea.'

Geraint's grandfather said, 'A wise woman you are, Gwen, letting Geraint go with Wil today. A woman who cuts the apron-strings ties her children to her heart-strings instead, and that is how it should be. And now what is this about Shafto?'

17

EVERYBODY turned up for the Shafto trial, including the national Press, among which opinion was sharply divided. This division of opinion could be represented by the *Daily Glass*, which saw Shafto as a hero victimized by pettifogging bureaucracy and red tape, and by *The Onlooker*, which saw him as a species of mountain vulture, descending from the heights to indulge in depraved looting. A fact of interest to both parties was that Shafto was the first person ever to be arrested in Snowdonia above the three-thousand-foot contour.

Geraint went along with his parents, and most of the village, to the magistrates' court. Many would-be spectators were unable to gain admittance and had to hang about outside; but Geraint and his parents were early and found seats in the packed well of the courtroom. Geraint waved to Betty Mai, sitting with her mother. Betty Mai jerked her chin and ignored him.

The hearing began. Shafto was charged with larceny of government property, obstructing a police officer in the execution of his duty, and with assaulting a police officer. He pleaded not guilty.

Police Sergeant Pugh was sworn and gave evidence.

He said, 'At four-thirty-five p.m. on Thursday, 28th December, I arrived with a stretcher party at the summit of Y Garn to take down casualties from a wrecked aircraft. The casualties were all deceased.'

The magistrate said, 'You need not go into all that, Sergeant; that will be the subject of a separate court of inquiry.'

'Yes, your worship. At four-thirty-nine p.m. I attempted to

take defendant into custody, a charge having been laid against him by Flight-Sergeant Andrews, and defendant struck me a blow on the nose. I then took him into custody. . . .'

Andrews took the stand and repeated the oath.

The magistrate said, 'Kindly tell us in your own words of the events which led to your laying this charge.'

'Well, sir, there isn't much to tell, really. The defendant arrived at the wreck after we had got to it first. I saw him nicking—er—that is, stealing petrol. He was filling his cigarette lighter.'

'I see,' said the magistrate. 'Not a great quantity of petrol, then?'

'No, sir,' said Andrews. He added virtuously, 'It was the principle of the thing.'

'I see,' said the magistrate again.

The magistrates' clerk whispered.

'Well, now,' said the magistrate. 'Will you please be a little more specific? Did the defendant open a container of petrol and fill his cigarette lighter from it, or what?'

Andrews said, 'Well, no. I mean—there was this petrol leaking from an engine—the starboard outer engine. That man—that is, the defendant—went over and held his lighter in the stream of petrol.'

The magistrate said, 'Do you mean to say that this petrol was running to waste on the ground?'

'Well, yes, sir. You couldn't do anything to stop it.'

The magistrate said, 'Do you mean to tell me that after this man and his companions had been scouring the mountains on an errand of mercy you had him arrested for filling a cigarette lighter from a stream of petrol which was going irrevocably to waste?'

'Well . . .' said Andrews.

'Be so good as to answer my question,' said the magistrate testily.

'Yes, sir. I did have him arrested. And I would do it again if I had to.'

The magistrate snapped, 'This court is not interested in your hypotheses, Flight-Sergeant.'

The magistrates' clerk whispered.

'Stand down now,' said the magistrate. 'I may recall you later. We had better hear the corroborative evidence. Call Leading Aircraftman Jeffrey Mannering.'

After the preamble Mannering said, 'I was a stretcher-bearer, see? This bug—I mean, the defendant, I said to him, well, I arst him to give me a hand getting the bodies on the stretchers, and he says he wouldn't. "You dirty dog," I says to him, and he says, "Go jump off the mountain," and then he gets out his lighter, but it doesn't work, and then he goes and fills it from the petrol escaping from the engine like Flight told you.'

'Defendant refused to assist you with the bodies of those unfortunate people?'

'That's right,' said Mannering cheerfully.

Before the clerk could say anything the magistrate said, 'I think we had better hear what the defendant has to say about all this. Cadwaladr—— Good heavens, what is this? Be so good as to ask defendant to stand.'

Shafto stood, glowering.

'How do you pronounce your second name?'

'O'Faolain,' said Shafto.

'O'Phweelan. I see. Your full name is Cadwaladr O'Faolain Shafto?'

There was a murmur from the court.

'Gor!' said an airman in front of Geraint.

Geraint looked at Betty Mai, caught her eye and winked. She blushed, that old, all-inclusive blush.

'The court will be silent,' the magistrate said severely. 'Defendant will take his place.'

Shafto gave his full name again, while the magistrate glared round the court; then Shafto was sworn in.

'Now then. Let us hear your version of these events. One moment. Are you represented by a solicitor?'

'I am not,' said Shafto.

'You are aware that you were entitled to be so represented?'

Shafto said, 'Oh, get on with it, can't you?'

Surprised, the magistrate said, 'Do not take that tone here or you will find yourself regretting it. Now then, what have you to say to these charges?'

Shafto said, 'Oh, I took that petrol all right, I am not denying it. And I hit that copper when he tried to arrest me. Why did he want to try and arrest me for a fiddling little thing like that? That's what I want to know. The stuff was pouring out all over the place. How can you steal stuff that's pouring out all over the place? You said so yourself.'

He paused and glared indignantly at the magistrate, who sighed and said, 'Am I then to change the plea to one of guilty?'

Shafto said, 'If you like. It's a lot of fuss about nothing.'

'Enter a plea of guilty,' the magistrate instructed with relief.

Geraint felt his father shift beside him and stand up.

The magistrate said, 'Why is that person standing? Do you wish to say something?'

Wil said, 'I wish to speak on Mr Shafto's behalf, sir.'

Shafto raised his eyebrows.

The magistrate said, 'Well, we will hear what you have to say.' He said to Shafto, 'Stand down,' and then, 'Mr Usher, kindly bring that gentleman to the stand.'

After the preliminaries the magistrate said to Wil, 'Do you wish to speak in Welsh or in English?'

'I will speak in English,' said Wil. 'I shall be able to manage.'

He stood there rock-like, imperturbable.

'Very well. Now we have heard evidence to the effect that defendant openly filled his cigarette lighter with petrol from the aircraft in question, and he has admitted doing so. He has changed his plea to one of guilty, and he has admitted striking the police sergeant who attempted to arrest him. Now then, what is it that you wish to say?'

Wil said, 'Mr Shafto and my son and I were helping the police, isn't it? It was the police who called us out to help in the first place. We are not paid for going into the mountains, and we do not want to be paid for it. But Mr Shafto likes to make a bit of a competition out of it. He was very keen to get to the wreck before anyone else, and he was very disappointed to see that the R.A.F. had reached it first. I think he took all that a bit too seriously, but who is to say that a man should not be keen? It makes him press on instead of resting, and it might have saved those men's lives if the circumstances had been different. Mr Shafto lost his temper, but he had done his best. He did not steal the petrol for gain. He did it as you might put your fingers to your nose and pull bacon.'

'Pull bacon?' said the magistrate. 'Oh, I see. What a revolting expression! Are you saying, then, that defendant took this petrol and struck the police sergeant as a gesture of annoyance at not being first at the wreck of the aircraft?'

'Yes,' said Wil. 'That is exactly what I am saying. I think he was a bit tired, too, and that might have made him even sharper-tempered than usual.'

'I was not tired,' roared Shafto. 'I am as good a man as you in the mountains any day.'

'Be silent!' said the magistrate. 'I shall not tell you again to observe proper respect in this court.'

Mr Williams from the police also added a testimony in Shafto's favour: he was of previous good character, and he had helped the police in mountain-rescue work before without any untoward incident.

The magistrate conferred briefly with his clerk and then said, 'My only problem here is to decide on a just penalty. The defendant has changed his plea to one of guilty. Certain facts have been adduced in mitigation. . . . I am not bound to take into account defendant's behaviour in refusing to help the stretcher-bearer when requested, except in so far as it throws light on the character of the defendant. But I am bound to take into consideration his behaviour in this court, which has been conspicuously lacking in respect. Finally, and most weightily, the police must be allowed to perform their duty unimpeded. It matters not in the least whether a person finds himself arrested on a charge which appears to him to be trifling; he must submit. It is for the courts to decide the matter then. It is also for the courts to impose penalties which will deter individuals from obstructing the police in the execution of their duty.' He turned to Shafto. 'You will go to prison for one month.'

'Bloody hell,' said Shafto.

Shafto was released from prison on a Tuesday, and on the Wednesday he called for Wil as usual in his van.

'Well, did you have a good time?' asked Wil.

'A nice little holiday at Her Majesty's expense,' said Persimmon Hughes. 'Wasn't it, Shafto?'

Shafto slammed the van into first gear and moved off.

'Holiday?' he said. 'They made me work, sewing mailbags. Terrible job, wears the ends of your fingers. But I had a good time last night: free beer all night from the gentlemen of the Press.'

Madog Parry said, 'Well, you got your picture in the papers.'

As they drove up the top road it was a wild morning, March roaring along, rags of cloud below them like old grey dusters blown by the gale. The men went into the big cabin and sat down, Shafto acknowledging shouts and banter from the other workmen while Wil looked through the little window-pane to Snowdon's summit, pale golden in a watery sun.

Wil said to Shafto, 'We should be hearing soon about those music scholarships.'

Shafto mused, the glowing tip of his cigarette almost burning his nose.

He said, 'They reckon competition is very keen. I don't know, but I can't see the two of them getting a place.'

'No,' said Wil. 'It would be too much to expect.'

They chewed over this for some time.

Finally Shafto said, 'My missis tells me there is a *Noson Lawen* in the village tonight. Betty Mai is singing. You going?'

'Well, of course,' said Wil. 'Geraint will be playing, isn't it?'

Foreseeing a quarrel, Persimmon Hughes said hastily, 'Come on, lads. Let us go up now.'

They went up to Patagonia and sat in the fire cabin while Persimmon Hughes and Shafto smoked another cigarette.

Shafto said, 'How has that old crack been behaving itself while I have been away?'

The others looked at one another.

'Well,' said Madog Parry, 'we haven't been up there for three weeks or so. We have been working down here by the roadway. I suppose it is all right.'

A raven called from Crud y Gwynt, the harsh croak blown to them on the wind outside.

'We'll go up and have a look,' said Shafto decisively. 'Has Iolo Jones inspected it?'

Wil said, 'He is supposed to go up on his routine rounds. He says it is safe: no further movement.'

'There is nothing like seeing for yourself,' said Shafto. 'You lot would just wait for it to come down on your heads; they're made of the same stuff as the rock. Let us go up, then.'

They went up the hand-rope, the wind tearing at their clothes, and then walked along the top gazing at the crack, Shafto talking to himself, his words hurled away over the valley into the racing cloud below.

'What did you say?' yelled Madog Parry.

Shafto bellowed, 'There is ice down there still; you cannot even see the wedges for the ice. It is solid from wall to wall.'

Wil shouted, 'What do you expect? It has been freezing up here for months after the snow and then the heavy rain.'

Persimmon Hughes caught their arms and pulled them into the shelter of a projecting rock.

He said, 'What do you think?'

'Think?' said Shafto. 'What do I think? I have been telling you all along. It is dangerous, that crack.'

Madog Parry said, 'We had better ask Iolo Jones to have another look.'

Shafto said, 'Madog, you are right. Your legs are the youngest. You go down to the big cabin and get someone to go and ring for Iolo Jones. We will be on the roadway.'

Iolo Jones appeared during the afternoon, irritable and flustered.

'I am loaded down with work,' he said. 'Loaded down I am, and you crazy gang bring me all the way up here to look at that old crack. You will have the feet falling off me with the walking you make me do.'

'Now, Iolo,' said Wil coaxingly, silencing Shafto with a wink, 'we know that you are a busy man indeed. You are too conscientious, that is your trouble. We thought you would want to know about that crack; we thought you ought to know about it. Now you go along with Madog here, and when you come down we will have a nice mug of hot tea waiting for you in the big cabin, and a little drop of something in it from that flask which I can see making a bulge in Shafto's pocket. You look as if you might have a cold coming on; there is nothing like a nice hot mug of tea for a cold, especially when the mug has a drop of something else in it.'

Iolo Jones said, 'Well, all right, then. But don't you let anyone see you lace that tea. It is against the rules and you know it.'

'Medicinal,' said Wil firmly. 'Medicinal, that is different, anybody knows that.'

The inspector left with Madog Parry, and Wil went with Shafto and Persimmon Hughes to the big cabin, where many men were sitting, unable to work because of the gale.

Shafto said to Wil, 'That will cost you two shillings,' as he poured a secretive tot into a mug. 'You were the one to offer it to Iolo Jones, and you shall be the one who pays for it.'

Wil said, 'I will pay, though you are the one who is worrying about the crack. If I had not smoothed Iolo Jones down a bit he would be back in the office by now.'

Shafto said grudgingly, 'Oh well, give me a shilling then. I will stand half the cost of the whisky. But it is an imposition. Prussic acid, that is what I should be using to lace that Iolo's tea.'

When Madog Parry appeared with the inspector he looked crestfallen; the inspector was gobbling with fury.

'You have called me up here again to no purpose,' he raged. 'That crack is safe, do you hear? It is so safe I would make my bed underneath it; I would sleep like a baby on the very roadway of Top Hat.'

Shafto filled the mug with tea.

'Here,' he said hastily. 'Just you drink this.'

The inspector took a sip, winced, blew on the surface of the tea, drank a little.

'Well,' he said at last, 'I will say this: it is a good drop of tea. Now listen, you men. I have been working in the Bron Eifion since I was a boy, and I know what I am doing. If you have me up here on this sort of wild-goose chase again somebody is going to get his cards. I don't know how, but I will fix it, never fear. That crack is so safe I would go to bed under it. I have told you now. If you bring me up here again for nothing I will have somebody sacked.'

He finished his tea and strutted out of the cabin. The men looked at one another.

'He means it,' said Persimmon Hughes. 'We had better leave things as they are for now, eh?'

Shafto said disgustedly, 'A waste of good whisky. It makes me sick the way that Iolo Jones goes on. I am getting fed up all round. With the coal you know where you are most of the time. You can shore up the workings as the face is driven farther in. Even then you sometimes have roof falls. But I will never get used to this way of carrying on.'

Madog Parry said, 'Yes, but you cannot compare this with the coal. It is different entirely.'

Shafto said, 'It is a damned sight more dangerous.'

Towards the end of the working day Shafto became abstracted and silent. Eventually he came over to Wil.

'Wil Edwards?' he said.

Wil put down his hammer and chisel and stood up, leaning against the block of slate on which he had been working. The wind had dropped, and light airs from the south-west were bringing a spatter of rain; the wet surface of the slate gleamed like gunmetal.

'Well?'

Shafto swallowed and said with difficulty, 'I have never thanked you for speaking up for me that time in court. You did not have to say anything at all, but you spoke up for me. Mind you, I did not agree with you when you said I was tired. But I think you meant well, and I am grateful to you for it.'

He scuffed the toe of his boot in a drift of small, broken slate, and added, 'I have been thinking about it, and I do not want you to pay for that whisky. Here.'

Shafto dug in his pocket and held out a shilling.

Wil Edwards looked at him, nodded, and took the shilling.

Shafto said, 'A man has his pride, and I would not want you to take this lightly. I am the first man in Wales ever to have been arrested above three thousand feet, and that is no small thing. Keep that in mind.'

'No,' said Wil. 'No, I do not take it lightly at all.'

He turned the shilling over in his fingers and said, 'An apology can never diminish a man in my eyes. You are a big man, Shafto, and famous now with your name in the papers and everything.'

He spun the shilling twinkling high in the air, then caught and pocketed it.

He said, 'There is a little matter of a lost knife between us, but I am willing to let that pass. As far as I am concerned, this sets things right.'

Shafto clapped Wil on the shoulder, and they made their way towards the big cabin. Persimmon Hughes and Madog Parry followed, nudging each other and gazing as Shafto and Wil talked animatedly together.

'Well,' said Persimmon Hughes, 'I have tried since years and years to make those two see a bit of common sense, and now it has happened I can claim no credit for it at all. Just look at the two of them, clacking away there!'

Madog Parry said, 'Well, we know what to do if ever they start quarrelling again. Get Shafto put away in jail for a spell.'

18

THAT evening the sun set in a purple and marigold sky
away over the strip of shining sea. Geraint put on his
best suit and went downstairs. His mother was fussing
with Wil Edwards' tie, pulling it straight. She dusted down the
shoulders of his rather shiny blue suit.

'There, that is a lot better,' she said.

Wil said to Geraint, 'Your Taid is coming to the *Noson Lawen*
too. Go up and see if he is ready. You will have to start with him
well ahead of us. We will catch up with you on the way.'

Geraint ran upstairs and shouted, 'Taid! Are you really
coming to the *Noson Lawen*?'

The old man was combing his beard in the bedroom.

He said, 'I have sat about this house long enough, and I am
tired of it. Another month of sitting about and I should be
taking to my bed, and when a man does that at my age it is the
end of him. I am going to make a fresh start now, and blossom
out a bit. A real social butterfly I shall be. I am only ninety-one
and I feel as frisky as a calf, indeed. Come, I am ready. I have half
a mind to take my harp along, but I had better not, for fear of
putting you young people in the shade.'

Geraint walked slowly down the lane with his grandfather,
his hand under the old man's elbow and guiding him very
lightly, ready in case he should stumble; the violin case bumped
at Geraint's other side.

Geraint said, 'So Dad has made things up with Shafto.'

His grandfather said, 'Not that way round, boy. Shafto has

made it up with your dad. And I should think so too. You sound pleased about it.'

'I am,' said Geraint with feeling. . . . . 'Taid?'

'Well?'

'Taid, I am seventeen now. Am I old enough to be in love? Properly, I mean? I can't talk about it to Dad—I don't know why.'

Geraint's grandfather said, 'When I was your age, boy, I had been in love fifty times, and it was no more each time than a quick ducking under the water like a dipper diving from a stone and then up again, shaking my feathers dry. Then I met your grandmother and I was under for good, drowned and done for.'

Geraint said, 'Yes, but do you *have* to dodge about all the time like that? Fifty times and so on, I mean?'

The old man chuckled and said, 'It does me a power of good when I look back on it.' Then he said, 'No. To be serious, no. What have you got at the back of your mind, boy?'

'Betty Mai Shafto,' said Geraint simply.

His grandfather said, 'You are your father's son right enough, Geraint. When he was a little boy he said to me, "Dad, when I grow up I am going to marry Gwen Rowlands." I said to him, "Wait. You can marry her if you want to, but you may change your mind yet." He never did. He knew what he wanted, and there has always been only the one woman for your dad. You are the same, and when I see the way you talk and go about things I see your father in you. You both have your feet upon a rock, as the psalm says. Now poor Tom took after me. If I had been in your shoes I would have been in at Betty Mai's bedroom window by now.'

Geraint said realistically, 'And she would have broken the washstand over my head.'

'Yes,' said his grandfather. 'Come to think of it, so would your grandmother if I had tried any of that with her. I got her with the harp, for women were more romantic then, or I was a better player even than I thought, and that says a lot. I made a net of music, and while she was still struggling in it I put the question, and all she could do was look at me and nod. But from what I have heard of her these years, I cannot see you catching Betty Mai like that; she is musical herself, and different in other ways: high-spirited, she is, and self-willed. I hope you get her, boy, but if you do, then mark my words—it will be like going to bed with a rosebush. A sniff of the blossom and a jab with the old thorn.'

He walked on in silence for a moment, and then he said, 'And you will never tire of either.'

The *Noson Lawen* was held in the chapel hall, the far end of which had a dais and was curtained off as a stage. Perhaps a hundred people had assembled, sitting on uncomfortable chairs for this 'merry evening'. Geraint's parents had not succeeded in overtaking their son and his grandfather until they had reached the entrance to the hall. Wil waved to Shafto, who grinned back; Mrs Shafto gave Gwen Edwards a grudging nod. Geraint went backstage.

The *Noson Lawen* was a mixture of variety show, classical concert, and cabaret, with a dash of religion. The Master of Ceremonies was Owen the butcher's brother, a fat and egregious man, who introduced each item in the programme with flat jokes. The first item was a choral selection.

'Well now,' said the Master of Ceremonies. 'It is my great pleasure to welcome this evening our guest choir, the Ysgubor Ddu Youth Club Male Voice Choir. They are good, my word— they have to have lungs of brass to say that lot, let alone sing!'

The audience tittered politely.

'And tonight the Ysgubor Ddu etcetera—you know what etcetera means? And the rest. That is what I am looking forward to when I have finished: a rest!'

More titters.

'The Ysgubor Ddu—*hrmm*—Youth Club Male Voice Choir,

ladies and gentlemen, are going to sing a selection from—*The Creation*!'

Applause.

The choir sang; at the end of the selection Geraint's grandfather blew his nose, deeply affected.

'That was grand,' he said. 'Indeed, there is more to music than singing *Sospan Fach* at a football match with your belly full of beer.'

There followed a sketch, the substance of which was the meeting between two girls from the north and two young men from the south, the point of which hinged on various differences of vocabulary.

Geraint yawned from the wings during the applause.

His father said to Gwen Edwards, 'I thought that was good; one of those young lads sounded just like Shafto. I wonder when Geraint is going to play.'

In the wings Betty Mai appeared and stood next to Geraint. He nodded to her, his heart beginning to thump.

'Hello, Betty Mai,' he said. 'How are you?'

'Oh, it's you,' she said distantly. 'I didn't see you standing there.'

'My protective colouring. See you in a minute. I'm on just now.'

The Master of Ceremonies finished his introduction.

'Did you ever hear anyone as corny as that?' said Geraint to Betty Mai, and walked onstage.

He played *Sheep May Safely Graze*, and followed it with a gypsy dance. He could hear his parents clapping above all the others, and he noticed with interest that Shafto was clapping too.

The applause died down and Geraint rejoined Betty Mai. A mournful figure pushed past them. It was Billy Davies.

'Hello, Billy,' said Betty Mai.

'Recitation,' said Billy Davies. 'My dad shoved me into this, and I bet he will be sorry for it by the time I have finished. A recitation, I ask you! Oh, great God, I am on now.'

Billy Davies trudged into the centre of the stage and struck an attitude. He began to recite a long poem by Dafydd ap Gwilym.

Geraint said judiciously, 'There is nothing wrong with that. What was he grumbling about?'

Betty Mai said, 'Nerves. We are not all like you. I am shaking like a leaf.'

Geraint looked at her unbelievingly.

'Nerves? Do not tell me you are nervous.'

'I am quaking in my shoes, I tell you.'

Geraint said, 'Well now, that is strange. I am very nervous myself, but I try to hide it, and my nerves vanish when I get on the stage. But you! I would never have said that you were nervous.'

'And I wouldn't have said that *you* were.'

They looked at each other in sudden fellow-feeling. Geraint reached for Betty Mai's hand and held it for a few seconds, but she shook free and said impatiently, 'Don't. I'm on in a minute.'

Billy Davies completed his recitation, and there was loud applause.

'Well, what do you know about that?' he said as he came back to Geraint and Betty Mai. 'Listen to them.'

'You were very good,' Betty Mai said. 'Oh dear, I feel terrible.'

Geraint said, 'You'll rock them in their seats. But whatever you do, don't sing that *Indian Love Call*—remember? We don't want all the electric-light bulbs to blow up.'

Betty Mai, accompanied by Mrs Davies at the piano, sang *Ar Lan y Mor*, a lovely and plaintive air.

The audience clapped furiously and cheered.

'God,' said Geraint when she returned, 'that was wonderful. I could see them all sniffing and wiping their noses down there. You have a glorious voice, Betty Mai. Listen, do you remember I told you once that your voice was better than Nansi Williams' —I mean Nansi Griffiths'? I meant it, you know, but you would not believe me. When I say something I mean it.'

Betty Mai said quietly, so that Billy Davies could not hear, 'But you went up the mountain with Nansi.'

Geraint said urgently, 'And why did you play that trick on

me that time at the fair? Running away with Maldwyn and that Peter! I know why you got me to try on his hairy old sweater and why you stuck your nose into it: you were trying to make believe I was Peter. And then when you had your chance you ran off with him. I hope you enjoyed yourself, that's all.'

Betty Mai stamped on Geraint's foot with the heel of her shoe. She said nothing, watching impassively as he hopped on one leg and held the other foot, cursing.

'Quiet there!' the Master of Ceremonies hissed in an aside. He said to the audience, 'I tell you, those young people in the wings—you would be surprised, the billing and cooing that goes on. And now . . .'

Geraint hopped to a chair.

'I can't walk,' he said.

Billy Davies came over, grinning.

'I can't walk,' Geraint repeated. 'Oh, the little cow!'

Billy Davies said, 'Better not let her hear you say that or your other foot will be having the treatment too.'

He peered at Geraint, who had removed his shoe and was examining his foot.

'Was it a stiletto heel?' Billy asked.

'How the hell do I know what sort of heel it was? She has broken every bone in my foot, that is all I know. It hurts like hell.'

The male-voice choir were singing a hymn as a finale, *O Llefara Addfwyn Iesu*, while Betty Mai watched and listened demurely, her back to Geraint and Billy.

'Look at her,' said Billy Davies with admiration. 'Butter wouldn't melt in her mouth. Look, I don't think you could call that a stiletto heel, though it is not far off. . . . Beautiful legs she has.'

'Somebody dropped a piano on my foot,' Geraint told his father as Billy Davies helped Geraint into the minister's car to give him a lift home.

The doctor came the following morning. Geraint had broken the second toe of his left foot. After the doctor had attended to it Geraint found an opportunity to speak privately to his grandfather.

'Betty Mai stamped on my foot, Taid,' he said aggrievedly. 'I told Dad somebody dropped a piano on it because I didn't want him to start any more bother. But it was Betty Mai.'

The old man said, 'A lovely voice she has. She stamped on your foot? Well, what did I tell you? A sniff of the blossom and a jab with the thorn, you would be getting.' He cackled and added, 'Trouble is, sometimes you cannot see the roses for the prickles.'

19

ONE afternoon in April, an afternoon of startling sun-
lit clarity after heavy rain, and with still more rain to
come, Madog Parry came scrambling down from the
top of Patagonia with Persimmon Hughes, the elder man lagging
behind, out of breath. Shafto and Wil Edwards looked up from
the roadway on which they were dressing slate.

'The crack!' Madog Parry gasped. 'It is beginning to work!'

'Come on,' said Shafto to Wil.

They ran past Persimmon Hughes, who sat down and wiped
his brow. Then he looked fearfully up towards the top of the
gallery and stood quickly, moving to the end of the gallery away
from the overhang.

Madog Parry called to him, 'Coming up again?'

'Not me,' said Persimmon Hughes. 'I will be waiting here and
getting my breath.'

Madog Parry followed Wil and Shafto. The two men were
standing looking down into the crack.

From its depths there came a sound like the creaking of
timber and cordage when a full-rigged ship heels in a wind, a
slow, ominous sound composed of many lesser movements.

'The old mountain's voice,' said Wil. 'Listen to the old
mountain groaning and grumbling down there.'

'Did you take any measurements?' Shafto asked Madog Parry.

'The depths of the wedges? No, not yet. As soon as we heard
it beginning to work we came down to you. Old Persimmon was
blowing blue lights out of his backside.'

'Just listen to it,' said Shafto. 'The mountain in labour. I will tell you what it is saying down there; it is saying, "Iolo Jones, Iolo Jones. I told you so, you monkey's get!"'

Wil said, 'Anyhow, we must send for Iolo. I will take the responsibility. Go on, Madog, away with you now and send for Iolo Jones. Tell them to say I sent you.'

When Iolo Jones finally arrived at the top of Patagonia he was incapable of speech. He sat down and panted for a couple of minutes, staring down unseeing to the Twll Mawr; Wil saw the gleam of green water far down there as he and Shafto waited for the inspector to regain his breath.

Madog Parry winked solemnly behind the inspector's back.

'Man, devil,' said the inspector at length. 'That Madog Parry has just about made me run all the way up here with his hands in the small of my back pushing me.'

Wil Edwards said, 'You told us that you would have someone sacked if we brought you up here for nothing. Well, I am the one who has sent for you. Remember that. And now if you can hear that crack working above the sound of your own puffing perhaps you would be good enough to tell us what you think of it.'

They listened.

'It is working a bit,' said the inspector eventually.

Shafto said, 'You don't say? If I heard that sort of noise in a coal-pit all you would see of me would be a puff of dust.'

Persimmon Hughes joined them.

'Well, I have come up,' he said, and peered fearfully into the crack. 'What do you think of it, Iolo?'

Iolo Jones said, 'Get the measurements, that is what we must do. A crack like this could go on working for months, years even. If the wedges are moving down the crack again, then it will mean closing half the Bron Eifion. We do not want to do that if it can be avoided. Myself, I still think it is safe.'

The depths of the wedges were measured.

'What did I say?' asked Iolo Jones triumphantly. 'It has not widened an inch! Safe as houses, that is. I have told you, I would

make my bed under it and sleep as sound as a sucking infant.'
He paused and then added judiciously, 'Still, perhaps you were
right to call me up here. I will take no action.'

Shafto said, 'You fat pig, you.'

Iolo Jones took a step backward, away from the crack.

'What did you say?' he gobbled.

Shafto said, 'For two pins I would pick you up and chuck you
into the Twll Mawr, except that your dirty carcass would
pollute the water. You hear that crack grinding and groaning
like that and you say it is safe! I wonder why to God we have
you wished on us. You are a man to back your hunch against
all reason, and I say you are a fat fool.'

Iolo Jones said, 'You will get a week's notice for this, Shafto.
Just you wait.'

Shafto said, 'Get knotted, you bald-headed bladder of lard,
you. What do I care for your threats? I will give myself a week's
notice, and I will get a job in the glass factory. They want men,
and they can have me for a start. Now you clear off before you
have an accident. If I lose my temper any more I might just
slip and bang into you somewhere by the edge there.'

Geraint's toe was better. He had never conceived that so
small a member could cause so much pain, or could immobilize
a person so completely. But it was better at last. He had been for
a walk without a stick, and the toe had given no trouble.

His father was home when Geraint returned from his walk,
and was talking animatedly with Geraint's grandfather.

'I was telling your Taid about the crack on top of Patagonia,'
Wil Edwards said to Geraint as he entered the parlour. 'It is
working. It sounds terrible.'

Geraint's grandfather said, 'Oh, sometimes they do. They can
go on for months making a row like a thousand elephants all
having triplets. But it does not always signify anything. Deep
down, the ice has melted at last, and the rock is settling.'

'Aye,' said Wil. 'But when I was coming home with Shafto I

remembered all that blasting they did on Moonlight. A good while ago, that was. But I remember thinking then that they would be undercutting the rock. You know the way the grain of that rock goes on the surface. It goes steeply down and back, on the slant. Now then, there is a huge weight of rock between the crack and the edge of Patagonia, and nothing to hold it except what's underneath, and that big quartz outcrop much farther down. If that blasting on Moonlight has cut far enough back the whole lot from Patagonia to Moonlight could come down: Patagonia, Monkey Brand, Top Hat, Jim Crow— the lot, right down to the top of the incline. I am not talking about a little fall. I am talking of half a million tons coming down, and that would be no joke. There would be five hundred men in the path of the fall, and enough slate to make a tomb for them as big as Caernarvon Castle.'

'It could go on working for months,' Geraint's grandfather repeated.

'I know that,' said Wil, exasperated. 'Everybody keeps on saying that. But what if it doesn't?'

On the Saturday morning Geraint rose early, took his mother and father their tea, and said, 'I am going to see if I can catch a trout or two this morning.'

Gwen Edwards said, 'Good. Now see that you do. I could fancy some trout for supper. They might cheer your dad up too. He has done nothing but moan about that Shafto leaving the quarry.'

'Next week he goes,' said Wil lugubriously. 'The place will not be the same without him.'

His wife clicked her tongue and said, 'You two have spent years doing nothing but fight, and now you are sorry he is leaving!'

'I will not deny it. I have been thinking of taking a job at the glass factory down at Ysgubor Ddu, where Shafto is going. But I cannot do it. It is easy for a man like Shafto, from the south.'

Gwen said, 'Well, others have left the quarry and gone to the factory. You might be better off, and you would have a steady wage and a much better pension.'

'Not at my age,' said Wil. 'There would not be much to choose. And, anyway, I cannot leave. There is freedom up there. In a factory a man is nothing more than a slave. I have made up my mind. I am staying at the quarry; but I shall miss Shafto.'

Geraint stood waiting for the empty cups. He took them and said, 'I will rinse these for you before I go, Mam.'

He went downstairs and washed the cups and saucers. Then he took out his fishing tackle and walked down the lane, striking to his right over the fields and up the path to Llyn Eifion. At the lake he turned briefly and scanned the horizon; in the clear air he could see the smoke of a ship at sea away beyond Anglesey. He thought with amazement how once he had been afraid of this view, how he had forced himself with an effort of will to look at it. He turned again and gazed over to where the great ridges sprang up Snowdon's flanks, towards the Pass of the Arrows, seeing again in imagination the cave above Lliwedd where the brave knights of Arthur leaned on their shields. The morning was chilly by the lake, but Geraint was warm within himself as his eyes rested on the range of peaks, the snow still covering their shoulders. He glanced upward to where a buzzard wheeled in the bright April air. It was a small country, and from where the buzzard hung it could all be seen: the windswept peaks of all the mountains in Snowdonia, the streams shining on their flanks, the waters collected and multiplied in the lakes, then bustled in a dozen miles over the impermeable rocks to the sea by way of the rivers: Conway, Anafon, Ogwen, Seiont, Gwyrfai, Llyfni, Dwyfach, Dwyfor, Glaslyn, every watercourse bounded by some of the oldest mountains in the world, their summits mirrored in the abiding lakes.

A small country, he thought. When the giants of the Himalayas and Karakorums and Rockies and Alps were thrusting up in fire and steam and thunder, these hills of Snowdon had been

215

formed ages before, were even then being worn down; the colossal pressures which had formed the slate had ceased, the glaciers finished their roaring and grinding, had scooped out the lake hollows and the river beds and left, here and there in the valley bottoms, the fertile glacial drift superimposed on the barren rock, waiting for the bone or antler or flint or tractor plough of an aeon hence. Soon the salmon would be leaping in the rivers again this year, as they had done a million years before the little, dark, narrow-headed men nosed up the creeks of the Conway in their dug-out boats and saw fish leaping in the river. A small country, Geraint thought, but it held a world within it, a world in time and a world in place, and both worlds were his. And then he knew that if he left it it would only be for a time. Coming to terms with his own ability and capacity, he said to himself aloud, 'I know. I will be a teacher, and I will come back and teach the violin.'

He would never be able to play like Yehudi Menuhin, but did it matter? No; if he made as good a teacher as Mr Griffiths he would be doing well enough. So that was that.

He took five trout, enough for supper, and then went at his leisure down the path. Away past the school he saw Billy Davies walking down the village street, and the toy shape of an abandoned lawn-mower on the front lawn of the minister's house. One day, in a few years, Billy Davies would have his own trim house in a Midland suburb of England, with a neat patch of shaven lawn at front and back, which he would keep tidy with a little motor-mower.

Geraint followed Billy into the village to catch him up for a chat. Pausing in the street, he looked for Billy among the morning shoppers. He saw Betty Mai coming towards him about a hundred yards distant, a shopping basket on her arm, and was going to meet her when Billy Davies came out of the post office, saw Geraint, and hurried over.

Billy said excitedly, 'Just the man! Mrs Howell said that if I met you I must tell you there is something you will want to have in a hurry, because it came after the morning delivery. I think she is the limit with that 200-watt lamp she keeps for looking through envelopes.'

Betty Mai joined them.

'Hello, Billy,' she said, ignoring Geraint. 'Did you see my dad going past your place to the wood early on? He took his gun out. First time for years. Have you heard any shooting?'

'No,' said Billy. 'Never mind that. You had better go into the post office with Geraint. There is a letter for you too. Mrs Howell says it is urgent.'

Betty Mai hurried into the post office, followed by Geraint. They stood behind Mrs Owen and waited impatiently while she bought stamps.

Mrs Owen said, 'Thank you, Mrs Howell.'

She turned, sniffed at Geraint, smiled at Betty Mai, and waited.

'News, you have,' she said. 'Mrs Howell was telling me.'

The postmistress reached below the counter and held up two identical buff-coloured envelopes.

'Royal Institute of Music, it says on the outside of the envelopes,' she said slyly. 'I thought you might want to have them now instead of waiting for Monday's delivery.'

They snatched the envelopes and tore them open, reading hastily.

Geraint said slowly, 'I have won a scholarship.'

Betty Mai said, 'So have I.'

They walked dazed out of the post office, hearing Mrs Howell's voice dimly, but not taking in the words. They paused outside where Billy Davies was waiting.

'Billy,' said Geraint. 'We have both won scholarships.'

'Well, congratulations indeed,' said Billy. 'I think that's wonderful!'

Betty Mai suddenly said, 'Oh, Geraint!' and flung her arms round his neck, hugging and kissing him, her tears wet on his cheeks. Passers-by stopped, gaped, whispered.

Geraint kissed Betty Mai long and heartily.

When he released her she sighed and said, 'Oh, Geraint,

Geraint, we shall be together at Liverpool. Oh, Geraint, I was only teasing you that time with Peter, and I am so sorry I hurt your poor toe.'

Geraint lifted her off her feet and whirled her round, laughing and yelling.

'Such carryings-on!' said Mrs Owen.

There was a long roll, like thunder, but the skies were clear. It was like thunder, but longer, a dull booming ground-bass with ear-splitting cracks and reports above it.

Madog Parry, who was waiting for opening time outside the Prince of Gwynedd with a group of cronies, said, 'Great God, it is the Bron Eifion! Come on!'

Men were running up the village street in a babble of voices. The thunder went on.

Wil Edwards dropped his newspaper on the kitchen table and said to Geraint's grandfather, 'Listen. The rock is falling. It is the mercy of God that it is Saturday. I am going up as fast as my legs will take me. When Gwen comes back tell her I have gone. That Iolo Jones will be going up as well, and I have a thing or two to say to him.'

The old man said, 'Yes, you must go,' and stayed silent, listening until his son's running footsteps had died away in the lane, hearing instead his own footsteps clattering to the cottage on an August day all those years ago after another rock fall; seeing again the little weakly figure of his son Tom standing at the cottage door. Tom had said, 'Dad, the doctor has brought Mam a baby boy, and she is crying upstairs.' He had pushed past Tom and run up the stairs, and his wife had said, 'Oh, sweetheart, I thought they had killed you,' and he had seen the baby's tiny, wet-looking black head on the pillow beside her. Tom had crept upstairs and put a small hand in his father's, and the woman had said, 'We shall call the baby Wil.'

The old man called, 'Gwen. Gwen,' but nobody came, and he relapsed into silence and reverie, time running the other way in his mind, like the footsteps.

Mrs Shafto emerged from the hairdresser's, a white towel

over her shoulders, her hair a mass of rollers and her face the same shade as the towel.

She said, 'Oh, sweet Jesus, I am a widow now, and so is Iolo Jones's missis.'

A knot of people collected round her.

'What do you mean?' someone asked, as Betty Mai ran across the street, followed by Geraint and Billy Davies.

Mrs Shafto said, swaying, 'I do not know what it is about, but my man said this morning that he was going up to the Bron Eifion with Iolo Jones; but he told me to tell Betty Mai he was going shooting. Oh——'

Mrs Shafto fainted.

'She will be all right in a minute. The shock, see?' someone said.

The thunder ceased.

Geraint said to Betty Mai, 'Come on, we must hurry. They will look after your mother.'

Billy Davies said, 'Dad has gone to Liverpool on the train. I will take you up in his car. Hurry now.'

They drove out of the village in a stream of cars and vans heading for the quarry, passing running, shouting people. They caught up with Geraint's father at the intersection of the lane with the bottom road.

Geraint said, 'Stop, Billy, there's my dad.'

Wil Edwards climbed into the car and said, 'Well, Betty Mai, your dad was right. The rock has come down. It will be a sight worth seeing, I can tell you.'

Betty Mai was sitting silently, her face pale and tear-streaked; she was twisting a handkerchief in her fingers. Geraint had an arm round her shoulders.

Wil pushed Geraint's fishing tackle out of the way to make more room for himself and said, 'I would like to see Iolo Jones's face. That is why I am going up.'

Geraint said, 'Dad, Shafto was up at the quarry with Iolo Jones when the rock fell. I don't know what it is about.'

They took the bottom road and stopped near the main sheds inside the quarry gates.

Wil Edwards said, 'Shafto was here, all right. There is his van.'

They got out of the car and looked past a number of parked vehicles to where Shafto's van stood, people swirling around it. Geraint looked up into the quarry, and caught his breath.

'Look!'

A great wound now slashed down from Patagonia, a clean scar at the top, cutting down Patagonia, through Monkey Brand, through Top Hat and Jim Crow. On Moonlight there was a vast fan-shaped heap of rubble, subdivided by a quartz outcrop which split it neatly in two; below it the rock detritus extended across The Haymarket and down to the lips of the Twll Mawr. To the right, the upper section of the gravity incline was obliterated except for a few girders of the engine shed protruding like twisted steel claws. Small dolls were climbing among the huge blocks of rubble; along an undamaged section of roadway on Moonlight Geraint could see the jib of a mobile crane moving, the rest of the crane hidden from view by the slope.

'Great Lord,' said Wil Edwards. 'It is like using a power hammer to kill a pair of ants. The quarry will be out of production for months. Come, we will help to search for them. Betty Mai, you had better wait in the car or let Billy take you home.'

Betty Mai shook her head. 'I am coming too,' she said.

They walked up the incline till the rubble began. A man shouted to Wil, 'It is your mate Shafto and Iolo Jones. They are in there somewhere; they were seen coming up.'

Madog Parry and Persimmon Hughes were scrabbling in the rock at the top of the incline.

'What were they doing up here?' said Wil.

Madog Parry said, 'Wil. You got here. We thought they might be somewhere on the incline.'

Other parties of men were searching at random, while far above them the manager was supervising the work of the crane. Two more cranes were moving into position on Jim Crow and Top Hat, the under-manager in charge.

Wil shook his head.

'It is hopeless,' he said. 'Even with the cranes it is hopeless. It will take five years to shift all this lot.'

They heard above them a short, muffled explosion. Geraint jumped and held Betty Mai tightly, expecting another fall of rock.

Persimmon Hughes said, 'That was a gunshot.'

Betty Mai said, 'Mam told me my dad took his gun with him this morning. It must be Dad!'

Wil shouted, 'Shafto is alive! Hurry!'

He leaped upwards among the rocks. Madog Parry kept pace with him. Persimmon Hughes was next, then Geraint with Betty Mai and Billy Davies.

They paused a hundred feet below the quartz outcrop.

There was another shot. They ran and stumbled and clambered upwards. People were coming from all directions, shouting and jabbering.

Wil bellowed, 'Keep quiet, you fools!'

There was silence. Somewhere a stone shifted under a man's boot. Then they heard a faint sound, a cry from the depths of the rock at the foot of the outcrop. They worked their way forward. Wil shouted, and the reply came at once. He bent down at the foot of a crannied heap of great stone blocks and yelled, 'Shafto. It is Wil Edwards.'

Shafto's voice came, 'And about time, too.'

'Is Iolo Jones with you?'

Iolo Jones shouted, 'We are both in here. Help, for God's sake.'

Somebody said, 'That is Iolo Jones. He is frightened out of his wits by the sound of him.'

'So would you be,' said another man. 'And so would I.'

Wil said, 'We must get the cranes on the job. But we cannot pull the rocks away blindly; if something shifts the wrong way it will squash them. I am going in to have a look.'

Persimmon Hughes said, 'You are mad. That lot might move at any time and you would be done for as well.'

Wil said, 'I am going in,' and he walked forward, scaled a block of stone, wriggled into a crevice between it and the one above, and was lost from view. There was silence save for the scraping of Wil's boots, fainter and fainter. Then the sound of voices, muffled and unintelligible.

Persimmon Hughes said, 'I wish to God Wil would come out of there.'

In five minutes more Wil emerged, his clothes streaked with dust, his hands grazed.

He did not speak at first, but walked round the mass of rock, regarding it intently.

Then he said, 'The cranes can lift off that lot like taking down a tower of kids' bricks.'

He turned and grinned triumphantly down at the others. Behind him there was a slight grinding sound, then a crunch. The gap through which he had wriggled was no longer there. They heard a small clatter of falling stones. Wil glanced over his shoulder at the rock, and smiled tautly.

Shafto shouted, 'Hurry up there.'

Wil yelled back, 'Oh, shut up, Shafto.' He said to Madog Parry, 'I could not see them, but I got close enough. Neither of them is hurt at all; not a scratch. It is a miracle. They are under the base of the outcrop, where there is an overhang.'

The manager arrived.

He said, 'Good God, don't tell me those men are alive!'

Wil said, 'They are fine, sir, if we can only get these stones away from them one by one, taking it very easy with the cranes, isn't it?'

The manager breathed heavily.

He said, 'Get those cranes here, then, double quick.'

At twelve-thirty all the rescuers were given coffee and biscuits. The cranes worked slowly. Each huge block of stone had to be secured with chains. If there was no way of passing chains under a block, then it had to be dragged sideways from the top of the main mass with great care, so that it would disturb nothing else when it fell. Betty Mai sat with Geraint, her hand in his, and watched numbly. Commands were shouted, the jibs of the cranes lifted, the great blocks swung away one by one and were set down; the cranes manœuvred this way and that to find the safest way of working. Block after block was removed. From time to time there would be a rumble; work would cease and men begin shouting into the mass of rocks; each time a reply came from Shafto or Iolo Jones.

At four o'clock wreaths of mist began to creep up from the lake.

Geraint said, 'We seem to have been here for ever.'

Betty Mai did not speak.

The men finished passing chains round an enormous block, signalled to the crane-driver. The cable tightened, the chains lifted, stayed; the jib of the crane started to dip.

The manager shouted, 'Make him let go, there! It's pulling the crane over.'

The crane-driver slackened off, then moved the crane forward to the broken edge of the roadway above, lifting the jib as he went. The cable tightened again, the chains lifted.

The manager said, 'Make him move back. If the edge of the roadway gives——'

Wil Edwards said, 'Let him be, sir. He knows what he is doing.'

The block moved slowly and easily upward; the jib swung round and the block was deposited lightly on the roadway.

Someone gave a faint cheer.

Wil walked forward, peered down.

He said, 'Hello, Shafto. Hello, Iolo . . . Great God!'

Wil turned to the manager and said, 'Come and look.'

People crowded forward.

The manager said incredulously, 'They—they have got a bed in there.'

He scratched his head in perplexity, then shook it. Finally he said crisply, 'Get the rest of those blocks out from the front, and be quick about it. I want to talk to those men, by God, I do.'

Betty Mai peered down and called, 'Dad, are you all right?'

She could see Shafto's grimy face. He was holding a shotgun. Behind him, sitting on a small camp-bed, his head in his hands, was Iolo Jones. He looked up.

'I am going to have Shafto for every crime in the calendar,' he said to the manager. 'Every crime in the calendar.'

'You want to think twice about what you do,' Shafto said. He called up to Betty Mai, 'I only just fired a warning shot, like, and the whole lot came down. If it hadn't come down today it would have come down tomorrow, or Monday. And if it had come down on Monday there would be four or five hundred corpses in this little lot. You think of that, everybody.'

'I am going to have you, Shafto,' said Iolo Jones hysterically, giggling a little. 'Every crime there is in the book I will have you for.'

'Belt up,' said Shafto. He called upwards, 'Iolo Jones said this lot was so safe he would make his bed under it. And that is just what he did. I made him carry it up here himself, too.'

The crowd had ebbed away. Shafto and Iolo Jones were heading for the police station with the manager and Mr Pritchard, who had got a case at last. Wil had followed with Madog Parry and Persimmon Hughes and Billy Davies; the mist had thickened, hiding the rubble.

There were two voices in the mist.

'The mist is thick.'

A rustle, a creak.

'We must go.'

'In a minute.'

'Mmm.'

A sigh.

'I like the blossom better than the thorns.'

'What?'

'Oh, nothing.'

A long silence, and then the slow sound of footsteps on the rock.

23.129558

80p

(fichum —
re Snowdonia)